# Mistletoe & Magic

# Mistletoe & Magic

## Wisteria Cove
### Book 2

**Erin Branscom**

*To Shanna,*
*Thank you for always showing up for me and being such an encouraging friend. I treasure our friendship. 25 years now! Which still shocks me, because aren't we still 18 and 22? From Chili's lava cakes to jamming out to Britney Spears. I treasure all of our memories. I hope every single person can find a Shanna Burns in their lifetime.*

# Content Warning

This book includes "on-page" adult content and language
unsuitable for minors.

# Chapter 1
# Ivy

The breakup wasn't even the worst part. The worst part was that he kept my dog. *My Lola.* "I miss her," I rant as my sister Willa turns her old tan Jeep Wrangler with the heater that barely works half the time onto the winding road that leads into Wisteria Cove. She had picked me up at my townhouse in Boston when my boyfriend Derek and I'd had a fight and he'd told me to leave.

The asshole had even been nice enough to pack a bag for me and set it by the door before I woke up. He wanted me gone so his new girlfriend could move right in. Ultimate betrayal.

"I was the one who took care of her and did everything for her. She was supposed to be a gift from him. And Derek just— what? Gets to keep her like *I'm* the one who cheated? Why are Lola and I being punished because Derek can't keep it in his pants?"

"It's not right," Willa replies, shaking her head angrily on my behalf. "He's an actual reindeer turd in human form. But can I point out something hilarious? You're sadder about losing the dog than losing him."

Damn. She's right. I love my dog. But I definitely fell out of love with Derek.

I fall back against the passenger seat headrest with a dramatic groan, the fluff from my hood poofing up around me like I'm drowning in a marshmallow. "I knew it was over for a while, and I just didn't want to add it to my list of failures. What am I going to do now? I've had so many jobs in the last five years. No one takes me seriously in Wisteria Cove anymore.

My ex is a sleazy, emotionally constipated, controlling criminal defense attorney who is threatening me with legal action if I try to take Lola. And my best friend—now his new girlfriend—wasted no time moving in with him before I was barely even out the door."

I'd wanted to lose it when I opened the door with my bags, thinking Willa was here to get me and realizing instead it was Kristin, my best friend who had been screwing Derek the whole time we were together.

The way she wouldn't meet my eyes and had turned with her bags and said, "I'll come back later."

"Go fuck yourself, Kristin!" I'd yelled at her as she scurried down the street like a rat. Girl code doesn't mean a thing to her. Just take whatever you want, I guess. I should have known when she stopped coming to girl's night out that something was up, but I realize now that was when she would have been meeting Derek.

Derek's betrayal didn't hurt as much as Kristin's did. I felt humiliated because I would confide in her about Derek and she would listen. All along she was screwing him, and I trusted her. I told her everything, and she pretended to support me and encouraged me to break up with him. Now I know why.

"Ex-best friend," Willa corrects. "Also, she's a massive turd, too. I think we should hex her."

"Yeah, she is. She can have Derek. I honestly should have left him sooner. I'm an idiot for not figuring this out and leaving when you guys tried to warn me." I pull out the thermos and take a long sip of peppermint cocoa that Willa brought for me because she's literally the best and has her own cafe in her very own bookstore.

I know what Willa is probably thinking. She and my other sister Rowan repeatedly tried to tell me to leave Derek and that he was bad news. I never listened. And the truth is, I thought maybe I could help Derek. Sometimes I'd see glimmers of the person he could be. But then he'd flip back to the asshole that he always was. He would make me feel so badly about myself and subtly suggest that he was the only person who would ever tolerate me. And if I broke up with him, he would just be another failure, like all of the jobs I've had. Sometimes I can still hear Derek's voice in my head, telling me nobody would want me or put up with my shit.

So, I stuck it out, hoping that it would get better. It only got worse.

"Kristin didn't take your man; she took your problem, and I actually can't think of a better consequence for either of them than each other," she says disdainfully as she makes her way back to Wisteria Cove.

I nod, because that's all I have in me. I am so tired of fighting with Derek and his treatment of me. But it also feels like I'm going back home to Wisteria Cove with my tail between my legs.

"It's all going to work out. And now you get to be a nanny to Junie. It's a great job for you until you can figure out what *you* want to do. This is actually great. You are amazing at so many things," Willa says as she holds her hand out for the thermos to take a sip.

"I don't know... Are you really sure Remy is okay with all this? I mean, don't get me wrong—being a nanny for Junie sounds absolutely amazing. And not to mention living at the tree farm at Christmas. It sounds magical and all that. But Remy is just...I don't know. I need to think about something long term. I guess I could do that while I'm there..."

And honestly working with Remy would be...a dream. He's so freaking mysterious and hot. He's got the whole grumpy single swoony dad thing down. And I would love to work with Junie. This truly would be a dream job for me.

"Remy's mom was at the bookstore with me when you called me and said that this is perfect timing for everyone. She said that Remy really needs your help," Willa says as she hands me back the thermos.

Donna is Remy and Finn's mom. She's also an incredibly famous author, like Nora Roberts-famous, and has written over a hundred bestsellers in the past few decades. If towns had grandma's, she'd be Wisteria Coves. Our very own royalty. We all love her so much. I guess if Donna says it's okay, it must be okay.

But I'm still not completely convinced. "It's just that every time we've been at things together, Remy barely talks to me or acknowledges me. It's like he doesn't even *like* me," I say as I glance out my window at the neighborhood, where every house looks dressed for a storybook holiday.

Porches are wrapped in garlands and big red velvet bows. Wreaths hang on every door. Windows glow with paper snowflakes taped on some of them, and I can see trees inside, twinkling and proud. Snow dusts the sidewalks, just enough to sprinkle it. A pack of kids waddles in puffed coats, bundled like marshmallows, dragging bright red sleds. Their laughter skips across the street and lands in my chest.

Someone's chimney sends up a ribbon of smoke that smells like cedar and comfort. The air slips in through the crack in my rolled-down window and brings pine, a hint of sugar, and something buttery that has to be coming from the corner bakery. It wraps around me like a memory of mittened hands and a mother's scarf tied snug under my chin.

Across the way, a neighbor lifts a strand of lights and the bulbs blink one by one, soft gold. The whole world feels softer, whispering that I am exactly where I am supposed to be. Coming home to Wisteria Cove feels right.

Willa breaks through my thoughts and smirks. "Donna may have mentioned that he's been extra grumpy with the holiday season approaching at the tree farm, so he definitely needs your help. Besides, Junie is a great kid. You always have fun with her. Plus, Remy is not bad to look at. Maybe you two of you can work out your issues together over the holidays. If you know what I mean," she wiggles her eyebrows.

"I'm not emotionally ready to handle a hot, grumpy single dad, Willa." I say dryly.

"Oh, so you admit he's hot," she smirks.

All right, I've *always* had a crush on Remy. Age gap is one of my favorite romance tropes, and Remy definitely gives off the vibes. He's thirty-five and smoking broody perfection. He's only nine years older than me, so my fantasies of Remy have always been chef's-kiss perfection. Of course, I am not telling Willa any of this. Or that I named my favorite vibrator Remy.

Nope, she doesn't need to know any of that. And this might be exactly why I'm having second thoughts about working with Remy. Because it's not just second thoughts, it's some seriously dirty thoughts. Working for someone I've had a crush on for so long is likely to bring on complicated emotions. And I'm feeling complicated enough these days.

Willa lives in a cabin out on Remy's tree farm with her boyfriend Tate, who works as a manager for Remy. She and my other sister, Rowan, would tease me mercilessly if they knew I had a thing for Remy, and I *most definitely* have a thing for Remy. I think any hot-blooded woman with a beating heart would have a thing for him.

First of all, he's tall—at least six foot two. Derek was maybe five foot eight. I'm not crying over a man who isn't even six feet tall. Remy's got that dark hair, brooding storm-gray eyes, sexy jawline. And he's built with buff arms like a bodybuilder, only I know for a fact he got that body naturally working his tree farm.

Yeah, I'm a goner for Remy Bennett. Even though he's always been that unattainable book boyfriend that you dream about and never a reality. Until today. Today he's a reality. And a great distraction from Derek and his bullshit.

"I think you two would be good for each other," she smirks. "And you know Donna is right. This is a good opportunity for you both. Remy needs help, and you need a job with a place to stay. Win-win."

"I'm not like you and Rowan. I don't have my shit together like you two. I'm a mess," I say quietly. "What if I let him down?"

"I don't know why you think that," she says, glancing over with a look of concern. "You are totally smart, cool, and a knock-out. So what if you haven't found your passion yet? Maybe it's Remy." She cackles at the last part.

My sister Willa has always had a gift for spot-on intuition. My other sister, Rowan, is an apothecary and yoga instructor, who I fill in for occasionally. Both are really beautiful and successful. I don't have the same gifts they do; in fact, I don't have any gifts. People widely know and respect our mother, Lilith, as the town sea witch. Do they ride on brooms? No, but they all definitely have gifts.

I'm just Ivy. The girl who has had dozens of part-time jobs and can't seem to get her shit together and find herself. And today, getting kicked out of the town home that Derek and I shared and moving back to my hometown is just another failure I guess I can add to the list. Poor Ivy can't keep a job or a man.

I sit up higher in my seat as we pull into the drive for Bennett Tree Farm. It's like something out of a snow globe. big, beautiful red barn dusted with fresh powder comes into sight, surrounded by towering evergreens wrapped in string lights. A hand-painted sign reads "Cut Your Own Joy." I don't know who painted it, but I want to hug them. I glance back and realize maybe Junie did that. It's adorable.

"This is like...if Hallmark had a baby with a Pinterest board," I breathe. "Wow. Remy has done a lot to the place in the past few years since he took it over."

"Welcome to your new life," Willa says. "You're going to have so much fun here. I love living out here, too."

"I don't even know how to nanny. What if Junie decides she doesn't like me?" I say suddenly, feeling nervous.

"Last year, you made a giant gingerbread replica of Hogwarts for fun." She glances over and laughs.

"What?" I say with a shrug. I guess I am a big kid at heart.

"It's hilarious that out of all the jobs you've had, being a nanny is the one job you haven't had yet," she teases. "I feel like I'm dropping you off for your first day of school."

"All right, not fair." But it is ironic, I guess. I am notorious for having had a ton of part-time jobs everywhere. I've done it all. From dog walking, pet sitting, serving, bartending, cleaning houses...I've mostly done it all. Some would say I'm a jack of all trades, but I just haven't found what makes me happy. Willa is successful with her bookstore and coffee shop, Wisteria Books & Brews. And Rowan is opening up her own apothecary shop, Salt & Root, next to the bookstore, where she'll have a yoga studio on the top floor and her apothecary on the bottom. We've all been working and saving to go in on it together. It's going to be amazing when she finally gets it up and going.

We pull up to the one-bedroom cabin that Willa and Tate live in on the Bennett tree farm property, and head in and get Cobweb, her cat, to bring with her back to the bookstore.

"Can you grab her carrier?" she calls as she heads to the back of the tiny space.

"Yeah," I say as I look around and find Cobweb curled up on their bed on a blanket in their cozy, rustic home.

Outside, the cabin glows like a lantern through the trees. A wreath hangs on the red front door, woven with cedar, eucalyptus, and a few sprigs of wisteria, that our mom likely gave her, tied with a bright red ribbon. A stack of split logs is tucked beneath the overhang, dusted with snow. Stockings hang from boat hooks Tate mounted into the beam, knit in cream and red. The Christmas lights throw a soft glow across the room, catching on the framed black-and-white photos of Wisteria Cove and the little watercolor of the harbor that Willa loves.

The tree stands near the big window, tall and full, dressed in a mix that is pure Willa and Tate. Hand-cut paper snowflakes from the bookstore craft night. Cinnamon salt dough stars. A driftwood star crowns the top, sanded smooth by years in the water. Bright red ribbon winds through the branches, and tucked between needles are small bookish ornaments: tiny open novels, a miniature typewriter, a copper bookmark charm. Cobweb, their black kitten, patrols the skirt of the tree like a tiny shadow, occasionally batting a felt acorn and then pretending innocence.

On the dining table sits a long runner of linen, scattered with pinecones, taper candles in mismatched brass holders, and a bowl of oranges studded with cloves. The kitchen is strung with a simple strand of lights over the open shelves, reflecting off polished copper pots. A kettle rests on the stove. Mugs wait with candy canes hooked over the rims. Every corner has a touch of them. A stack of well-loved Christmas records near the record player. A basket of knit throws by the couch. A jar of wish papers on the coffee table for guests to write a hope and toss into the fire. The whole cabin feels like a held breath and a warm hug, the kind of place where you can hear the snow hush outside and the quiet promise of the season settle in your bones.

"Come here, Cobweb," I whisper as I stroke her fur and pull her up to my chin and kiss her soft head. "You're a good baby, aren't you?"

She meows softly and snuggles into me. "Time to go to the bookstore, Cobweb."

The front door opens, and Tate comes in. "Hey," he calls to me as he pulls the door closed behind him and glances around.

"Hi," I call back, waving with Cobweb's paw.

In an instant, Cobweb is off of me and over in Tate's arms. He strokes her fur and murmurs to her. "Where's Willa?"

"Right here," she calls as she comes out of the bathroom and goes to him, wrapping him in a hug and kissing him. Those two are endgame and goals.

I grin at them; they're so cute. Crazy cute. I knew Derek wasn't for me when I saw how good it was for Tate and Willa. And I want what they have someday.

*Someday.*

"What are you guys doing here?" he asks me, still holding Willa.

"Today's Ivy's first day as Junie's nanny," Willa says as she grabs the cat carrier and loads up Cobweb. "I've got to get to the bookstore. Mom's watching things for me, and she's probably rearranging everything as we speak. Can you take Ivy up to the house with you on the side by side?"

"He hired a nanny?" he asks, giving me a confused look.

"Ummm...well, yeah. What do you mean?" I ask nervously, feeling my emotions roll over me.

Tate shrugs, "I didn't realize he hired someone. Actually, you know what, this is great. He's been having to miss a lot of work, and he's been really stressed out lately. This will be a big help to him."

I shrug. "Donna said it was okay, and I assumed—."

It's about that time that I realize that Donna probably set us up. I should've known. Great.Heat crawls up my neck. My smile feels pasted-on, and I picture Remy walking in and finding me here, uninvited, like a stray cat who wandered into his kitchen. The old worry flares fast.

*You do too much.*

*You're in the way.*

*You read the room wrong.*

I think of my suitcase by the door, how easy it would be to zip it, mumble an apology, and disappear before anyone has to say it out loud. I can already hear the story I will tell myself in the car. *No harm done. You tried. It was a misunderstanding.* Only it wouldn't feel like a misunderstanding. It would feel like proof.I try to breathe. The house feels warm and safe, and for a second, I let myself want it. I want to belong here. Then doubt slides in again, quiet and sharp. If he didn't say *yes*, if he didn't say he wanted me here, then I'm trespassing on the softest parts of his life. I glance toward the doorway, half expecting Remy to appear with that guarded look he wears.

My chest tightens. I could make a joke. I could spin this into something breezy and charming. That is the old reflex. Smile. Minimize. Make yourself smaller so no can hurt you when their jabs land.I straighten instead. If I am going to be here, it has to be because he wants me here. Not because his mother nudged the chess pieces around and called it fate. The thought steadies me. I can ask him. I can risk the answer. My heart knocks against my ribs like it's trying to get out, but I lift my chin anyway.*Please let him want me here.* And if he doesn'tt, let me be brave enough to hear it.

* * *

Tate drops me at the end of the drive with a quick squeeze to my shoulder. The taillights fade, and the quiet of the Bennett Tree Farm settles around me. It smells like pine and cold and the faint sweetness of sap. Gravel crunches under my boots as I follow the path toward the house. Remy's place sits back from the lot, sturdy and square, the kind of farmhouse that looks like it has weathered a hundred winters and plans to meet a hundred more. There is a stack of split logs under the eave, neat as a picture. A child's pair of glittery purple mittens is clipped to the railing with a clothespin, forgotten and waiting. My chest pinches at the sight.

I slow on the last step and just stand there, taking it in. The windows glow honey-gold. Somewhere out by the trees, a saw hums and then stops. Wind moves through the rows and the whole farm stirs. I search for signs of chaos or company. No extra cars. No boots scattered on the mat. No music. Only quiet and light.

My breath fogs the air. I rub my palms against my jeans nervously. Donna said it was fine. Maybe she meant well. Maybe she nudged me right where I am supposed to be. Or maybe I am about to knock and regret this.I study the door like it holds an answer. The paint is scuffed near the bottom, the handle shines from a thousand turns. Home. That is what it looks like. Not imposing. Not grand. Just a place where people hang up their coats and stay warm.

I raise my hand to knock and hesitate. What if he is not expecting me. What if he looks surprised, and I hear that pause people make when they are trying to be kind. I picture my suit-case by the step, me backing away with a laugh that is not real. I could call Tate. I could be gone in three minutes.I knock anyway. Gentle first, knuckles to wood. The bell gives a small chime. Silence answers.I wait, listening hard. Heat ticks in the baseboards. I knock again, a little louder. My heartbeat counts off the seconds. I can smell woodsmoke drifting from the chimney, and something like cinnamon if I let myself believe it. I rest my palm against the door to steady myself. The wood is warm.

Please let him want me here. The thought moves through me like a prayer I have not said in years.I knock a third time and press closer, ear tilted to the quiet. "Remy," I call, softer than I meant to. "It's Ivy."

"Maybe they're not home," I say aloud, because talking to myself is a hobby at this point.

The front door opens, and Donna looks out, with her pencil tucked behind her ear. "Ivy!" she calls and opens her arms for a hug. "There you are. Come on in." Donna is probably in her mid-fifties if I had to guess. She has a silver bob of hair, bright green eyes, and they are the kindest eyes I've ever known. Donna has been friends with my mom since before I could remember, and she's always been kind to me and my sisters.

I give her a hug and a big smile. "Hey, Donna."

She looks out and waves as Tate drives away toward the big barn at the front of the property. "I'm glad you're here. Junie will be so excited to see you after school."

Of course she has school. I forget tiny people go to school.

I glance past her at the house, and it's a complete disaster. It still has Fourth of July decorations everywhere and bags of fall decorations in bags along the wall like they never got put up or got put back in a hurry. But I'm guessing they never got put up. And now it's the middle of the holiday season. There are piles of things everywhere with boxes, bags, and random ornaments and streamers in weird places. And it's chaos.

"As you can tell, Remy desperately needs your help," she says with a grimace. She moves to the dining table where a notebook waits, open beside her laptop, pages flagged with sticky notes. She lifts her coffee, her lipstick stamped on the rim like a signature, and takes a sip while her gaze sweeps the room. I glance around, too. The boots by the door. The cereal bowl abandoned on the counter. The stack of unopened mail. She looks weary and also determined, like a general taking stock before a battle.I hover near the chair and tuck my hands into my sleeves. "I am happy to help. I just want to be clear on what you want me to do.""Good," she says, and the word sounds like relief. She picks up a pen and draws a neat line down the center of a fresh page. "You are here as Junie's nanny first. Not a housekeeper. Not a maid." She writes NANNY on one side and OTHER HELP on the other. "Let us start with Junie."She ticks items as she talks, her voice settling into a rhythm. "School bus comes at eight-ten. Drop-off is at three. After school snack. Homework check. Play time. Bath and bed by eight if she is melting, eight-thirty if she is wide awake. She loves stories. She will try to talk you into two. You can give her as many as you can tolerate." Donna looks up, eyes kind. "You can handle that." "Yes," I say. "That part I can do." I love to read, and I know that Junie does, too."Good. Now, Remy." She writes his name in the margin and taps it with the pen. "He works until he cannot see straight. You are not his housekeeper, but if you can help keep the day from falling apart, that will help Junie." She marks a few bullets. "Light cooking is welcome. Family dinners are not required, but they make life easier. Toss a load of Junie's laundry in when it piles up. Wipe counters if they are sticky. That sort of thing.""So nanny first," I say. "Light household support second.""Exactly." She circles both columns. My shoulders loosen a notch. "Thank you.""Where you will live." She flips to another page. "There is a small bedroom down the hall across from Junie's. Fresh sheets are on the bed, and there is a dresser. Closet, too. The bathroom is shared. If this does not feel right after a week, there is a studio over the garage that can be made comfortable, but I would like you close to her at first." "That's totally fine," I say. The thought of being near Junie steadies me."Money." She closes the notebook and reaches into her tote. She sets an envelope on the table and slides it toward me. "Your first week's pay in advance. A prepaid card for groceries and household items. A little cash for incidentals. Don't use your own money. If you need more on the card, I will add it."I blink. "Thank you. That is more than fair."She smiles back, then sobers. "Two more things. Boundaries and communication."I nod, tense again."Remy is not caught up on this plan," she says gently. "That is on me. He would never ask for help and he is stretched too thin to see straight. I will talk to him tonight and make that clear. In the meantime, you are allowed to take up space here. You are not a secret, and you are not a burden. If he bristles, it is only habit. He is a good man who loves his daughter. He will adjust."My stomach flutters, but I breathe. "All right.""Communication," she continues. "Text me if you have questions. Call if it is urgent. Here are the school numbers. Here is the pediatrician. Junie has no allergies beyond a mild dislike of broccoli. The EpiPen in the kitchen drawer is mine. Don't worry about it." She writes her number again on a sticky note and sticks it to the edge of the notebook like a mother hen planting a flag.I listen and let the plan wrap around my nerves like a blanket. This, I can do. Structure feels like kindness.From down the hall comes the distant clank of the heater kicking on. The house settles around us. Donna tucks her pencil behind her ear and slides the notebook toward me. "Look this over tonight. Add notes if you think of them. In the mornings,

Remy leaves by six if the trees need him. You can be up by seven. Make Junie's lunch or let her buy. She is adventurous on pizza day."I tuck the envelope and the card into my bag. "I'll make it work.""I know you will." Donna picks up her coffee again, then sets it down without drinking. She studies my face as if checking to see how I'm feeling about all this. "I'm not trying to push you into the deep end. I'm trying to give you the job you'll be good at. Help Junie feel steady. Help Remy remember that life is not only work and worry.""I can do that," I say quietly.Her smile warms. "I picked you because you are sunshine with a spine. Remy needs both."I let out a breath I didn't know I was holding. "Where do you want me to start today?""Start with the school pickup," she says. "Take Remy's truck. Keys are on the hook by the door. Use the card for whatever you need. If you run into anything strange, call me."She finally lifts the mug and finishes the last swallow. The lipstick print touches her lip in the same place. She looks less weary now, like sharing the weight lightened it. She squeezes my hand. "You are not here to clean up our mess. You are here to keep our family whole."I nod. "Understood.""Good." She collects her tote and her laptop, then pauses at the door. "Welcome home, Ivy."The word home lands soft and bright in my chest. I tuck it away and head for the hook by the door, keys chiming, a plan in my pocket and a little girl to meet at three.

I watch her speed down the driveway, and I turn and take in the house that looks like a tornado went through it. Glitter everywhere, toys, and half-completed art projects. Dishes piled high in the kitchen sink, and the dishwasher was also full and open. I think every single dish he owns is dirty. I survey the rooms and sigh. Well, Remy definitely needs help. The house is beautiful and updated. But the house appears sad and colorless. Basic. Not homey at all. However, Junie has her artwork proudly displayed on the fridge. I open the fridge, and it's full of old takeout containers and condiments. I can't really see any ingredients here to make meals. The freezer is about the same with some frozen food, quick meal stuff. I quickly make a list of my top favorite meals I can make and what I would need from the store and take a quick walk through the rest of the rooms. Junie's room is tidy, with a few toys out. She has a twin bed with stuffed animals around it and the unmade bed as if she had gotten up in a hurry. Her laundry basket is overflowing, so I take that and pull it towards the laundry room and get a load going.I walk down the hall to what looks like Remy's room at the end of the hall. I've never seen a sadder beige room. No personality at all. Plain. Also, an overflowing pile of clothes in the corner. He apparently doesn't like to do laundry or has no time. I bet it's the latter because from what I've seen and noticed about him, Remy's a great dad. Every time we've been at dinners and other places, he's always taking care of Junie, and she always seems like a happy and solid kid.I head out and get in Remy's truck since Derek was nice enough to keep the car he had leased under his name that I paid for. I make my way to town, jamming out to Taylor Swift—*I can do it with a broken heart.*

Because fuck Derek.

I can do anything with a broken heart. And honestly, I'm not so sure my heart is broken. I feel free.I get to the market and pop in and get everything on my list and some extra fun things for Junie. This kid and I are going to have a blast. I glance at my watch. Perfect. I still have plenty of time to get home, get everything put away, and get the house cleaned up.I quickly grab a peppermint mocha from the coffee shop on the edge of town and make my way back outside of town to Remy's tree farm. The wheels crunch over packed snow as I pull up the long, winding drive, with a bag of groceries bouncing in the passenger seat and my drink sloshing dangerously in the cup holder.

Bennett Tree Farm stretches out in front of me like something off a vintage Christmas card with evergreens dusted in powdered-sugar snow, the wooden sign at the entrance hand-painted and slightly crooked, like it's been there forever and doesn't need to prove anything. Row upon row of trees stand tall and proud. A row near the barn has branches twinkling with half-lit strands of bulbs, as if someone started decorating and never quite finished. I bet he could use help at the tree farm, too. And luckily for him, I have plenty of retail experience.But it's the house that really gets to me. It's beautiful, don't get me wrong. It's a classic white farmhouse style with navy shutters, a wraparound porch, and a wide front door the color of cranberry jam. There's even a swing hanging from one of the porch beams, creaking slightly in the winter wind. But something about it...

It doesn't *feel* like a home. Not really. There's no wreath on the door. No twinkle-lights in the windows. There's no holiday-themed mat in front of the door. The curtains are all drawn, and no one shoveled the driveway. It looks lonely. It looks like a place someone's *staying*, not somewhere they *live*. A place to sleep, eat, and exist. When I dream of having a home someday, I want all the cozy vibes. I want to dance in the kitchen with upbeat music always on. I want to leave love notes on the fridge and forget a mug on the windowsill. I want to make memories and have traditions. This house has so much potential for *life*.

My fingers tighten around the grocery bag, full of cookie dough ingredients, hot cocoa mix, and the ingredients to my top three favorite dinners that I hope they love.

This family's been through something. I can feel it in the walls, even from inside the truck.

And I don't know how long I'm staying here. I don't know if Remy Bennett even *wants* me here.

But I know one thing for certain. I'm going to make this place feel like it has Christmas magic again. It will be filled with the smell of fresh cookies, warmth, and glittery chaos. I'll string lights and hang mistletoe in inconvenient places. I'm going to make that little girl feel like she's the star of her own holiday movie. And maybe I'm going to make the grump in the flannel shirt remember what joy feels like. Even if he fights it every step of the way.

Because I have a feeling he will.

# Chapter 2
# Ivy

Music croons softly from the speaker in the corner, one of my favorite Christmas playlists of classic Bing Crosby melting into Mariah Carey like peppermint cocoa swirling in whipped cream. It's impossible not to get into the holiday mood with this playlist on. The washing machine hums from the mudroom, and I'm folding the last of Junie's socks into a little rainbow-stacked pile on the now-cleared-off dining room table. The same table that a few hours ago was buried in unopened mail, a half-empty toolbox with tools scattered, empty boxes, and a pinecone wreath craft still in a stage of assembly.

But not anymore. Now, this place smells like vanilla, orange peel, and clean linen. The fireplace crackles. I've got cookie ingredients laid out in neat little bowls like a Food Network witch who moonlights as a domestic goddess. The recipe's sitting in its little cookbook stand.

The second I hear the school bus brakes screech out front, my heart flutters. I don't know what's wrong with me, but this little girl has already carved herself a place in my heart that I didn't even know was empty. I want to be the best nanny that I can be to her.

The door bursts open. "IVY!!" Junie squeals when she sees me waiting as her backpack hits the floor with a thud, followed by the pitter-patter of snow-booted feet slamming into the hardwood. She launches herself across the room like a joyful human cannonball, flying straight into my arms.

"Oof!" I laugh, catching her with a spin. "There's my mermaid pirate!"

She buries her face in my shoulder, sinking into me with relief. "What are you doing here?"

I pull back just enough to smile at her. "Well, turns out I might be your new nanny. According to your Nana and your Dad." I add that last part, hoping it's actually true.

Junie gasps, eyes going wide with excitement. "Yes!!"

Then she looks around the kitchen and takes in the ingredients and recipe laid out. "Wait. Are we making *real* cookies?"

Her voice squeaks up two octaves, and her whole body wiggles with joy. She grabs my hands and jumps up and down, her puffy coat bouncing like she's a tiny Christmas marshmallow.

I nod, laughing. "That's the plan. But only if you go hang up your backpack and wash your hands first, you tiny tornado."

She's already halfway to the mudroom. "I'll do it! I'll be so fast! Don't start without me!"

"I wouldn't dream of it," I call after her. "I've been excited for this all day." I've spent time with Junie at the bookstore, and at family dinners because Donna and my mother are best friends. But I've never been with her at Remy's house.

While she's hanging up her coat and putting away her stuff, I pull out the last surprise: two matching Christmas aprons with dancing gingerbread pirates with candy cane swords.

When she returns, I hold one up with a grin. "Look what I got us!"

Her jaw drops. "We match?! That's the coolest thing ever."

She spins as if she's on the runway at a Paris bakery fashion show, then squeals and throws her arms around me again.

"You're the best witch-nanny EVER."

I press a kiss to her hair and whisper, "And you're the best cookie co-captain I've ever had."

She giggles, eyes sparkling, cheeks rosy from the cold and excitement.

We turn to the counter together, sleeves rolled up, Christmas music humming behind us like a scene straight out of a holiday movie.

And in that moment with flour in the air, joy buzzing between us, I swear the house already *feels* different. Lighter and warmer as if someone just opened a window and let Christmas back in.

I have a chicken casserole bubbling in the oven, golden cheese crisping on the edges just the way I like it. I've already folded the last load of laundry and sorted out all the bathroom linens that I'm currently washing and sorting. We made it into a game. Junie called it "Potion Ingredient Sorting," and I awarded her wizard points every time she folded a pile.

After dinner, we dance around the kitchen with the broom, cleaning up while Junie sings along to the "Jingle Bell Rock" remix like it's her Grammy debut.

Now the dishes are done, the counters are sparkling, and the floor is crumb-free. And there's a plate in the fridge labeled in Junie's handwriting because she insisted on adding a heart and a skull next to it. Just picturing Remy coming home is making me super nervous.

The house is glowing and cozy. I lit a brand-new candle I bought in town at one of my favorite witch shops as soon as the kitchen was spotless. Cinnamon, fir, and clove, with just a little enchantment woven into the wax. This house needs all of the magic it can get right now to bring it back to life. It flickers on the kitchen island now, casting a soft light across the room. The overhead lights are off, with only lamps to make it warm and golden.

Junie's curled up next to me on the couch in fuzzy socks and Christmas pajamas covered in dancing narwhals. She brushed her hair, and it's still damp from her bath. She brushed her teeth, and her face smells like bubblegum toothpaste and lavender soap.

We're watching *The Grinch*, and she's quiet. Not because she's tired, but because she's relaxed. Just the way every little kid should feel after a long day at school with a yummy dinner in her belly.

I wrap the blanket tighter around us and rest my cheek against the top of her head. Her body melts into mine like she's been waiting all day for this exact stillness.

Outside, snow falls in soft, steady flakes, coating the trees and the porch swing and the truck parked in front. Everything is hushed and wrapped up.

I breathe in the scent of her hair and the candle and the casserole still lingering in the air. Home. Yes, that's what this feels like. I had this at my house growing up.

This house felt cold when I got here. Not just in temperature, but in spirit. Like it was waiting for something. Or someone. Now? It feels better.

What would make it even better is if we decorated for Christmas.

* * *

I didn't mean to fall asleep on his couch. Really. My eyes are just resting, that's all. I feel like I've lived a dozen lives today, starting out in the Boston townhouse. And honestly, despite how it began, it ended up being a great day. Things feel a lot better now.

The house is quiet now. Junie went down easy after the movie, her tiny voice sleep-slurred with dreams and pirate songs. I read her three picture books. Okay, probably more like five. I can't say no to reading to a kid. And then she curled into her blanket with her stuffed narwhal and whispered, "Can you stay forever, Ivy?"

She said it like it was the most natural thing in the world.

That part might've been what made my heart swoon a little. Okay, a lot. And it caught me off guard. I brushed a curl out of her eyes and told her, "Let's get through this first week, okay?"

I think I passed out somewhere between "I'll just rest for a sec," and "I wonder if Remy has ever actually smiled."

Now the room is darker, the candle still flickering. My hand loosely clutches my phone. I blink against the fuzziness of sleep and stretch my legs before I realize something feels different. Someone is watching me. Someone tall and quiet. Someone who smells like snow, pine, and something sharp and clean and male.

I sit up with a small gasp, nearly dropping my phone. My heart jolts like a firework.

Remy Bennett is standing inside the kitchen, big and broad in every way. I knew he'd be home at one point, but nothing prepared me for the actual moment of us coming face to face. Alone in his house in the dark, at night.

He looks like a woodsy romance novel cover come to life. Flannel sleeves rolled to his forearms, jaw shadowed with end-of-the-day scruff. His hair is messy and windblown, and he's looking at me like he's trying to solve a problem he didn't know existed until he opened his front door.

"What are you doing here?" His voice is rough and low. "Where's my mom?"

I blink, my mouth opening slightly before my brain catches up. "She said she had deadlines, and that you knew I was starting today. Which I can tell that...you obviously did not."

His brow furrows. He stares like he's not sure if I'm real or just part of a really inconvenient dream.

"What exactly did she tell you?" he asks, as if still catching up.

"She said today was my first day as your new nanny," I reply, standing now. My joints pop, and I smooth my shirt down over my leggings nervously. "Said you needed someone, and she was behind on her book."

"She hired you to be my nanny?" He looks surprised, with a flash of irritation in his eyes.

"Pretty much. It was more of a classic Donna drive-by. One minute I'm in Boston with Derek, the next minute I'm up here with Junie. She said you wanted me."

That earns me a flicker of something on his face, but it passes quickly.

"As your nanny, I mean," I reply nervously.

*Geez, Ivy, get it together. He definitely doesn't want me. I'm not sure he's even an actual human. More like a grumpy cyborg.*

He steps farther into the living room, glancing toward the hallway. "She's asleep?"

I nod. "Out cold. Brushed teeth, bedtime stories, the full shebang. She was a champ. You've got a great kid, Remy."

He rubs a hand over the back of his neck, suddenly looking tired in a way that has nothing to do with physical labor. "I just wasn't expecting someone else to be here."

"I figured Donna was up to something," I say gently,

standing and moving to the doorway to the hallway. "I should have tried calling you to confirm."

He checks his phone and grimaces. "Wouldn't have mattered, anyway. Dead. Left it in the truck while I was loading orders."

There's a long pause. Not uncomfortable, just heavy. Like the silence between people who are strangers but also...not. Not really. Remy and I cross paths plenty. We've spent holidays with our family group, and I've seen him and Junie often. He's just never really talked to me like this before, and I've never been in his space like this.

Willa and Tate have told me about Remy's legendary pizza nights; however, I've never received an invitation. I've always been on the fringe with Remy. He keeps me at a distance, and I've always wondered why.

"Look," I say, breaking the quiet. "I didn't mean to overstep. So I'll pack up and head over to Willa's. It's late, but I don't think they'll mind letting me crash on their couch until morning."

He blinks as if I've spoken another language. "You're not going anywhere. It's freezing out there."

He says it in that low, steady voice, firm and no-nonsense, the kind that does not need to get louder to make you listen. The words slide under my skin and heat coils low in my stomach.

*Okay, Remy.* Apparently the quiet, broody tree farmer has a commanding streak, and my body is very much on board. Noted. Fantasies updated accordingly.

"I don't want to impose," I repeat, unsure of how this is supposed to go.

He doesn't answer, just looks around the room. At the folded laundry. The clean counters, empty sink.

"Where are your bags? He asks.

"Doesn't matter. I'm just going to walk to Willa's. I'm sure she can just give me a ride to my mom's..." I turn and a hand gently holds my arm and keeps me in place. My skin tingles under his hand.

"Bags," he demands, staring at me, not giving in.

"They're by the door. I know you don't really like me," I continue nervously, running my mouth like an idiot.

He freezes, and I continue... "I can just head out. I'll figure it out."

"What did you just say?" he asks.

"I...I'm just gonna go. It's fine. Tell Junie I had so much fun tonight, and I'm sorry I couldn't stay." I turn toward hook where my coat is hanging.

"Why do you think I don't like you?" he asks, searching my eyes.

I stare into his and take a deep breath. "I don't know, Remy. I'm just gonna go. I'm sorry for the mix up."

"You should stay," he says, voice low. "I have a guest room. It's not fancy, but it's clean and it's got a full-sized bed. Finn stayed there before he moved to town."

I blink. "You sure?"

He nods once. "Yeah. It's late. No reason for you to wake up Willa and Tate."

I open my mouth to say something, but he's already stalking toward my bags. He grabs the heaviest one, picks it up like it's nothing, grabs the rest without a word and heads down the hall.

Just like that. No argument or a thank you. Just Remy, alpha hottie Bennett, carrying my bags like a man on a mission, leaving me no choice but to follow.

The guest room smells of cedar and stale energy. Not bad, just...untouched. Like time paused here a while ago and no one pressed play again.

It's cozy in the way before someone moves in. Blank walls. A full-sized bed tucked under a sloped ceiling. A little bathroom with a white curtain around the old-fashioned claw foot tub. There's a heater in the corner, already humming to life as soon as Remy flips the switch.

"I haven't been in here in a while," he says. "The heat usually kicks in after a few minutes."

I nod, hugging my arms close. "It's great. Thank you."

He disappears into the hall and comes back with a stack of folded linens in his arms. They look freshly laundered, crisp and warm from wherever they've been hiding. So, Remy does do laundry. He hands them to me, and for a second our fingers touch.

It's barely anything. Just skin brushing skin. But something flickers through me. I thank him quickly and glance away, trying to ignore the sudden heat crawling up my neck.

He says nothing, just watches me. And when I glance back up, I see it. Not annoyance or frustration, but loneliness. It's there in the tired set of his jaw. The quiet ache hiding behind those gray eyes. There's sadness in him, too. The kind that settles deep. But underneath it...something else. A pull I can't quite name.

I tilt my head, surprised by how much I want to understand him. What is he carrying that makes him so lonely? Why do I feel like I want to know more about him?

"Ideally, I'm out the door by six most mornings," he says, voice low. "Junie's bus comes at eight-ten. Are you okay with getting her up and out?"

I nod, relieved that he's letting me stay on. "Of course."

He gives a quick nod back, like that's all the confirmation he needs.

"Thanks...for everything," he adds, and just like that, he's already moving toward the door.

I watch him go, with the way he fills the doorway without even trying, his shoulders broad and his posture tense. Even his walk has weight to it, like he's bracing for something that might never happen.

And then he's gone, the door clicking gently behind him.

I'm alone again. I let out a long breath and set the linens on the bed. The mattress squeaks a little as I strip off the stiff old sheets and replace them with the soft flannel ones he gave me. Snowflake print that's faded, but cozy.

The heater rattles in the corner, yet it's still cold.

I find an extra quilt in the closet and toss it on top of the bed, then add another. It feels like nesting. Like carving out a pocket of warmth in a life that's still unsettling.

The shower is a little too chilly, but I crank the water up, anyway. The pressure's decent, and the mirror fogs in seconds, and I wrap myself in a towel and brush my teeth with my feet curled against the cold tile floor.

When I finally crawl into bed, I'm wearing layers and burrowed under enough blankets to survive a blizzard. My phone buzzes once on the nightstand, but I ignore it. The silence is heavier now.

The heater hums, and snow falls outside the window in slow, patient rhythms.

I close my eyes, not sure what tomorrow will bring. Not sure what this job is becoming or how I ended up in Wisteria Cove with a single dad and a little girl who already feels like someone I'm meant to take care of.

But I know one thing. That man is carrying too much. And for the first time in a long time, I think maybe I'm exactly where I'm supposed to be.

# Chapter 3
# Remy

The door to my guest room clicks shut behind me, and I stand in the silence for a beat before heading down the hall. My feet feel heavy on the cold wood floor, my limbs twice as tired as usual from the long day.

The order backlog and more snow on the way had me working a double. I'm behind on everything and have so many things I still need to take care of here at home. Most days, I feel like I'm juggling plates, and they're all crashing down one by one. I can't get ahead or keep up, no matter what I do.

But then I did a double take when I walked into the kitchen earlier and looked around. It was like Mary Freaking Poppins had been here. For a second I wondered if I was in the wrong house. I'm grateful for my mom and Finn's help, but I know I rely on them too much during my busy season. I need help. They both have their own jobs and lives and can't be running to help me with mine all the time. It makes me even angrier with myself that I can't keep it together.

I pause in the doorway of Junie's room. Because she likes her door cracked, the hall light spilling across the rug, I gently nudge it open and lean against the door frame. She's out cold, hair fanned across the pillow, arms wrapped around her stuffed narwhal, cheeks flushed. The blanket's pulled up to her chin, and there's a little smile playing on her lips like her dreams are made of candy canes and mermaid treasure maps and all the things that make her happy. I can't wait to hear all about them tomorrow.

I step inside and crouch beside her bed. Carefully, I press a kiss to her forehead and brush a strand of hair from her eyes. She shifts but doesn't wake. The room smells clean, like lavender, maybe. The mermaid night-light glows softly in the corner. She never organizes her bookshelf that way on her own, even though she wants me to. It's in rainbow order with every spine lined up as if someone had taken the time to sort them. Like someone cared enough to do it right.

*Ivy.*

Her dresser drawers are closed. No socks spill out and no clothes on the floor. I open one quietly and see everything folded, small and neat. She laid out her outfit for the morning at the foot of the bed. A soft red sweater. Jeans. Glittery socks.

I don't even know where Ivy found those socks. I stand there for a second longer than I mean to. Then, I quietly pull the door almost shut and turn toward the kitchen, the knot in my chest lighter than it was when I came home.

I haven't eaten since this morning, and I didn't even realize it until the smell of something delicious hit me the second I stepped through the front door. I figured it was left over from whatever they had earlier.

I open up the fridge and see a plate wrapped in foil. A little sticky note slapped on top in pink marker with a skull and heart drawn below it.

**"FOR DAD. Eat it or we hex you. -Junie and Ivy**

I let out a laugh. Then, I peel back the foil and close my eyes. Chicken casserole, and it smells like heaven.

The counters are clean, and the sink is empty. The table is bare except for a candle I don't remember owning. There are no piles of mail or dirty dishes stacked next to the sink. The floor's been swept. Hell, the rug even has vacuum lines on it. I don't remember the last time this room felt like something more than a space we just pass through on the way to doing something else. Right now, it feels like coming home to an actual home. Hell, she did this in one day.

I heat the food and eat standing up, one hand braced against the counter. I barely taste it. I just inhale it like a man who's been starving and didn't know it. Every bite unravels a little more tension from my spine. The long day melts off of me.

I finish, rinse the plate, and tuck it in the dishwasher that, somehow, is empty, all the dishes done and put away. Then I lean back against the counter, cross my arms, and look around. I thought about telling her tomorrow that I didn't need her. That I didn't need anyone. I should be able to take care of my house and kid.

But I need someone who can pick up the pieces when I can't. Someone who can remember to fold the towels, keep the library books from being overdue, and make dinner that doesn't come from a box in the freezer.

Junie needs Ivy here. She deserves this, and I know I realistically can't do it all. And it makes me mad that I can't. I wanted to give Junie everything and not have her feel like she was missing out on anything. But I know I can't. I can't give Junie the Christmas that she deserves or the home that feels like this.

I never thought help would show up like this, all light and warmth in a way that cuts right through me. She's smart, sure, but that's not what gets to me. It's the way she shines, the way

Ivy brings life into every room she walks into. I wonder idly what happened to her bonehead boyfriend.

Frankly, I don't care as long as he's gone.

I've caught myself watching her at her mom's table, or in the bookstore, and sometimes I almost believe I could have that kind of brightness in my life.

But she doesn't belong here, not in this quiet ruin I've made of things. Not in the wreckage of everything I've failed to give Junie since her mom left us. She deserves more than shadows, and that's all I seem to have left.

But she's here. And somehow...everything feels lighter after just one night.

I grab my phone, which I had thrown on the charger in the kitchen, and step out onto the quiet back porch. The cold slaps my face, but I like it. It helps me focus. Helps me push past the part of myself that wants to crawl back into my shell and ignore what's happening.

I scroll to my mom's name and hit call. I know she'll pick up because she usually stays up late writing, like the night owl that she is. That was part of the problem. Having her come here early in the morning was hard on her. No wonder she advocated for Ivy so hard. She picks up on the first ring. "I was wondering when you'd get around to thanking me," she says, voice bright, cheerful, and entirely too smug.

"I believe you forgot to loop me into your plan," I tell her. "I thought you were staying with Junie tonight."

"I have a book due. Ivy stepped up."

"You hired her without checking with me. I could've just taken Junie to the barn with me."

"I did it because, you know, Junie needs this. Visiting the barn occasionally is fine. But I am guessing she had a fun time with Ivy, even though you don't want to admit it. She needs to be at home and have a routine and be on a schedule," she says in her authoritative mom voice.

"That's not the point," I mutter, pacing the porch. "I don't need a stranger in my house."

"Ivy's not a stranger; she's family. She's known Junie for a long time. And more importantly? *You* need her."

I silently fume because she's right.

"She did lovely tonight, didn't she?" Donna asks. "I bet she even got Junie to go brush her teeth without a fight, didn't she? And Ivy is a wonderful cook. I bet she even made a great meal? And now Junie is fast asleep?"

I close my eyes and sigh. "Yeah. She seems good."

"Then stop fighting it."

"She's not permanent," I argue.

"She doesn't have to be. Why can't she stay through the holidays? Help you get your feet back under you? You're barely getting by, Remy, and you know it. You can't keep going like this."

I run a hand through my hair. "I don't want Junie to get used to someone who's just going to leave."

"You're overthinking this, son. It's a win-win. Ivy needs this, Junie needs this, and God knows you need this. Just embrace it," she says, sounding tired. I know she's also burning the candle at both ends right now, which is why I feel guilty that I had asked her to help so much.

I run a hand over my face and stare up at the stars.

"She's not Sloane, sweetheart. You've got this farm and Junie to think about," she says quietly.

"I won't let us get burned again," I say adamantly.

She sighs. "You always were a stubborn old goat."

I grunt.

"Let her stay," she says. "You don't have to marry her. Just let her keep you from drowning."

"Fine," I grunt. "But if she does anything out of line, she's gone."

My mom laughs, "Yeah, like Ivy would. She's a saint."

"I gotta get to bed. Talk to you tomorrow, Mom."

"Go easy on her!" she calls before ending the call.

Inside, the house is quiet again. Peaceful and lonely. The usual.

I shower, hot water sluicing down my back until the tension finally breaks and my body feels like jelly. I scrub off the sawdust and sweat, the pine sap, and the guilt. I dry off and crawl into bed without checking my phone again.

And for the first time in a long time, I don't feel like the weight of the world is going to crush me in my sleep.

I just feel... tired. But not alone. I drift off to sleep, staring up at the ceiling and wondering what Ivy must think of me. An older single dad who can't get his act together, whose wife left him. Yeah, I'm a real winner here.

* * *

The phone rings while I'm wrapping a pallet of trees to send to Boston. I glance at the display, and my stomach tightens when I see that it's Junie's school.

I was wide awake at four a.m. So I got up and out the door extra early, getting ahead of the day so I could get home earlier to Junie tonight. Plus, I didn't want to run into Chaos, aka Ivy, who kept me wondering about her down the hall from my room.

I couldn't stop thinking about what she said about me not liking her. Why would she think that? I've always thought Ivy was easily one of the most beautiful and special people I've ever met. Way out of my league, but a great person. She's always been great to my kid, and she's like a ray of sunshine to my pitch black. We're just opposites.

"This is Remy Bennett." I answer, worry filling me that something might have happened to Junie.

"Hi, Mr. Bennett, it's Ms. Clarke from Wisteria Cove Elementary."

Junie's teacher. My gut tightens more. "Everything okay?" I ask hesitantly.

There's a pause. "Junie's fine. But..."

I brace myself. "But?"

"There was an incident at recess. Junie was, uh...baiting seagulls."

I blink. "What?"

"With gummy worms," Ms. Clarke says, her voice a mix of disbelief and resignation. "And...she caught one with her bare hands."

I pull the phone away from my ear for a second, stare at it, then bring it back. Surely I didn't hear that right.

"It did bite her, but not hard. She's fine. The bird is fine. We're...mostly fine." She clears her throat. "But we had to file an incident report, and we wanted to let you know."

My hand comes up to cover my face, but I can't stop the laugh that escapes.

"She also named it Sully," Ms. Clarke adds, like that's an important piece of evidence in the story. "We were hoping you could talk to her about this again."

I put my head in my hand, chuckling into my palm, trying to keep it together. "Thank you for calling and letting me know. I'll talk to her."

When I hang up, I let the phone drop onto the counter and scrub my face with both hands, shaking with laughter. My kid is never boring, that's for sure.

"Something funny?"

I look up, and Ivy is standing inside the door, cheeks pink from the cold, a little puff of breath hanging in the air before it vanishes. The knit hat with the ridiculous pompom sits crooked on her head, and her hair spills out around her shoulders in loose waves that look warm even when the room is not. Snow crystals cling to a few strands and catch the light. Her eyes find mine and go soft. Her mouth curves, full, and I feel something shift under my ribs.

She is bundled in a simple coat, zip half done. Black leggings tucked into worn boots that have seen their share of salt and slush. Nothing fancy, yet she looks amazing. She steps farther in and the scent of cold air and something sweet moves with her, like sugar and pine.

The way she tucks a strand of hair behind her ear should not take my breath, but it does. The way her green eyes flick over the room and then come back to me like I'm the answer she was looking for—that's what does me in. She's adorable in her hat and the too-long sleeves.

She's breathtaking in the way she carries herself, steady and open, like she belongs anywhere she decides to stand. It does not matter what she's wearing. She could walk in here in that sweater or in a dress or in old flannel, and I would feel the same punch. She's just...Ivy. She steps into my space and knocks the air right out of me.

She hefts a big brown paper bag from a grocery store onto the counter and beams. "I brought you some things, and I'm looking for your Christmas decorations, and I can't find them anywhere. I thought Junie and I could make the place a little more festive after school."

She continues, and I can't really follow everything she's saying because I watch her walk around and take in the shop, smiling and chatting away, and I can't take my eyes off of her.

"Decorations are in the shed behind the house," I say, my voice coming out gruffer than I mean. Then I clear my throat and say, "I can get them later and put them in the garage if you want to look through them. I don't have time to decorate."

She tilts her head, studying me for a beat, like she can read the shift in me. "You don't want to help?"

"I've got a lot to do." It is not a lie, but it is not the reason. The real reason is her. Being around her makes my thoughts drift to places they should not go. To things I can't have. It did not start last week or even this fall. It started the first time she laughed at Junie's knock-knock joke and then bent to tie Junie's boot because the lace kept dragging through the slush.

It started the night I saw her in the bookstore window, head tipped toward Willa as they worked together.

It started in quiet ways that stacked up. The way she listens with her whole face. The way she notices the small things that make a day easier and then does them without asking for credit.

The way she talks to people like they matter. Even when they don't deserve it.

Derek the dickhead did not deserve any of that sweetness. I watched her try to make that mess work with a man who did not look up when she walked into a room. I saw her get smaller every time he brushed her off. That is the kind of thinking she brings out in me. I notice everything.

So I stayed back. Out of respect and self-preservation. Because it is one thing to want someone you cannot have. It is another to want them while they are standing beside a man who does not see them, and to pretend you feel nothing while you watch. I kept my distance because Junie needs steady, and I don't invite storms into my house. I kept my distance because if I let myself reach for Ivy once, I don't know that I would stop.

So yes, I have work to do. There is always work. But the truth sits right under it. If I don't put space between us, I'll start imagining a life I don't get to have, and I am not sure I could hide it if I did.

She smiles a little, but there's something in her eyes, something that says she knows I'm keeping her at arm's length. "All right. Junie and I can handle it."

I nod and stare at her, my eyes cutting away before it gets weird.

"What were you laughing at when I walked in?" She asks as she stands close enough for me to notice that she smells really good. She leans in and smiles at me that practically makes me come unglued. Her big green eyes meet mine, and her head tilts a little.

I lean back against the counter, still trying to get the image of my kid wrestling a seagull out of my head. "Junie was baiting seagulls at recess."

"Baiting them?"

"With gummy worms." I confirm.

Her lips twitch as if she's already trying not to laugh. "Oh, no."

"And she caught one. With her bare hands."

Ivy gasps, and then she laughs, a full, warm, head-tipped-back laugh. "You're kidding."

"She named it Sully."

That does it. She doubles over against the counter, giggling so hard. "Oh my God, I love her."

My heart surges when she says that.

I shake my head, still smiling despite myself.

Ivy straightens, cheeks flushed from laughing, eyes bright. "She's a great kid. I really love being with her. I promise I'll do a good job as her nanny."

Something in my chest shifts. I've heard people say nice things about Junie before. Her teachers, my mom, neighbors and friends, but not like this. Not with the warmth that Ivy has.

I watch the curve of her plump lips still tipped into a smile, her cheeks flushed from the cold. Her dark red hair catches the light from the window. She's beautiful. God, she probably doesn't even know how beautiful she is.

And that's the problem. I *know* how beautiful she is. I can't be catching feelings for the temporary nanny.

I pull my gaze away, busying myself with the tangled set of lights on the counter. The last thing I need is her thinking I'm standing here staring at her like some idiot.

She nudges the bag towards me and smiles, then turns and heads toward the door. I keep my eyes on the counter, not watching the way her hips sway or the way her laugh echoes a little in the shop when she turns to head out.

"See you tonight," she says over her shoulder, like it's already a given.

"Thanks," I call gruffly.

I don't let myself think about how easily she could fit into our life here. How easily she fits with Junie. Because if I do, I'll forget all the reasons I told myself to keep her on the other side of whatever invisible line I've drawn.

I don't need someone getting too close. I don't need Junie getting attached to someone who might not stick around. And I sure as hell don't need the distraction of the prettiest woman I've ever seen, standing in my shop, talking about decorating like it's the most important thing in the world.

I pull the bag closer and see a homemade lunch she's packed for me. A double-thick sandwich that looks gourmet, chips, a container of cut up fruit and carrots. One of my favorite energy drinks and a bottle of water are at the bottom.

Whoa. I've never had anyone do anything like this for me before. My mom isn't much of a cook, so we mostly do takeout and frozen meals. I can cook, but mostly I'm too tired to cook here lately.

I try to focus on my work and eat my lunch, which is amazing. Keep my hands busy, my mind on the orders, the deliveries, the thousand other things that have to get done before the holiday rush.

But really, there's just one thing on my mind.

*Ivy*.

# Chapter 4
# Ivy

**I**'m cutting an apple for Junie's after-school snack when I ask the question. "So, what are your favorite holiday traditions that you and your dad have?"

She swings her legs under the table, chewing the piece of cheddar cheese I sliced on her plate. She swallows, then shrugs. "We usually do pizza night on Fridays, but Dad's too busy now."

"I've heard about your legendary pizza nights," I say, smiling. "But what about during Christmas? What do you do for fun?"

Another shrug. "We don't really do much. Not like the other kids in my class do."

The way she says it makes something pinch deep in my chest. Casual and matter-of-fact. Like she's already decided not to expect more. The kid lives on a Christmas tree farm and doesn't have a magical Christmas? Unreal. We have to change that.

I lean my elbows on the table. "Well, what if we did something really special this year? Christmas is basically the perfect excuse for having so much fun."

Her eyes light up, cautious but curious. "Like what?"

"Like everything. Hot cocoa. Homemade marshmallows are the best, and you can do almost any flavor. Movie marathons. Cookies in ridiculous shapes. Staying up way too late to watch for Santa. Driving around to see the best lights in town. Snow angels. Drying oranges to hang over the windows so the entire house smells amazing." I'm breathless; I'm so excited thinking about it all.

Junie leans forward and asks me dreamily. "Can we do all of that?"

"Absolutely," I say, already heading for the craft cupboard. "I have an idea. We're going to make a *map*."

She perks up even more. "Like a treasure map?"

I shrug. "You know what? Yeah, like a treasure map. Why not? We can call it whatever you want."

I organized this cabinet earlier today and repurposed old yogurt containers for paintbrushes and made it so Junie can find things for her art projects easier. This kid loves to do crafts, and I wanted to make everything easier for her to find.

Ten minutes later, the dining table is covered in a giant sheet of beige butcher paper that runs from one end to the other. Markers, glue sticks, scissors, and every color of construction paper I could find are scattered across the surface.

Junie's in charge of drawing the treasure chest at the top of the page with gold coins spilling out with little snowflakes mixed in. I work on big bubble letters: **The Bennett Family Holiday Treasure Map**.

Every time we think of a tradition, Junie practices copying it down in her careful, crooked handwriting, complete with pictures, so she knows what's what.

*Christmas lights tour*
*Hot cocoa and homemade marshmallows*
*Cozy fires with story time*

*Christmas movie marathons with popcorn*
*Bake cookies for the neighbors*
*Make paper snowflakes for every window*
*Gingerbread house contest*
*Snowball fight (if weather cooperates)*
*Decorate the tree with only the weirdest ornaments we can find*
*Ugly sweater party*
*Make a snowman*
*Orange slices hung across the windows*

When the list is done, we make little paths between each tradition, winding like a pirate map. I add tiny doodles as we go with mugs of cocoa, candy canes, holly berries. Junie draws a giant Santa hat on the treasure chest and announces it "done."

We march out to the garage, armed with flashlights, and dig through the stack of boxes marked **Christmas** in thick black marker that Remy left for us. Some lids are dusty. The tape is peeling. I pop one open and find an avalanche of ornaments, some shiny and new, some clearly from decades ago when Remy was little.

Junie gasps like she's discovered buried gold. "We have so much stuff!"

"We have *everything*," I say excitedly. "And we're going to use it all."

Over the next few hours, the house transforms. We hang garland along the staircase and wrap the banister with twinkle lights. Junie finds an old box of ornaments shaped like tiny sleds and hangs them in a row across the mantle. I set a big bowl of pinecones on the coffee table and tuck in sprigs of greenery.

We put on Christmas music at almost full volume. I teach Junie how to slice oranges thin for drying, and I explain to her how we're going to thread them with twine between strands of white lights. They glow like little suns once we hang them across the kitchen windows.

We drag the boxes from room to room while I arrange wreaths and fill mason jars with cinnamon sticks and cloves. She insists on wearing the Santa hat we found in one box, even though it keeps slipping over her eyes.

By the time we finish, the house doesn't just look different. It *feels* different. It's as if Christmas had been waiting in those boxes all along.

We stand back in the living room, side by side, looking at the decorations everywhere.

Junie grins. "It looks like a Christmas wonderland. We just need a tree."

I grin back. "That's because it is. We can ask your dad about that."

She hugs me, "Thank you, Ivy. This is going to be the best Christmas ever."

* * *

It's past nine when I finally head down the hall to my room. I'm tired in a satisfying way that comes from making something beautiful.

I take a quick shower to wash off the dust and glitter from the day. My cheeks are still warm from all the laughter, my hair smelling faintly of oranges and cinnamon.

I climb into bed with my phone and call my mom. She answers on the second ring.

"Well, if it isn't Buddy the Christmas Elf herself," she says.

I laugh. "I think I might be. This nanny job is...honestly, it's amazing."

"I talked to Donna earlier," Mom says, voice softening. "She says you're doing great. Junie called her and couldn't stop talking about how much fun she's having with you decorating."

The words hit something tender in me. "Yeah, she was excited to talk to her Nana tonight. I'm glad she's having fun."

"Donna sounded impressed. Said you've already made a difference."

I smile into the dark, pulling the blankets tighter around me. "It doesn't feel like a job. It feels like...I don't know. Like I'm exactly where I'm supposed to be."

"Well, I'm glad you're happy, sweetie. Have you heard from Derek about getting your things and Lola?" she asks.

I close my eyes at hearing his name. "No. I wish I could get my stuff, and that he'd let me have Lola."

"Well, hang on, honey, let me see if I can work some magic," she says in an ominous tone.

"Oh, Mom," I laugh.

* * *

I can't sleep because I have so much running through my head.

I pull on socks and pad down the stairs, careful not to wake Junie. The house is dark except for a few lamps and lights, their soft glow spilling across the living room and catching on the garland we hung along the banister. The oranges we strung over the windows look like tiny lanterns, and for a second, I stand there and just...breathe it in. The place feels different now. Like someone poured Christmas into all the corners that used to be empty.

I head into the kitchen, open the fridge, and grab the milk. Hot cocoa always helps me sleep. I set a pot on the stove and hum to myself as I wait for it to heat.

That's when the door opens. Cold air rushes in, carrying the scent of snow and pine. I turn, startled, and there's Remy, stepping in from the mudroom. He's in a hoodie and worn jeans, boots dusted with snow, his hair mussed from the wind. There's a streak of sawdust on one sleeve, and he smells faintly of fresh-cut wood.

For a moment, I have a thought of what it might feel like for him to come home and kiss me and pull me into his arms.

I shake that off and pull myself together.

He stops just inside the kitchen, his gaze moving past me to the living room.

I follow his eyes. He's taking it all in with the lights, the garland, the oranges glowing in the window like he's not sure what he's looking at.

"You were busy," he says finally. His voice is quiet, not gruff exactly, but cautious.

"Yeah, we had a lot of fun," I shrug as I try not to stare at him too long.

*Be cool, Ivy, be cool.*

He stares at me and takes in the house, his eyes landing on different things like he's cataloging it in his mind.

"She said you don't really do much for Christmas, so...I thought we could decorate and make some plans."

His gaze shifts to me, and he looks guilty. "She told you that?"

"She wasn't upset about it." I glance at him over my shoulder. "But she's had a lot of fun."

He just stands there, hands in his pockets, watching me like he's trying to figure out my angle.

"You didn't have to do all this," he says."I know." I shrug and lift the mug to my lips. "But I wanted to. We had fun."He shakes his head when I nudge a second mug toward him. No thanks. His gaze tracks the cup in my hands instead. I take a sip and the steam curls against my mouth. He steps closer. Slow. Deliberate. My breath sticks.Without a word, he reaches for my mug. His fingers skim mine and a spark jumps in my stomach. He brings the cup to his mouth, blows lightly across the surface, then drinks from the same spot I did, eyes on mine the entire time. Heat climbs my throat. My knees go traitor soft.He lowers the mug, slides it back toward me, and our fingers brush again. The room feels small and bright. I am suddenly very aware of my mouth, and the way he is looking at it."Careful," he says, voice low. "It's still hot."I'm not at all sure he means the chocolate.I clear my throat, trying to be cool, but there's literally no cool in me right now. Zip. Zilch. "Junie and I made a Christmas tradition map," I tell him, turning back to my mug. "You can save it for next year, too."

His eyes widen briefly, and he looks away. I wonder what he's thinking.

"She loves the oranges," I add. "She kept standing back to admire them like she was looking at fireworks."

That earns the smallest tug at the corner of his mouth. It's not quite a smile, but it's enough to make me want to keep chasing it.

"She's a great kid, Remy." I say softly. "You've done a good job."

He stares into his cocoa for a long moment. "Yeah, she is." His voice is quieter now, almost reverent.

We stand there in the soft glow of the lights, sipping cocoa. I sneak glances at him when I think he's not looking. It's unfair how sexy he looks without even trying. Every time I'm around him, I feel like I notice something new about him and...I love it. His dark lashes, that perpetually serious expression. But tonight there's something else underneath it. Something almost... unguarded. Like he's thawing.

He catches me looking, and for a heartbeat neither of us looks away.

"Are you cold?" he asks, nodding toward the flannel shirt I threw on over my pajamas.

I shrug. "I'm fine."

"I'll check the heater. Sometimes it gets colder in your room," he says.

"Thanks," I say.

He takes another sip of cocoa and says, "Thanks...for today. For keeping her happy."

Something warm blooms in my chest at the words. "Anytime."

He sets his empty mug in the sink and glances toward the living room again. His eyes linger on the garland over the front door, the wreath over the mantle, the twinkle of the lights. I don't know whether he likes it. He heads down the hall without another word, and I watch him go, his broad frame filling the doorway. He moves like a man carrying too much, but tonight... maybe it's just a little less.

The room is warmer now. I curl under the blankets, my hair still smelling faintly of oranges, my chest still warm from cocoa and the smallest crack in Remy Bennett's armor.

He's not exactly warm yet, but we'll get there.

But maybe...just maybe...I've started the fire.

# Chapter 5
# Remy

My brother Finn's truck pulls up just before sunrise, and he strides into the barn like he's on a mission. He claps me on the shoulder, steals my wrench, and starts inspecting the tree shaker like he's the supervisor and I'm his employee. "You look less feral today," he says, eying me. "Did you finally sleep over four hours, or is it because of your new nanny everyone's talking about?"

"Be quiet and help me fix this."

I grumble with frustration at the machine that stopped working. I can fix most things, but Finn can fix *anything*. He builds what he cannot buy and turns rough boards into furniture that belongs in a magazine.

He laughs, works in silence for a minute, then glances toward the main house and asks more seriously, "How is Ivy doing with Junie?"

"Fine." I ignore what he's implying and check the order board. We are behind, but not in the weeds, thanks to my getting a head start today with Ivy here, who helped Junie get on the bus this morning.

Finn's mouth tips into a smirk. "Saw she turned your house

into a literal Christmas snow globe last night. Junie sent me and Mom pictures from her tablet."

"I noticed," I say, pretending to be chill. But I more than noticed; I freaking loved it. Coming home to a home-cooked meal and a house that looks and smells great is a dream come true.

The tree farm was our uncle Carl's, and a place that I've always loved. As a kid, I came here as often as I could and worked alongside my uncle until I went off to college. And on every break, I was back here helping him. I loved being around him. He was pretty exceptional. He got sick and died a few years ago and left the farm to Finn and me. Finn had no interest, so I bought him out, and now it's all mine. Finn's out here all the time using the back barn to work on his woodworking projects, and I love having him around. Working on the farm here reminds me of our uncle and brings back good memories. It feels like he's still here sometimes.

"How's the new house?" I ask, trying to change the subject, because I know he is itching to give me even more crap about Ivy and get under my skin, as brothers do. He recently purchased our friend Tate's childhood home and has been slowly renovating it. Tate took a job out here as the tree farm manager and moved into a cabin on the back of the farm with his girlfriend, Willa, Ivy's sister.

"It's going. Not as fast as I'd like—been busy with Rowan's new shop," he says, and then catches himself and gives me a sideways look because he knows I could give him crap about Rowan. But I won't. I've got too much on my mind to give him crap and shoot the shit.

Rowan is Ivy's sister and is opening a new apothecary shop next to Willa's bookstore, Wisteria Books & Brew.

"It'll get there," I tell him. "I'm heading out to help Tate with today's load. Appreciate your help."

"I'll come down and help. I got a little bit of time this morning before I meet with the painters and Rowan," he grunts as he twists some bolts into place.

I nod and zip up my coat and head out into the cold, Finn following me to the truck. The tree lot stretches in rows of green, neat and waiting. It should make me feel calm. It usually does. Today, though, my thoughts keep going back to Ivy. I wonder what she's doing and what they have planned for after school. What dinner she's going to make. I shake myself out of it and remind myself that this is temporary. I shouldn't get used to it or get too excited.

Luckily, we have enough work to keep busy. Tate, Finn, and I load two fresh pallets onto the flatbed for Tate to deliver to a store in a nearby town. By the time we're finished and heading to the farm store, Junie is on the bus and on her way to school, and the sun is fully up, casting a clear, pale light across the porch of the small farm stand building from which we sell just about every tree farm souvenir you can think of.

I hit the brakes and back up. There are bins of vintage ornaments I don't remember setting out or owning. The chalkboard sign is neat, as if someone took the time to hand-letter it perfectly. *What the hell?*

The door to the farm stand swings open, and Ivy steps out, a bright green scarf looped twice around her neck, hair in a messy knot. I catch myself wanting to reach over and release it and run my fingers through that dark red hair that catches my breath every time I look at her.

What is she doing here at the farm store?

She's dragging a display table by herself, and it's heavy. She braces her boots and nudges it an inch at a time.

Finn jumps out to help her. He turns and yells with a smirk, "You gonna help or keep admiring the view?"

I shake my head and glare at him as I climb out of my truck.

"What are you doing?" I clip as I watch her make herself at home, decorating the farm store.

She looks up, her bright green eyes catching me off guard. "Rearranging. Your flow is weird. Customers bottleneck at the candle shelf and never make it to the hot drinks, which is now cocoa since the cider urn was on life support. Finn's going to fix it."

"My flow is what?" I ask, confused. And we don't have a candle shelf. What is she talking about?

"Come see." She waves us in as if we work for her. And I follow because, honestly, I'd follow Ivy anywhere. She could rearrange my trees out in the grove, and I'd probably let her. But I'd definitely gripe and complain about it and not admit it to anyone.

Inside the farm stand, the air smells like oranges and chocolate. She has pulled the old wire racks into a long loop that actually makes sense. Small items like stuffed reindeer and Santas are displayed near the register in woven baskets, which makes me even feel more inclined to buy them with the heavier things against the walls. Someone cleared the counter. The ancient tip jar has a ribbon tied around it and a small sign that says 'Thank you' in Junie's handwriting, accompanied by a snowman doodle.

A big circular candle display is in the middle, with candles in boxes around it. Where the hell did those all come from?

I hate that I dropped the ball in not making this look better. I have two highschoolers from town who help part-time, but they just run the cash register and keep the drink station filled. I haven't been able to really make this space look better, but Ivy did this in one morning. And I'm not a bit surprised. She's the most efficient person I think I've ever met, and I didn't expect this from her.

Finn whistles, impressed. "How did you know to do all of this?"

"I learned it from working retail," she says, straightening a row of mugs that say Tree Hugger. "And common sense. I like to shop, so I organized it based on how I would want to shop."

I pause at the far end of the counter. The cider counter isn't there anymore. It is an actual station set up in the corner now. She found the good carafes, and they're shiny and clean. There's a stack of paper cups and a jar of candy canes. The electric kettle is set on a wooden board, not teetering on a milk crate, which before was probably a safety violation. Handwritten labels sit in clear frames. Classic cocoa. Peppermint. There is even a bin of mini marshmallows beside a bowl of the fancy homemade ones, in bags labeled with flavors and ingredients. The old outlet along the wall that wasn't working is now open, and a fresh plate lies next to it ready to be fixed.

"Did you mess with that outlet?" I ask, alarmed.

"I texted Finn to check the connection and replace it. It wasn't working."

I look at Finn. He shrugs and gives me a grin, baiting me. "She was persuasive with homemade marshmallows and dinner."

She is *not* making him dinner.

Heat fills my cheeks. I don't like her asking Finn to help. I want her to ask me, dammit.

"You could have asked me," I say. It comes out sharper than I intended.

Her smile falters for a fraction of a second. "You were up hauling trees at dawn or whatever else you do. I didn't think it was worth bothering you over a minor issue. Plus, Finn wanted homemade marshmallows and a casserole."

Of course, she thinks I don't like her. I have given her every reason not to. It is not that I don't like her. That is the problem. I like her too much. And instead of saying something halfway decent, something that might make her feel welcome or seen, what comes out is the same defensive garbage I always fall back on. My jaw locks. The words snap before I can soften them.

"This is not what we agreed on," I say, sharper than I mean to be. "You are the nanny. You are not supposed to help with the business." Her face flickers. I hate that I did that. I hate that I know why. If I let her get any closer to the parts of my life that keep me upright, I am not sure I will know how to keep my hands off her. So I push. I make it cold. I watch it land and pretend it is necessary.

Finn coughs into his fist. "Asshole."

Ivy studies me as if she is deciding which version of me is standing here. The cooperative one. Or the asshole one. And I hate that I'm being an asshole right now. The place looks freaking great. And I'm grateful. I'm just surprised, and I don't like that she talks to everyone but me.

"I am not trying to step on your toes," she says. "I'm trying to keep customers from tripping over everything in here. Plus, I've done everything I need to do at the house, and I'm bored until Junie comes home from school. I like doing this. Please let me help," she pleads, with stormy green eyes that do things to me.

"Look," I say, jaw tight. "If you need something, you ask me. This is my shop, not Finn's. If you keep overstepping, you're fired."

"Understood." She nods. "So do I have approval to make it not a fire hazard?"

Finn glares at me and shakes his head.

I exhale and rub a thumb over the edge of the counter. The new layout works. I know it. She did in one pass what I put off for months, and pride stings.

"Fine," I mutter. "But stop subcontracting my family for repairs."

"Your family is great," she says, light again, giving Finn a hug. "Thanks for helping, Finn."

I stand there watching this like I'm going to crash out watching him touch her. Finn smirks at me over Ivy's shoulder and wiggles his eyebrows. I narrow my eyes at him.

She brushes past me to hang a strand of lights under the shelf. The scent of her shampoo hits me. Orange and something sweet, I can't figure out. I step back and close my eyes as if the smell is dangerous.

"Careful," I grumble. "That ladder isn't very solid."

"Don't worry," she says, climbing anyway. "Finn is spotting me."

Finn grins up at her. "I am the best spotter on this side of Wisteria Cove."

I'm going to murder him if he keeps grinning at her like that. I don't want him spotting her. I don't want him to do anything with her.

I hate how quickly they get along. She did not ask me to help. She did not even look to see if I would help. And she's barely glanced at me. It's like I'm not even here. She made that comment the other day about my not liking her. Why would she even think that? Maybe it's her who doesn't like me. And I get that. Hell, sometimes I don't even like me.

I grumble and head to the back to grab more twine, so I have something to do. Then, I circle out the side door and come back in, as if it was always my plan. Ivy is down from the ladder, taping the cocoa flavors to the front of the counter. Her eyes are bright, and she hums along to music she has playing.

"You know this is temporary," I say. It sounds like a reminder to her, but really...it's a warning for me.

"I know," she says in a singsong voice, still not looking at me. "Through the holidays."

"Through the holidays," I repeat dryly.

She lifts her chin. "Plenty of time to make it magical for Junie."

I want to say something, but she's right. This is about Junie. Not about me. Not about me wanting her. Junie deserves this. And I can't mess it up for her. Junie's had enough people let her down in her life. Especially her own mother.

Ivy climbs back up, moving too fast, her hands too loose on the wrung of the ladder. The legs wobble, tilting the whole frame. She stumbles. Her gasp is soft but loud.

I move without thinking.

One second she's flailing, and the next, she's in my arms.

Her body collides with mine, so soft, warm, and real, that I freeze, my hands instinctively tightening around her waist. She smells like cinnamon and cold air and whatever lotion she uses that's been driving me quietly insane for days.

My heart kicks hard in my chest. She looks up at me, startled, cheeks flushed, and for a beat too long, neither of us moves. Or speaks.

I blink, like that'll shake it off. "You are a walking red flag, Ivy," I mutter, shaking my head as I set her gently back on her feet. My palms are still burning. I wipe them on my jeans, trying to play it cool, but I curl my hands in on themselves. I'm not sure if I'm trying to keep hold of the sensation of her warmth in the center of my palms, or I'm trying desperately not to reach for her again. But God help me, I am so screwed.

I set her down and step back, giving her room to stand on her own. Her mouth opens. Then she smiles slowly and surely. "You call them red flags. I call them ten fun facts you did not know about me."

Finn, fixing the outlet, laughs.

I should shut this down and send her back to the house. Instead, I hear myself say, "Name three."

She taps the marker against her lips as if she's thinking. I should not watch her mouth. I do anyway, wishing I were that pen.

"One. I can parallel park a truck and trailer in one try," she says with a confident smile. "Two. I can make homemade marshmallows that taste like a campfire and a fluffy cloud had a baby. Three. I can get your kid to brush her teeth and go to bed without a fight."

My reply dies somewhere behind my teeth. I set the twine on the counter and look anywhere except at her. "Good, she needs extra brushing if you're making marshmallows with her."

"This looks so much better than the shitshow you had going on in here," Finn says, helpful as a shovel to the face.

"I noticed," I say.

We fall into work, and Ivy keeps moving. She loops ribbon through the wreath display, then shifts a crate three inches and somehow makes the entire wall look better.

Ivy goes to get Junie from the bus and brings her back to show off the farm stand with a snack she prepared for her. Junie is holding Ivy's hand and talking her ear off, and Ivy is listening intently. She immediately runs to me and wraps me in a big hug when she sees me. "Hi, Dad. Ivy says I can help out in the store with her, but then we have to go do dinner and take my bath."

"Hey Juniebug. She did, did she?" I say as I glance over at Ivy, who is already chatting up customers and helping them. Great. More smiles for everyone but me.

Customers trickle in. A dad with two kids who want the tallest tree on earth. A couple arguing about Balsam versus Frasers. Ivy sells cocoa to all of them, listens, laughs, then sends them to me with a nod that says, trust him. It puts people at ease. It puts me on edge. She's in my space, and I hate it. Okay, I hate how I turn into an even bigger doofus when she's around. Like I forget how to talk and walk. And everything comes out of my mouth sharper than intended.

Junie hands out coloring sheets to all the kids with Christmas trees on them and upsells all the treats and toys alongside Ivy. I'll admit, everything is going great. And it feels great having Ivy and Junie around.

When the rush dips, Ivy slides a cup across the counter toward me. "Taste test."

I fold my arms. "I don't have time for taste tests."

"You have time for this one," she says with a grin and meets my eyes. "Peppermint. With the marshmallows that taste like an ice cream blizzard."

Tate walks up and takes one and moans like a dramatic idiot. "Holy. That should be illegal."

I lift mine and take a sip. It is stupid-good. I don't give her the satisfaction of a full reaction. She sees through me, anyway. Her smile is small. Pleased, but not gloating.

"Stop improving things," I say under my breath.

"Why," she says softly, giving me a look like she's challenging me. "Are you going to fire me?"

Oh, there are a lot of things I'd like to do to Ivy. Firing her is not one of them.

"You should sell more of these marshmallows. They're amazing," Tate tells her, and I give him a dirty look that tells him not to encourage her.

I look through the front window instead. Snow flurries drift across the lot. The tree rows blur into a watercolor of green and white. For a second, I imagine this whole place the way she sees it. A place of happiness and traditions.

Junie pulls papers out of her backpack. "We made a star map in class," she tells her, breathless. "It looks like our treasure map, but in the sky."

Ivy crouches to her level. "Then we need star cookies tonight. With extra edible glitter."

Junie spins. "Daddy, can Ivy sleep over forever?"

The room tilts. I tug my cap low to hide whatever crosses my face. "We'll talk about it later, bug."

Ivy stands and smooths Junie's hat. She moves back into the flow of customers as if she has been here for years, and it's her personal farm store. She is everywhere at once. Handing out napkins, ringing up a wreath, and telling a story that makes an old man linger to hear the end. She is bright enough to make people gather. She's captivating enough to make them stay.

It is good for the farm. It is good for my kid, and that terrifies me. Because when she leaves, we're left without the brightness. We're left in the cold.

Tate nudges my shoulder. "You gonna keep pretending she's not doing you a favor and turning this place completely around?"

"I know she is," I snap. The words taste like surrender. "That's the problem."

He laughs softly. "Finn called it when he said you were allergic to help."

I watch Ivy tie a candy cane to a bag with a neat red bow. She catches me looking. For a heartbeat, we hold our gazes. Something flickers, and I look away first.

Through the holidays. That is what I told my mom and me. We can't get used to this. Ivy will leave us, too.

But as Ivy flits through the farm like a Christmas fairy, Junie orbiting her like a planet that has finally found its sun, I cannot shake the thought that letting her in might be the biggest mistake I make.

Or it might possibly be the only thing that saves us.

# Chapter 6
# Ivy

"Junie," I say, laughing at her Christmas tree made of candy canes, "no more candy canes. We have to go home and eat our yummy dinner."

She groans. "I want to stay and help Dad and Captain Tate."

It's adorable she calls Tate that. He used to be a commercial fisherman, but now he is fixing up his father's old boat that the town pitched in and bought for him, and he's going to do boat tours.

Everything about this kid is great. This nanny job might be my favorite job so far.

At the door, Junie launches herself at Remy, who's still talking to Tate near the cash register. He catches her, squeezing her tight.

"Ivy has something yummy in the slow cooker," she announces proudly. "It's pot roast. We have to go home and eat now."

Finn strolls in just as Junie says that and grins. "Can I come? I want pot roast."

"No," Remy says flatly, without even looking at him.

"Damn, me too." Tate grins at Junie. "That sounds good."

Finn raises his brows at me like, 'Did you hear that?' I did. And maybe it's nothing. Or maybe... it's interesting. Remy sounded almost jealous.

I smile cheerfully. "Plenty for everyone. I even made two loaves of homemade bread."

Back at the house, everything is warm and glowing. The garland, the dried oranges, the wreaths, all the decorations in place—the only thing missing is a tree.

"When can we get a tree?" Junie asks, shrugging off her coat, also noticing what's missing.

"We can ask your dad," I say, giving her a little nudge toward the sink to wash her hands.

The pot roast has been simmering all day, and the thick slices of homemade bread I'm going to warm in the oven and slather with yummy butter are making my mouth water just thinking about it. Junie eats like she's been starving, chattering about school and how she wants to add "build a snow fort" to the tradition map.

"We can add anything you want," I promise, and she smiles.

After her bath and bedtime story, she's tucked in and snoring before I've even turned off the light.

When I come back downstairs, Finn's coming through the front door.

"I hope it's not too late to stop by," he says, stepping inside and stamping snow off his boots. "I'll take you up on that dinner."

"Perfect, because I have a favor to ask you," I tell him as I get our bowls and food ready. I tell him about the little charms I've been making Junie. Tiny stars, snowflakes, and hearts she can collect each day on a charm necklace until Christmas. "I need a box with twenty-four little compartments to make an advent calendar for Junie."

I ladle pot roast into a bowl and set bread between us. The kitchen smells like thyme and warmth. Outside the window, the porch light throws a halo on the drift by the steps.

He grins. "Done. I love making stuff like that. I'll work on it this weekend."

"Thanks so much. And for all your help with the shop. How are you and Rowan? I know you've been helping her at Salt and Root."

Finn has been helping my sister get her new apothecary shop up and going next to Willa's bookstore.

Finn picks up his spoon. "She came by the lot at lunch," he says, like we were already in the middle of the story. "Came over to tell me she had a list of repairs she needed me to help with. Also brought me a thermos of hot tea that is supposed to help with my virility. Should I be concerned?"

I laugh and smile into my glass. "That sounds like her. But also, her teas are really good."

"She and I spend nearly every day together. But she only sees me as her friend. I'm friend zoned for life with your sister."

He finally takes a bite, chews, and keeps talking. "I don't get it, Ivy. What is wrong with me? I'm right here. I'm available. But she's on a dating app, looking for the love of her life, she tells me."

I set my elbow on the table and rest my chin in my hand. He does not seem to notice that he hasn't touched his bread. "I don't know why. Maybe she's afraid getting involved will ruin your friendship."

"I wish she would ruin the friendship," he says, then thinks. "I want to be more than her friend."

He looks at the bowl like he is trying to gather his thoughts. "She is going on all these dates, and then we go to lunch the next day and talk about the dates. And honestly, while I love our lunches, I *hate* her dates."

"I heard you've been going on dates, too," I say softly.

He nods like that's the only answer. "Yeah, because I thought if I went on dates, I'd forget about her like that. It turns out, it makes me crazier about her."

Something loosens low in my chest. He is not asking me questions. He is telling me who she is to him, one small scene at a time. The room feels warmer for it.

He drags a hand over his jaw. "I know she will say she is fine, but she is worried about those permits. She pretends she isn't, but when she is thinking too hard, she taps her thumb against her bottom lip. She did it twice today." He looks up. "Do you think I should go with her to City Hall? Or would that feel like I am crowding her?"

"Go if she asks," I say. "Offer if she doesn'tt. Let her choose. Bring coffee with the splash of cream and a cinnamon bun she never admits she wants."

He nods, stores it away. The heater ticks on. He finally reaches for the bread and tears it in half, then passes me a piece.

He keeps going like he can't help it. "She makes everything feel like it matters."

My mouth curves before I can stop it. I tap my finger against the rim of my glass. "Wow," I say, and let it land, light but true. "You really like my sister."

He goes still, then his mouth tips in the smallest smile. He looks down at his bowl and pretends to chase a potato. "Yeah," he says, quiet, as if the word is a secret he has been carrying around for a long time. "I do."

"Aww. Well, for the record, I'm rooting for you two to get together."

"Don't tell Remy." He groans. "I'll never hear the end of it."

I smile. "I won't. And you don't have to worry about that. Remy doesn't even want to talk to me."

Finn tilts his head, genuinely confused. "That's funny. He seems very different when you're around."

I blink. "What do you mean?"

He shrugs, "He's probably not going to say it, but you're practically his favorite person right now, helping out like this. You're a miracle worker."

I roll my eyes. "Right. He seems more annoyed with my being here than anything."

He looks at me and says, "You've done so much around here. I know he's grateful that you're here. He's just a grumpy asshole sometimes," he says, then laughs and adds, "Okay, most of the time."

The front door opens, and the cold rushes in with Remy. He shakes snow from his shoulders, hangs his coat, and steps into the kitchen. He sees me sitting here holding my mug and Finn eating, and glares at him for a second.

The second he sees the slow cooker, his brows lift. "That smells good."

"It is," I say, looking anywhere but at him. Because, fine—if he wants to ice me out, I can, as well. Two can play this game. That's what I should be doing anyway, keeping everything professional and distant. I can't afford to lose this job, too.

He cuts a piece of bread from the loaf and slathers it in butter, then takes a bite like he hasn't eaten in days. His eyes close, and he lets out an inaudible sound, half sigh, half groan that makes my stomach do an odd little flip. I don't need to add to the fantasies.

Damn it, Remy.

"Good?" I ask, taking a sip from my mug.

He nods once, still chewing. "Really good. Thanks."

Finn smirks at me as he takes a bite. I ignore him.

"Must be nice having someone make these homemade dinners and make your house look like a winter wonderland even if you don't even like Christmas," Finn teases.

Remy ignores us and takes a bite of his pot roast, and his eyes close in euphoria.

After a few minutes, I ask, "Why don't you like Christmas? How can you own a Christmas tree farm and not like Christmas?"

I am genuinely confused.

Remy looks up, frowning. "I like Christmas."

"It doesn't seem like it. You're like the Grinch who works at the North Pole."

Finn practically chokes on his bread as he laughs. Remy just shakes his head, rolls his eyes, and goes back to eating like he's done with the conversation.

The room quiets again, and I suddenly feel the weight of the day settling in my limbs. And maybe a little something else. A flutter I'm not ready to name, not after the way Remy looked at me just now, like I'd poked at something he didn't want touched.

I rinse out my mug and place it gently in the dishwasher.

"I think I'm going to head to bed," I say, softer now.

Finn gives a wave, still smiling. Remy doesn't look up.

That's fine. I'm too tired to decode whatever's going on behind that unreadable expression of his.

I plan to retreat to the quiet of my room, grateful for the excuse to be alone. To breathe. To think. And if my thoughts were to wander to Remy, to the way his voice rumbles when he's annoyed, or how his jaw clenches when he's trying not to react, well...at least I can do that with the door closed.

As I turn to leave, Finn grins, "Have fun tomorrow. Do you have big plans? Rewire the barn lights, label Remy's moods, and rezone the tree lot?"

"Ha ha, Finn. Good night," I call as I head down the hall.

I can still hear the low rumble of Remy and Finn's voices. I don't linger to listen.

Remy's a grump. And if he's miserable, it's no one's fault but his own.

Still...that little sound he made over dinner? I'm not forgetting that anytime soon, especially when I have to use my vibrator to keep me warm tonight and think about him.

* * *

I'm bundled up because it's still cold, the heater humming weakly. I should have asked Finn to look at my heater. Not even bothering with grumpy Remy. I feel that if I ask him for help, it'll set him off. I learned with my ex, Derek, that asking for help always makes things worse.

I'm staring at a picture of Lola on my phone—big brown eyes and floppy ears and her speckled fur. She's a blue heeler mix Derek got for me when she was a puppy. He didn't know what breed she was and didn't like her when she grew into the rowdy little cattle dog she is. After I trained her and worked with her, he decided she was 'okay.' But he always made comments that he'd rather have a doodle or some other type of dog. I've always loved dogs, and one of my favorite part-time jobs was dog walking.

I miss her so much, it physically hurts. Before I can talk myself out of it, I open a new text.

**_Ivy: Hey. Can I please have Lola? I miss her._**

It takes two minutes for the little dots to appear.

**_Derek: Not happening._**

I stare at the screen. Okay, jerk.

**_Ivy: At least let me pick up some of my furniture and things. I couldn't take everything with me._**

***Derek: Also, no. And if you don't call your psycho sisters and mother off, I will sue your entire family.***

I blink.

***Ivy: What are you talking about?***
***Derek: Ask them.***

The dots vanish. He's gone.

I drop my phone onto the blanket, and my heart feels sick, and I whisper. "Great. I'm never getting my dog back."

I jab Rowan's contact and put her on speaker.

She picks up on the third ring. "What?"

"Hi to you, too. Did you guys do something to Derek?"

"Not yet," Rowan says in her usual calm, vaguely menacing tone.

"What do you mean, not yet?"

"I mean exactly what I just said."

I flop back against the pillows. "Rowan. He just accused you of being a psycho and threatened to sue our whole family."

She hums, unimpressed. "I'm honored."

"I'm serious. Did you do anything? Did you show up at his apartment? Hex him?"

"Again, no," she says, then adds, "But I'd love to do lots of things to Derek."

I squeeze my eyes shut, afraid to ask. "Such as?"

"Take him on a little field trip to a graveyard."

"That's it?"

"Alive," she clarifies. "Bury him up to his neck. Give the crows something to chew on."

I pinch the bridge of my nose. "Rowan, gross."

"Or," she continues thoughtfully, "super glue all his dresser drawers shut. Put a single sardine in his car's air vent. Replace the cream in his Oreos with toothpaste."

"You've put a lot of thought into this."

"I like to be prepared," she says, her voice all Wednesday Addams-satisfaction.

I sigh, smiling despite myself. "You're terrifying."

"You called me," she reminds me.

"I did. And since I have you...what's up with you and Finn?"

There's a beat of silence. "...What are you talking about?"

"That pause was guilty," I singsong. "You're not telling me something."

"Your phone's cutting out," she says immediately. "I can't— hello?—can you hear—"

"You're in your yoga studio; I can hear the clicking of the heater," I point out.

Another pause. "You're imagining things."

"Uh-huh. Sure."

"I have to go," she says, her voice low and deliberate, like she's ending a business deal.

"You like him," I say before she can hang up. "And you're terrible at pretending you don't."

Click.

I stare at the phone, then laugh, shaking my head. My sisters are absolute chaos in three different flavors.

And apparently, still haunting my ex.

* * *

When I wake up, I take a minute to remember where I am. The room is beyond cold, the radiator clicking like it's trying but failing to do its job, and for a second, I think maybe I've dreamed all of this—Junie, the farm, Remy's permanent scowl.

Then the smell of pancakes hits me. I'm confused because I've been doing all of the cooking.

I shiver as I pull on slippers over my thick socks and head

68

toward the kitchen, hair still a mess from sleep, and stop in the doorway.

Remy's at the stove in a faded red flannel, sleeves shoved up his forearms, spatula in one hand. Junie's sitting cross-legged at the counter across from him in flannel pajamas with little candy canes all over them, her hair pulled into a braid so neat it could win an award.

"You made pancakes?" I ask, like it's the most shocking thing I've ever seen Remy do.

Remy doesn't look at me, just flips a pancake onto a plate and slides it across the table toward the empty chair. He doesn't even use words, just the tiniest chin tilt toward it, like *that's for you.*

"Thanks," I say softly, but he's already turning back to the stove.

Junie takes a giant sip of orange juice and grins at me over the glass. "He made a mess."

I follow her gaze and try not to laugh. The counter looks like a bag of flour exploded. There's a trail of batter drips across the stove top, and eggshells in the sink.

"It's okay," I say, hiding a smile. "I bet they're super yummy."

Remy flicks her a look, more amused than annoyed. "You made the mess."

"You cracked the eggs everywhere," she says matter-of-factly.

It's so cute watching them together. He's been working a lot this week, and it looks like he might actually have a day off.

I sit, take a bite of the pancakes that are fluffy and perfectly cooked, and hum my approval. "These are *so* good."

"Junie is the best helper," he says, like that explains everything.

"What are your plans today?" I ask Junie, still not trying to focus on Remy.

"Nana needs me to help her with her decorating," Junie says as she wipes her mouth on her napkin.

"How about you?" Remy asks, bringing his coffee mug to his lips.

He needs a shave, and probably a haircut, but he looks damn good. Rugged and hot. I'm distracted and shake myself back into the moment.

"I overslept and missed my ride into town with Willa. But I can see if my mom can come get me," I shrug.

"What do you need to do in town?" he asks as he leans back against the counter and watches me. He does that, and it's not in a creepy way, but it makes me feel like I should have tried harder this morning instead of throwing my wild hair up in a messy bun and throwing on a hoodie.

"I need to run a bunch of errands," I say as I take another bite and close my eyes. These are delicious pancakes.

He slides over a small plate of bacon, and I smile and help myself to a piece.

I realize there's a lot I don't know about Remy. I know his mom very well, and we grew up in the same town, but he's older than I am, so we weren't close growing up. When I was nine, he was eighteen and already away at college. Finn is younger, so I got to know him better. Remy moved back here when Junie was a baby about four years ago.

Donna sweeps in with the cold and the smell of coffee, kisses Junie's cheek, and starts gasping like the house is a museum. "Look at this garland. Who staged this, elves?"

"Me and Ivy," Junie says, tugging her along. "Come on, Nana, I'll show you." She points at every decoration. "Isn't Ivy great?"

"She's wonderful." Donna winks at me, then she turns to

Remy. "Can you take Ivy to town? I am going to take Junie. We have a lot to do. You two share a truck. Save gas. Fall in love."

"Mom," Remy warns, and the way he says it tells me he's used to her meddling and giving him crap.

Donna looks at me and back at Remy with a grin. "Fifteen minutes, Junie. Wear something that says festive. We're going shopping first."

I head to my room and hurry and get ready. I curl my hair, dab on a little shimmer, and pick the green sweater with the soft sleeves that make me feel like a present. I add jeans, boots that feel comfortable but look good, and tie on my favorite red scarf. I love this time of year and the romantic rituals of dressing cozily. The small decisions that feel like a celebration. By the time I tie the scarf, my cheeks are warm, and my nerves are frazzled, and I can hear Junie below telling Donna again how great I am. I feel the same about that kid.

I grab my coat and my lip balm, check the mirror one last time, and breathe. Festive. Capable. Maybe a little brave. Then I head down to gauge Remy and what kind of mood he's going to be in.

He is out there in the cold, breath white in the frosty air, scraping the windshield in steady strokes. When he sees me, he doesn't say a word. He stomps over, ice scraper still in his hand, and opens the passenger door. The cab is warm. He does not look at me, his face as unreadable as ever, but his hand stays on the door until I climb in. For a second, I just sit there, baffled and soft all at once, because he left the glass half-frosted to make sure I did not have to touch the handle. I rub my gloved hands together and bite back a smile that blooms anyway. Actions, not words. With Remy, it is always that. He shuts the door carefully, goes back to the scraper, and I watch him through the fogging window with my heart doing its own small, traitorous thing.

The heater hums loudly as we pull out of the driveway, snowflakes drifting lazily through the air.

It's quiet for a while, just the sound of the tires crunching over snow and ice, until a familiar guitar riff comes through the speakers.

My head snaps up. "You listen to Taylor Swift?"

His jaw twitches like he's trying not to react. "It's Junie's playlist."

"Sure, it is," I tease, grinning. "Can I pick the music?"

"No," he clips.

"What are you gonna do? Fire me?" I tease. "You need me here, and you know it. I'm a big help, and I keep things interesting."

"That you do," he mutters and turns onto the highway, glancing over at me and down my body, but not in a creepy way. It almost looked like Remy was maybe...possibly...checking me out.

I connect my phone to his aux cord and play eighties hits and serenade him. He glares at me and says, "fired."

"I'd love to see you try, Remington Bennett," I challenge.

And that actually adds a spark to his eyes as he purses his lips and focuses on the road.

Before I can say anything else, he actually sings the next line, low, quiet, and better than I'd expect from a grump like Remy Bennett.

For a second, I just...stare. My fingers are warm inside my gloves, but my cheeks feel hotter than they should in the truck with hot Remy.

We fall into easy conversation after that, and there's a tiny spark of something you can't name yet.

He tells me Junie's been begging for a dog. "Keeps drawing little pictures and leaving them on my pillow. Yesterday was a doodle of a dog with a giant red bow around its neck."

"Subtle of her." I laugh, but it fades too fast. "I didn't get to bring my dog with me when I moved here."

His eyes flick toward me, quick but sharp, before going back to the road. "Why not?"

"My ex would not let me take her."

He does not say anything at first. His hand shifts on the wheel, knuckles tightening a shade against the worn leather like he is tucking that away.

The ride goes quiet. Peaceful, the kind of quiet that happens with Remy sometimes, even when I am not sure what to do with all the space between us. Trees blur past in dark rows. The heater hums low. Some old song plays soft on the radio, all warm guitar and memory.

"You said your ex would not let you take your dog," he says finally. His voice is low, like he is not sure he should ask.

I nod, eyes on the window. "Yeah." A beat passes. "He kept my dog. Took my furniture. Kept the house. Slept with my best friend for the sweet little bonus round."

The words land heavy. Too raw. I wish I could grab them back. I almost say *forget it. Sorry. Never mind.* I glance over instead.

His face is unreadable, but his hands are not. One grips the wheel until the tendons stand out. He pulls a breath through his nose, sharp and controlled.

"That guy is a piece of shit," he says quietly.

I let out a breath I did not know I was holding. It leaves me soft around the edges. "Yeah," I say, voice smaller now. "He really is."

We don't talk much after that. The silence shifts, though. It is not awkward. It feels like he took a corner of the weight and set it on his side of the truck without asking me for permission. The road hums under the tires. The song changes. I look out at the trees, and for the first time in a while my chest does not feel like it is holding its breath.

* * *

When we hit Main Street, garland wraps the lampposts, each with a big red bow. Wreaths hang on shop doors, and the bakery window fogs over with steam from the ovens.

As we pass the coffee shop, I point out every Christmas decoration in sight, rating them out loud.

"That one?" I say, pointing at a custom wooden Santa on someone's roof. "Nine out of ten. Loses a point for the saggy sleigh."

He huffs. "What gets a ten out of ten? Who makes these standards?"

"You'll know it when you see it."

We turn the corner and there it is, a twenty-foot inflatable snowman holding a candy cane the size of a telephone pole. I tilt my head and judge.

I yell, "TEN!" so loudly he actually flinches.

"Your energy is exhausting," he mutters, but I swear I see the edge of a smile before he turns his head.

"You have no idea. My stamina is out of control. You gotta get in shape to keep up with my enthusiasm," I tell him and watch his eyes darken a little with something that looks like desire and challenge.

I don't want to flirt with Remy, but flirting with Remy comes easy, and I can't seem to stop.

We run our errands in record time. He's efficient, tossing bags and boxes into the cart without hesitation. I pick up all of my supplies for Junie's advent calendar project. Remy says nothing, just tags along and towers over me as we walk. Once, I almost slide my gloved hand into his excitedly, but then I remember that he doesn't like me.

But damn, I wish he did.

When we load the supplies into the truck, a Christmas song comes on. Without thinking, I start singing.

He pretends to look exasperated, but I don't miss the smirk.

"Fired," he tells me again.

"Again, would love to see you try to fire me, Remington Bennett. I'm the best thing that has ever happened to you. You neeeeeeeeeeeeeed me," I sing to him and dance in my seat.

"Ridiculous," Remy throws the truck into reverse, resting one hand on the back of my seat as he twists to look behind us. It's such a simple move—practical, even—but there's something sexy about the way his arm stretches behind me, muscles flexing under the fabric of his flannel, his jaw set in concentration. I try not to notice. I fail spectacularly

Instead of replying, I reward him with my own lip-syncing rendition of *I Think We're Alone Now by Tiffany*. An eighties classic.

By the time we pull into the bookstore to park I've decided two things.

He might secretly be more fun than he lets on.

I wouldn't mind spending more time with him again. In a non-professional setting.

And I wouldn't mind seeing what else is hiding under all that flannel and gruffness.

# Chapter 7
# Remy

I am smiling at a receipt when I realize I have been smiling for five minutes straight at basically nothing. And I know why. It is the woman in my passenger seat who keeps treating errands like a holiday parade, as if we're having the best day of our lives instead of just running basic errands. Somehow Ivy has the gift of making everyone feel magic in the mundane.

With everything she does, she's sunshine.

The way she sings to the radio and waves at everyone we pass on Main. When I mutter the need to get going, she pats my arm and then waits by the truck for me to open the door for her.

"Thanks, Remington," she calls, cheerfully.

I give her a look. "Why do you call me that?"

"Why not?" she asks, giving me a smile that makes my lip twitch. "It's a sexy name." She says it in a teasing sexy voice that makes me feel things.

"No one calls me that," I mutter.

"Well, then I'll just need to find a suitable name for you, then," she says as she turns on her heels.

Wisteria Books & Brews smells like butter and cinnamon

and the best part of my childhood, books. Willa sees us as she's putting up a tray of fresh muffins and lights up.

"What are you two doing here?" she asks, looking back and forth at us, surprised to see us together.

Ivy says. "Hey, Willa. We need two cinnamon rolls."

"I'm her chauffeur," I say quietly as I look through her new books, hoping that sounds believable.

Willa laughs and shakes her head at us, as if we're both full of it, and packs up two containers of cinnamon rolls, sliding them across the counter. Ivy takes one, hands me the other one, and says, "For you, beast."

"I am not a beast." I give her a ridiculous look.

"You're grumpy like the Beast in Beauty and the Beast."

"I am not grumpy," I argue.

She lifts an eyebrow. "Your face says otherwise. Eat."

Willa watches us in fascination and gives Ivy a look with raised eyebrows. "Want one to go for Junie?"

"She's with my mom, but thanks. I'm sure she's getting plenty sugared up as it is," I say as I take a bite of the cinnamon roll and nod. "This is good."

"Thanks, fresh from the oven." Willa wipes down the counter in front of her.

Ivy makes a soft sound as she takes a bite and reaches without thinking and grips my bicep as she takes a bite. "These are still warm, Willa."

My gaze drifts to her mouth, and everything else blurs. Her touch still hums on my skin. I want her to touch me on purpose. She finds my stare and grins like she knows what I'm thinking. I look away, trying to focus on anything but her.

Willa breaks our moment with an excited clap. "Come see how Rowan's shop is coming along." She leads us to the tarp draped across the opening on the far side of the bookstore. She lifts the edge and jerks her chin. We duck through. "Your brother has been a godsend in helping her out."

My eyes adjust and then go wide with surprise. Brick wraps the room in warm red and clay, old and honest, warm and inviting. On the street-facing wall, a tall window has purple and green stained glass, and the sun shining through it throws amethyst across the floor and up the shelving like spilled ink. The color makes the whole place look lit from inside.

Floor-to-ceiling shelves line the walls, thick oak with black iron brackets. A rolling ladder sits on a rail, waiting for someone to kick off and glide. The shelves are empty but ready. I can see the rows of glass apothecary jars in my head. Roots. Leaves. Dried citrus. Amber bottles for tinctures. Little drawers with brass label frames wait beneath, all in a neat grid, each with an iron pull waiting to be explored by customers.

Overhead, a line of hooks crosses the ceiling on a beam. Bundles of lavender and rosemary will dry there, neat and green against the brick. There is a copper rail under the window for hanging tools. Mortars and pestles sit out already, stone and olive wood, their bowls scored with use. A brass scale rests near a slate slab, the pans clean and bright, the weights lined up like soldiers.

On the right, a massive table sits against the wall. Walnut, if I am guessing right. One live edge remains, while the rest has been planed smoothly. The joinery is clean, the tenons proud. It looks like Finn's work. A farmhouse sink of dark stone anchors the back corner, with a tall gooseneck faucet and a drainboard on both sides.

Rowan waves and joins us from the back room. She talks about paint and signage proudly to Ivy, who takes it all in and is excited for Rowan—so much so that it's contagious. I try not to stare, but I can't keep my eyes off of her.

Ivy steps into the purple light and turns in a slow circle. It paints her sweater and the curve of her cheek. She presses her palms to the walnut table and smiles like she just recognized a future. "This is magic," she says, and her voice is soft like she knows the room can hear her.

"It's a good space," I say, but that is an understatement.

I touch the edge of the table and feel the weight. I can already see Rowan measuring herbs, and labeling jars in that neat hand that makes everything look like it belongs. The picture settles into my chest and sits there, warm. My brother's hand is all over this place, too.

Rowan smiles proudly and confirms my thoughts. "Thank you. I couldn't have made any of this happen without Finn."

Willa drops the tarp back against the jamb and claps playfully. "All right. Keep it up and I will put you both to work."

I look at the table again. "Tell me what you need," I say.

Ivy bumps her shoulder to mine, a quick spark of contact. "See," she says to Willa. "He's a good beast. Underneath it all, he's a big softy. Like a cinnamon roll. Hard on the outside, but soft on the inside."

I roll my eyes playfully and tease, "It's time to go."

But I like her touching me. Normally I'm not a big touchy-feely guy besides hugging my daughter, but I love Ivy's touch. I want more of it.

* * *

The hardware store is next. The bell over the door gives out a sad little ring as we step in. She heads straight for the lumber aisle and inhales like she paid for the experience.

"You are sniffing wood," I say.

"It is aromatherapy," she says. "Cedar. Pine. Amazingness."

"I own a tree farm. You can sniff wood there anytime you like."

She turns, eyes bright, smile slow. "Say that again, Beast."

"No," I clip and mutter, "fired."

She laughs, and the sound slides under my ribs like heat. An older guy two aisles over pretends not to hear us and fails.

We collect wire, hooks, felt pads for the chair legs, a tape measure that I don't need, and a key ring shaped like a tiny saw that she definitely doesn't need but looks thrilled to own. Ivy hums in a low, cheerful way that makes the bland store lights feel kinder. She bumps my shoulder in time with the beat. I tolerate it. I like it.

The mercantile creaks like a ship. Ivy tries on a hat that features a small pom at the crown, studies herself, then studies me as if testing whether I will admit I like it.

I don't. She swaps the hat for a plaid scarf, crosses the floor, and lifts it toward me.

"No," I say.

When she loops the scarf around my neck, the fabric is warm and soft against my skin, but it's her closeness that hits me first like a quiet spark right at my throat. Her scent drifts up with it, a bright rush of oranges and something subtle, and it wraps around me just as much as the scarf does. It's distracting in the best way, making my breath catch without me meaning it to. Her knuckles graze lightly over my beard, brushing the rough stubble, and it's a jolt, not painful, but electric. The contrast between her soft skin and my scratchy beard pulls my attention sharp into the moment. I feel a pulse in my chest, a little too aware of the space between us. Then she tilts her head, eyes narrowing as if she's sizing me up, judging my 'craftsmanship.' It's playful, but it gets under my skin, too. Like she's seeing something I'm trying not to show. I don't say anything, but I'm caught between wanting to laugh and wanting to close the distance just a bit more. "Rugged Christmas lumberjack dream," she announces. She drops it into our basket. "Done.'"

"I am not buying this." I add, even though I'm still lost in this moment with her.

"Good," she says. "Because I am buying it for you."

"That is unnecessary."

I haven't been given a gift like this—a 'just because' kind of gift—in so long, I'm not sure what to say. Warmth trickles through me at the thought of Ivy doing this for me.

"It is happiness. Don't fight me on happiness, Remy. It's all I have left."

She pays in cash, pops up on her toes as if she is celebrating a minor victory, then holds the brown paper bag to her chest as if it is evidence of a life well lived. I am absurdly jealous of a scarf.On the sidewalk a gust of wind lifts and she tucks her chin into her collar. Someone tests the string of lights on the library fir, and the bulbs come up one by one like a slow inhale. A kid chases his hat, catches it, and holds it over his head like a trophy. Ivy claps for him, quiet and proud, like she has been waiting all day for that win. I feel it hit low in my chest, that soft pull she has. She claps for strangers, and it makes me want to protect the part of her that believes people are worth cheering for.

In the truck she finds an oldies station and starts singing the verses she half remembers. She taps the dash like it is a snare drum and tries to harmonize with a trumpet that does not want a partner. I should be annoyed. I'm not. She narrates the town like a tour guide who got bored and decided to be funny. I catch myself smiling where she cannot see it. My hand eases on the wheel. The air in the cab changes.

Every time she laughs, it slides under my skin and warms a place I try to keep cold. Every time she points out some small, good thing, I want to pull the truck over and let her collect all the good things, so she never runs out. I tell myself to keep my eyes on the road, to remember why she is here, to keep the lines straight. Then she hits the chorus wrong on purpose and looks at me like I better back her up.

I do. And I feel the shift, quiet and sure, like the truck has found a smoother lane and I don't want to leave it.

"Let's play a game," she says. "Like twenty questions. Get to know each other better. You go first."

"What makes you happy?" I ask after a stretch of road that feels easy.

She thinks. "Small things," she says. "Fresh pens that actually write. Dogs to snuggle. Bookstores that smell like paper and dust and stories. The first snow of the season. When a song turns a bad mood into a good one. Cinnamon rolls fresh from the oven."

"Those are good," I agree.

"What about you, Beast?" she says with a smile.

"First cut of the season," I say. "The saw biting clean. The farm before sunrise when frost makes the ground shine. Junie laughing and happy. Coffee I remember to drink while it's still hot."

She looks at me like I just handed her a gift. "You see the good stuff, too," she says quietly. "You're just grumpier about it."

"I am *not* grumpy." I balk.

"You are also not nearly as grumpy as I first thought."

I snort. "Tell that to Finn."

"Finn thinks you are a teddy bear with a tight schedule."

"That is slander."

"Prove me wrong," she challenges. And the way she looks at me when she says it makes my dick hard again. Damn it. This day has been nothing but that over and over again.

I don't have a response to that. She's not wrong. I have a schedule for everything.

Back at the house, she hops out and begins wrestling a crate of twine that's twice her size before I gently take it from her.

She carries the bags, instead, and hangs the scarf on my hook by the door before I can object. It looks like it lives there. I pretend I don't notice. But I am going to probably keep that damn scarf forever for a memory of today.

In the kitchen, my mom lifts one perfect eyebrow at the sight of us. "You both came back in one piece," she comments cheerfully, checking each of us out in surprise.

"The day is still young," Ivy says as she kisses her cheek. "Remington might be coming around to liking me."

I snort and roll my eyes but the tone is light. And she is the first person I have ever actually liked hearing call me by my full name. I'm starting to come around to it but I'm not admitting to anything anytime soon.

"Excellent," Mom says as she reaches for the bakery box Willa shoved at us last minute. "Show me this happiness."

Junie barrels in and skids to a stop. "You're back," she says to Ivy, like there was never any doubt. She slings an arm around Ivy's waist and looks up at her grandma. "Isn't Ivy fun?"

"She is wonderful," my Mom says, and then she looks at me like she is checking whether I will admit what everyone else already knows.

I pretend to study something on my phone. Ivy bumps my shoulder with hers and slides the scarf from the hook.

"Come here," she says.

"I'm here."

"Closer."

I step forward until she's so close I can practically count the dark lashes brushing against her cheek. The faint scent of her wraps around me like the scarf she's about to tie.

Her hands move quickly but carefully, looping the scarf around my neck, the tips of her fingers brushing against my skin. I feel the warmth radiate from her arms as she tucks the ends just right, fingers lingering a moment longer than necessary. She looks up then, her gaze locking with mine, the green of her eyes catching the soft light—deep and clear, like the forest after rain. I *could* move away. But I don't want to.

"Functional and festive," she says, laughing. "Beast, but make it approachable.'"

"I am *not* a beast."

She smiles up at me. "You are a good man who growls." Then she leans in and whispers, "It's kinda hot, too."

I should not like that. But I do. I feel ridiculous in a way that is not uncomfortable.

I realize my face hurts a little from all the smiling I swear I am not doing.

Ivy catches me looking. She holds my gaze a beat longer than polite. There is a warmth there that looks like an invitation and feels like a dare. My heart does something I would never admit in front of my brother.

"Thank you," I say. It comes out rougher than I expect.

"For what," she asks.

"For today," I say. "For making it feel easy."

"It is supposed to feel that way," she says. "We can do hard, too."

And then she fucking winks at me.

Oh, fuck me. *Literally.* I should not feel like this towards my daughter's nanny. And I don't want my mom or Junie to see us this way, either.

And is she flirting with me? Oh my God.

Ivy turns to Junie and asks about the decorations at her nana's. Junie takes her hand like that is the most natural thing in the world and pulls her toward the table. My mom catches my eye and winks. I roll mine and cannot hide my grin.

It's really hard to be grumpy. The scarf is warm. The kitchen smells of cinnamon and pine. The house sounds like it's full of family and love. Ivy is sunshine in boots, and I did not plan on liking that. I like it, anyway.

And the worst part? I had fun. More fun than I've had in... hell, maybe years. She somehow made me see Wisteria Cove with a fresh set of eyes. Lately, life feels like a day-to-day struggle. And today it felt...fun. Lighter and less stressful.

And damn, I want more. I crave more.

# Chapter 8
## Ivy

The rumble of the truck makes the window glass vibrate just enough to pull me away from stacking the last of the plates as I unload the dishwasher. I glance up, and Junie's messy little head pops into view over the couch, cheeks squished against the glass.

"Dad brought the trailer around," she announces like she's breaking some very big news.

I wipe my hands on my leggings and meet her at the door, feeling curious. "The trailer?"

"Yeah," she says, eyes wide with curiosity as she watches out the window. "Come on. Let's go see."

I shrug into my coat, following her, sliding my arms through too fast, and shove my feet into my boots. Junie's already hopping from foot to foot like she's waiting for the starter pistol at a race. When I open the front door, the cold air blasts against my cheeks, and there's Remy standing at the end of the porch steps, gloves on, coat unzipped just enough to show the flannel underneath. The wind teases his hair, and he looks... determined.

Junie bounces down the steps first. "Are we going to get the tree today?" She asks, looking hopeful.

He shakes his head once, gaze locked on me like I'm the only one in a three-mile radius. "Not today. Right now, we have something very important to take care of, and I need your help."

Her little shoulders drop in a disappointed sigh. "Like what?"

"We're going to get Ivy's things," he says, looking at me, his voice low but edged in steel. "Remember when I told you we don't let people hurt and steal from others? We're going to get Ivy's dog and her stuff back."

*Oh, shit. He's joking.*

Remy turns again to look at me, his gaze meeting mine with a look in his eye that is possessive and determined. "Get ready. We're going."

The way he says it, with hesitation or room for argument, hits somewhere deep. It makes me forget to breathe for half a second.

"Remy, you don't have to—" I start to object. I don't want to be Remy's charity case. I feel like he's done enough giving me a job, and if I push it, he might not keep me around. Derek sure didn't.

"We're going." He tips his chin toward the truck like that's the end. "Boots, coat, whatever else you need. We're leaving in five. Let's roll out."

The flutter in my chest is ridiculous. I'm used to men like Derek, who are manipulative, who make me feel like asking for help is some kind of weakness. I had to practically beg for anything I needed or do it myself. But Remy doesn't ask. He just...handles it. Like he's going to make things right and take care of everyone around him. And there's no room for negotiation. He just says it, and we do it. And...I like it. It's really hot. Next to Junie, Remy might just be becoming my favorite person in the world. I am obviously not his, but I think everyone who knows Remy knows that deep down he's a good man. And a great dad to Junie.

Junie slips her hand into mine and beams up at me as we walk back into the house. "See? Told you my dad likes you."

I laugh under my breath, but my pulse is still thundering as I head to get ready, realizing five minutes is not enough time. "Brush your teeth," I call to Junie and quickly get ready. Remy is a man of surprises, and I'm scared for this one but thrilled. I want my dog back.

Holy crap, I might get my dog back.

* * *

The rumble of the truck and the squeak of the trailer hitch cranks my nerves even tighter as we make our way down my street to my old townhouse.

"Are you sure you're okay with my dog staying at your house?"

He glances over at me and says, "Will she eat my kid or pee on things?"

"No, she is a very good and sweet girl," I promise.

"I love dogs!" Junie pipes up from the backseat with a grin. "Maybe she'll sleep with me."

"She loves to snuggle," I promise Junie with a smile. But my stomach turns in knots as we pull up, and Remy puts the truck in park. I don't want to see Derek again.

It looks like Derek has just pulled up and is checking his mail. Black wool coat pressed sharp. Scarf knotted with precision. Shiny black Audi parked like a mirror. He could be posing for a Boston magazine spread. When we ease to the curb, he looks up. The smile he gives me is all teeth and no warmth. It is not a smile. It is a warning.

My stomach drops the way it does on a bad elevator. Heat skims my face, then drains, leaving me cold under my coat. For a second I am back in that kitchen that does not belong to me anymore, watching him slide his phone facedown, telling myself not to make a scene. The phantom weight of Lola's leash burns in my palm. I hear her nails on the hardwood that last morning, the way she whined at the door when I could not take her with me.

Anger lifts first, clean and bright. It hits my tongue like copper. Nerves come right after, a thin, mean flutter under my ribs. There is a smaller voice that I hate, the one that asks if I look like someone who had to start over with two suitcases and a defeated heart. If I look like a woman who lost the couch and the bed and the dog and still somehow kept her soft parts intact.

I straighten. I make myself breathe. The glassy calm I used to wear for him slides toward me out of habit, and I push it away. I don't need it. Not here. Not with Remy's truck warm at my back and his steady presence like a weight in the world.

Derek's eyes flick over me. He smiles again, that knife-flat line, and tucks his mail under his arm like he is winning. My hands shake once on my lap and then go still. I lace my fingers together, so I don't ball them into fists.

I hear Remy's breath, a slow drag in and out. He does not touch me, but I feel him anyway, the way the cab gathers around his quiet. The way he becomes a place to stand. The shame that used to curl me small does not find a home this time. It burns off in the heat of my anger and the steady thud of my own heart.

"Ready?" Remy asks, voice low.

I lift my chin. "Yeah," I say. My voice holds. "I am ready."

Derek takes a step like he might come over. I open my door first. The cold hits my face, sharp and clean, and I climb out into it like it belongs to me.

For a second, Remy doesn't move, just stares at Derek like

he's measuring the distance between him and deciding how he wants to do this.

"I can do this," I say quickly. I'm more convincing myself than I am stating a fact. It's not working. I'm glued to the seat and can't find my feet to make them work to get out.

Remy's eyes cut to me, one brow lifting. "Wait here a minute. I'll be right back."

It's not a suggestion. Not patronizing either, it's protective in a way that makes my pulse jump. And normally I'd argue, but something tells me he's right, and I should wait.

He gets out, shutting the door with a slam that echoes across the small yard. No gloves. Coat unzipped just enough to see the flannel underneath. His shoulders roll as if he's getting ready for a fight.

Junie watches and asks, "Who is *that* guy?"

"That's my ex-boyfriend, Derek." I murmur.

"Is that the one Uncle Finn calls Temu?" she asks, confused.

"That's the one," I say, biting my lip nervously as I watch.

"Well, you definitely got an upgrade with my dad," she mutters.

"Hey! Your dad and I are just friends," I blurt. I roll my window down and listen; Junie leans in, too.

"Bennett," Derek says with fake surprise, straightening.

*Wait. Do they know each other? I rack my brain trying to remember if Derek had met Remy at a family dinner or something, but Derek mostly made me go alone to those.*

"Here to get Ivy's things," Remy says flatly. "You gonna move, or do I need to go through you?"

Derek laughs, but it's thin. "This is between Ivy and me. Maybe you should go back to your little tree farm. Couldn't hack it here as a lawyer, right?"

*Wait, what?*

Remy steps into his space, so close I can see Derek tense up and back up.

"Here's what's gonna happen. You're gonna stand right there while I take her inside and she gathers up her things, and you're not gonna say a word while she does it."

"She owes me—" Derek starts.

"She owes you nothing," Remy cuts in, voice sharp as a blade. "And if you so much as raise your voice at her, I'll make sure you regret it. In fact, don't even talk to her or look at her. If you do, this will go sideways quickly for you."

Derek's face twitches in anger, maybe fear, and then he retreats toward his car, muttering and pulling out his phone, pushing some buttons and placing it to his ear.

Remy turns back to me, expression softening in an instant. "Come on. We need to hurry. Let's get your things. Junie, you stay right here in the truck. Don't unbuckle."

I climb out, heart thudding so hard I can feel it in my fingertips. He meets me halfway, his hand brushing the small of my back as he steers me toward the stairs. That one warm, solid touch feels like more safety than I've had in months.

Inside, it looks like a completely different home. I recognize Kristin's things everywhere. There's an expensive-looking flower bouquet on the kitchen island. I pull out the card, and it says, "Happy three-month anniversary." Oh, that's cute. We broke up this week. Nice to know she's been fucking my boyfriend for three months. Also, Derek never once sent me flowers like that.

I look for Lola everywhere. "She's not here," I say to Remy, panic filling my chest.

"We gotta hurry," Remy says as he glances out the front window at Derek, who is pacing angrily on the phone and waving his hand at the house towards us. "I'll find out where she is."

We grab my stuff that was haphazardly shoved into boxes in

the guest room. Some of my things are broken, as if someone had tossed them in carelessly. I swipe an angry tear from my eye and pick up another box and carry it out to the trailer. I need to know where Lola is. I don't want to talk to Derek, though. I can hear him on the phone, and he's angry. I can't tell what he's saying, but I hear my name.

A sharp bark splits the air. Before I can react, a blur of dark gray and black fur comes barreling from the alley, dragging a leash. "Lola!" I crouch just in time for her to leap into my arms, tail wagging so hard her entire body wiggles.

I don't even glance at her. I can't. My focus sharpens on getting Lola into the truck, like that's the only thing that matters, and it is.

Kristin says nothing. Not a word. She just walks over and stands next to Derek like it's the most natural thing in the world, like she didn't burn every bridge we ever built.

I feel her presence like a cold draft at my back, sharp and unwelcome. The girl who used to help me fix my hair before job interviews. The one who cried on my couch whenever she had her heart broken. The one who swore she'd never hurt me.

She doesn't look at me. I don't look at her.

Lola wiggles free, bolts past me, and launches herself right into the passenger seat of Remy's truck and over into the back, as if she's breaking free from Derek, too. Her tongue is hanging out as if she's not had enough water.

Remy pauses mid-step, box in his arms, head tilting, looking surprised. "*That's* your dog?"

"Yeah." I smile proudly.

His brows draw together. "I was not expecting a cattle dog."

"What were you expecting?" I ask, grinning with relief at having her back.

He shifts the box to his hip. "I don't know. Maybe one of those little purse dogs you carry around in a tote."

I laugh. "Nope. She's the best dog I've ever had."

He glances at the truck, where Lola is now sitting proudly in the back seat like she owns the place, tongue hanging out, Junie staring at her in awe and wonder.

"It's Bluey," she says in awe as she pets her side. Lola responds by kissing her cheek and turning back to me, looking relieved to see me.

"She already likes Junie," I say, and from the steady thump of her tail against the seat, I know she agrees.

By the time the last box is in the trailer, my legs are tired, and Lola has claimed Junie's blanket in the back seat. Junie has poured a water bottle into a cup for her, and she looks more relaxed.

Remy and I walk back in and do one last walk-through, Remy watching the truck as I make my way through room by room. I realize nothing here matters to me. I have my journals, scrapbooks, photos. A wooden chest that my mom had given me. And I have Lola. That's all I need. Everything else has been tainted by Kristin and Derek, and I don't want any of it anymore.

The ride back is quiet at first. Junie conks out a few minutes in, her head tipped to the side, little hand still wrapped around Lola like she's her security blanket.

I stare out at the snow-slick highway until Remy breaks the silence. "I never understood why you were with him."

My breath fogs the window. "I think I just...wanted to be loved. In the beginning, he love-bombed me and said and did all the right things, but then he stopped. Then I realized I didn't fit in that world. I never would."

"What world are you talking about?"

"A lawyer's wife," I say as I watch out the window as we hit the highway to Wisteria Cove. "Cocktail parties, firm dinners, smiling at the right moments, uncomfortable shoes and outfits curated just right so the wives wouldn't look at me like I was trash like Derek loved to remind me I was." I glance at him. "I thought I could mold myself into that person, so he'd love me. Be the woman who fits."

He keeps his eyes on the road, but I see the way his jaw ticks. "Sounds miserable."

"It was." I watch the blur of pine trees, my voice softer now. "And after being back home in Wisteria Cove, with you and Junie, I realized I don't fit in that world at all. I don't even want to."

His gaze flicks to me, brief but intense. "What world do you want to fit into?"

I shrug, a little helpless. "Who knows? The problem is, I don't know where I belong."

He's quiet for a few beats, the only sound the hum of the tires on snow. Then, almost too low to hear, "Maybe you've been looking in the wrong places."

My heart stutters, but I don't press him. Maybe he's right.

The snow falls again, soft and steady, and for the first time in a long time, the search doesn't feel so impossible.

The hum of the tires on the highway is steady enough to make my eyelids feel heavy, but I keep them open, watching the snowbanks blur past.

Remy's got one hand on the wheel, the other resting on the console. His jaw's tight, like it always is when Derek's name comes up. I'd noticed it the first time how his shoulders went stiff, the way he measured his words.

"You and Derek seemed to know each other," I say softly, watching his profile.

His mouth flattens. "I know him well enough to know I don't like him."

"How do you know him?" I ask curiously.

He glances at me, eyes cutting over for just a second before they're back on the road. "When we lived in Boston, my ex-wife worked with him at his firm."

My fingers twist in my lap. "Junie's mom?" I ask as I glance into the back seat and make sure that she's still out cold, clutching Lola.

"Her name is Sloane. She's a criminal defense attorney at his firm. At least she was; I'm not sure if she's still there." He says, his mouth in a firm line.

"The name sounds familiar, but I'm not sure. He worked at a pretty big firm, and I can't remember very many of the other attorneys' names," I admit.

He nods and watches the road, our twenty-five-minute drive turning into a longer one with the trailer and the snow.

"When was the last time she saw Junie?" I ask, then shake my head, thinking that maybe I'm crossing the line. "Wait, you don't have to answer that. I'm sorry; that's none of my business."

"January. Of last year," he adds.

"As in two years ago?" I ask, my eyes going wide. No freaking way. I couldn't go that long without seeing my family if I lived less than an hour away from them.

He nods. "She likes to do this thing where she says she's coming to get Junie and tells her they have this fun weekend planned, and then Junie gets all packed up and excited and waits, and she never shows up. She always has a lot of excuses."

"And she works with Derek?" I ask, racking my brain as I try to remember her. Then it clicks. "Wait, does she go by Whitmore?"

He nods. "Yes. That's her maiden name."

"I've met her," I tell him, not even believing this right now. "I have seen her at Derek's work events. She and Derek don't get along. He doesn't have good things to say about her. She made partner before he did, and he didn't like that."

He shakes his head. "Sounds about right. Put it this way—she's a shark. Does whatever it takes to get what she wants."

"Wow," I breathe and say before I can stop myself. "I can't see the two of you together."

He looks over at me and gives me a look. "Who do you see me with?"

I shake my head. "I don't know, but not her. She's...scary."

"She's a powerful woman," he says and shrugs. "Good at what she does for a living."

"But not a good wife or mom?" I ask.

He shrugs. "We were only together a few years before she left."

"I didn't realize you were a lawyer, too," I say cautiously.

He looks over at me and gives me a funny look as if he thought I already knew. "I'm not a lawyer anymore."

"I can't see it, but I mean, I guess. You seem like you're where you're supposed to be at the tree farm."

His jaw quirks. "Yep. Gave it all up to give Junie a better life in Wisteria Cove."

"That's insanely impressive, and I bet you have some amazing stories," I say, looking at him, trying to picture him in a suit in a courtroom.

Did this truck just get hotter all the sudden?

"Wait...what kind of lawyer were you?" I ask, half teasing, half bracing myself for some wild answer.

"A criminal defense attorney." He says it flatly, like it's nothing. Like he didn't just have a badass career that he gave up for his child.

"Actually crazy that I didn't know this," I mutter, shaking my head. "Do you...miss it?"

His jaw tightens, eyes fixed on the snowy road ahead. "No. I wasn't happy."

Something in his tone tugs at me. The way he says he *wasn't happy*, like it's a state he can't seem to find no matter where he is. My chest aches. "Sometimes you don't seem very happy here, either," I say softly, before I can swallow it back.

He doesn't glance at me. Just keeps his hands steady on the wheel. "I think there's a lot we don't know about each other," he says finally, voice low.

And he's right. There's so much unsaid between us, it hums in the air like static. So much I want to know, and so much I want to tell him.

We've got a lot to learn. And I'm about to become his best student.

# Chapter 9
# Remy

Junie giggles and squeezes Lola tighter. "I like her so much, Daddy."

The dog licks her cheek, and Junie shrieks, delighted. My heart clenches with the reminder that Ivy is temporary, and I just did a crazy thing in bringing her dog here and making my little girl fall for her, too.

When Ivy doesn't work here anymore, she'll lose two things now. Ivy and the dog.

But with Ivy, I can't help but get involved. Especially when some asshat like Derek is screwing her over. It's just not happening.

By the time we get home and get everything unloaded in our storage area of the barn, Lola sits plastered against Junie on the couch, tail thumping happily, tongue hanging out. I glance over, and my little girl is all dimples and flushed cheeks with excitement, like Christmas morning came early.

I glance over, and Ivy's not much different. Both of them are so happy to have the dog here. Something feels lighter with Ivy. She seems to have let her guard down some.

And me? I feel like a kind of peace has settled in over us I can't explain. An easiness that feels...right. Scary, but right.

Ivy smiles and scratches the dog's ears. "Junie, I think my dog likes you more than me now."

For a second I just sit there, watching them. My daughter's smile and Ivy's soft teasing. Even the dog seems to feel like she belongs here already. Something in my chest eases that I didn't realize I was still carrying.

"Tomorrow morning," I tell them. "We'll go pick out a tree. You can choose."

Junie gasps again, practically bouncing in her booster seat. "Really? Any tree I want?"

"Really. Any tree."

Ivy glances over at me, lips curved, eyes shining. That look goes straight through me. "Thank you," she mouths. I nod before I get even sappier.

I carry the last of Ivy's boxes in before she can argue. She makes a face at me when I refuse to let her take it, but I set it by the wall in the living room, out of the way. Junie immediately takes Lola and races from one end of the house to the other, squeals echoing up into the beams.

"She is going to sleep like a rock tonight," Ivy says, shaking her head with a grin.

"Good," I answer. The truth is, I don't mind the chaos Ivy has brought into this house. It feels like a home when Junie is playing and laughing. Somehow, this house has gone from just feeling like a place we lay our heads down at night to feeling like a place where we can live. Have fun, make memories. And I have to catch myself and remind myself that this is the point. Not to just work non-stop and not be able to stop and enjoy it. And she's done this in a week. I can't imagine what would happen if she stayed longer.

Later, after Junie has had her bath and is in pajamas, I set up camp at the kitchen island with my laptop with receipts and invoices. The numbers blur, but I push through, needing to catch up on paperwork. My ears stay tuned, though. Ivy hums as she works through Junie's tangles in the living room on the floor. My daughter giggles and leans in, closing her eyes, looking content.

My throat tightens at the sight of them. Junie should have had this with her own mother. But she doesn't, I remind myself. Sloane made her choice. And no matter how much that hurt my daughter, I have to accept that. But I struggle when I see Junie struggle with those choices. Kids just don't understand. Sloane never wanted a family or to get pregnant. She told me after she accidentally got pregnant that she had thought it would just be her and me. Kids weren't something she ever wanted.

Had I known that, I don't know if I ever would have married her. I always wanted a family of my own, and I thought after she had her and held Junie, she'd be happy about her, but Sloane seemed to move further and further away from us, working non-stop, and eventually, she just stopped coming home. I needed help, and when my uncle passed away and I had the chance to move home to Wisteria Cove and run the tree farm, I took it. I knew my mom and brother would be here, and Junie would have more solid people around her that loved her. I know, deep down, that I made the right choice. Sloane didn't want to build a life here with us, or there, either. I had to do what was right for my daughter, no matter how hard that has been. When we moved here, Sloane told me she was relieved not to have the pressure of being a mother anymore. And I can never understand that.

Later on, the pipes clink loudly when Ivy shuts off the shower, as if something has broken. I go down the hall and knock. "Everything okay?"

"Well...no. I mean, yes. I don't know. Remy...I need your help, but I am in the shower, and I don't know what to do," she yells frantically through the door.

'I turn the handle and crack the door. "What happened?"

Her voice comes out high and panicked over the roar of water. "The shower knob came off! I can't shut it off—*it's freezing!*"

I open the door wider and step into chaos.

She's standing in the glass shower stall, soaked, clutching a hand towel that's doing its best to keep her covered. Water blasts from the showerhead, spraying off the tile and pooling across the floor. She's dripping, trembling, clearly trying not to cry or scream.

Without thinking, I grab a full-size towel from the counter, swing open the shower door, and step in. I barely register the freezing spray before I reach for her, keeping my eyes averted.

"Here," I say, wrapping the towel around her shoulders and pulling her gently toward me. "I've got you."

Her bare feet slip a little on the tile, and I catch her. She's shivering, light in my arms, the towel now soaked but holding for now.

I lift her out of the stall, keeping my eyes above her head like my life depends on it. Her hair is sticking to her cheeks, her arms gripping the towel tight as I lower her to the bathmat.

And then the towel slips.

She gasps. I freeze.

We both look at each other like we're standing on a live wire.

Her eyes are wide, cheeks flushed. She scrambles for the towel, laughter bubbling up out of sheer panic. "Oh my *God*, this is mortifying."

I turn fast—too fast—and nearly knock over a bottle of lotion, my own shirt soaked through, water dripping onto my face from my hair. "Didn't see anything," I say hoarsely, staring very intently at the broken faucet in my hand. I definitely didn't see her dusky nipples, hard and pebbled from the cold. And I didn't see the dip of her waist, or where her hips flare out. And of course I didn't notice— "Nope. Saw nothing at all. Promise."

"Liar," she mumbles, but there's laughter in it.

I crouch down and fumble with the shutoff valve, trying to focus on the task instead of the fact that she's behind me, half-naked and dripping, and I just had her in my arms.

This day is going to be permanently etched in my brain. Whether I want it to be or not.

The water is off. I'm soaking wet; she's soaking wet, and we're both breathing heavily as we watch each other, Ivy's towel now firmly in place. All of a sudden, we both break into laughter.

"Well, that was...something," she says with a grin.

"I had no idea that faucet was broken, I promise," I say as I meet her eyes.

"Well, now you've seen me naked. There's no need to tiptoe around me anymore. We *really* know each other now," she teases.

My mouth drops open. "I don't tiptoe around you."

"Well, you don't seem to like me, either," she says, her face twisting in a nervous grin.

I step closer to her, reaching behind her to grab another towel, and she stills and closes her eyes as I come close to her face. "You don't know what I like, Ivy."

Then I take the towel, use it to dry my face and arms, and head down the hall.

I leave before I do something I can't take back. Like kiss the hell out of her.

* * *

There is a stack of invoices on my desk and a dozen calls I should return before noon. Two wholesale orders need tagging. A baler belt that needs checking. I know every task waiting for me at the lot the way other men know the backs of their hands. Most mornings I feel the weight the second my feet hit the floor.

Today I don't. Today I feel the pull of my kid in a snowflake sweater asking about hot chocolate and which tree we will cut, and I feel the quiet nudge of the woman who put cocoa on the shopping list without making it a thing.

Ivy moves through the house like she has always known where things live. She tucks mittens in Junie's pocket and sets a thermos by the door. She catches my eye and smiles like she is letting me in on a secret. I think about yesterday, hauling boxes from the condo while Derek watched from the sidewalk, and how Ivy kept her chin level the whole time. I think about the way Junie slipped her hand into Ivy's without asking and how some knot in me loosened.

I take a sip of coffee and make a choice. The farm will not break if I step back for a few hours. Tate has the crews lined out. He knows the rhythm of December. He knows when to radio me if the line at checkout snakes past the firs or if a tractor coughs wrong. I trust him. I need to act like I do.

"Tree first," I tell Junie. "Then we can string lights."

Her grin is bright enough to melt frost. She bounces on her toes. The dog sneezes and wags like she understands the plan.

A month ago, I would have been out the door before sunrise, coffee in a travel mug, mind already at the lot, body catching up later. A month ago, I would have told myself I was choosing responsibility. Maybe I was. Maybe I was also hiding in the work because it did not ask anything of me that I did not know how to give.

Now I look at my daughter and the woman by my sink, and

I feel something I have not felt in a long time. Lighter. Like there is air where the grind used to sit. The work is still there. It will always be there. But today my kid gets a fresh-cut tree and a dad who is not just passing through the kitchen on his way to somewhere else. Today I let Tate steer for a while, and I stay where the good noise is.

A knock rattles the front door.

Junie races across the living room before I can set the mug down. She flings it open with all the force her little body can manage. Finn stands there in a neon green hoodie so bright it makes my eyes hurt.

"What are you wearing?" I cringe and look away as if he's blinding me.

"Uncle Finn!" she squeals. "You look like a tennis ball."

Finn groans, glancing down at himself. "What? No, I don't."

"Yes, you do," Junie insists with a huge, knowing grin. "And you better watch out for dogs. They'll chase you. Like Lola."

Finn gapes at her as if she's just betrayed him. "Who the heck is Lola?"

I lean against the counter, biting back a laugh at hearing my five-year-old give Finn crap, which is one of my favorite things to do.

"Actually," Junie adds with perfect seriousness, "Nana says you are a golden retriever. So it makes sense why you're dressed like that. You'll attract your fellow golden retrievers. And Lola is my new best friend, silly. She's outside with Ivy. But really, I think she's mine now."

I don't laugh. The grin dies in my mouth. The coffee turns bitter on my tongue. Junie says she really feels like Lola is hers now and I feel the floor tilt. I picture that glossy black Audi and a man who would keep a dog out of spite, and my kid standing in a doorway with empty hands. The thought hits like a cold nail.

I set the mug down. "Hey," I say, aiming for gentle and landing closer to firm, "we are taking care of Lola. She belongs with Ivy."

Junie's smile falters, small and confused. Guilt flares, but the line has to be there. I cannot let her build a world that someone else can yank away. I glance at Ivy. She reads me fast, puts a hand on Junie's shoulder, and nods like we are on the same page.

"Lola is my girl," Ivy says softly, "and you are her favorite person. That is a real thing."

Junie brightens a little. I take my mug again and stare into it like it has answers. I hate how quick I am to brace. I hate that I have to be. But I will not let my daughter fall in love with something that is not ours to keep. Not if I can help it.

"Also, will you guys stop calling me that?" Finn protests, glaring at me. "I'm *not* a dog."

Our mom teases Finn that he's got the golden retriever trope in him, whatever that means. She's tried to explain it a few times. But it makes Finn irritated, so that's all that matters. And this is just hilarious.

Ivy wanders in from the back porch, hair loose around her shoulders, eyes sparkling. Lola is hot on her heels, ready to see who is here. Ivy takes one look at Finn and snorts. "That sweatshirt is brighter than the Christmas lights. Honestly, you and your brother *are* the walking definition of golden retriever energy. The only difference is Remy growls if you pet him."

I scoff, but I like it. I wouldn't mind Ivy's hands on me. And I bet I wouldn't growl. I'd do *something*.

"Traitors. All of you." Finn kicks the snow off his boots and comes inside. Lola runs to him, tail wagging. He crouches to scratch behind her ears, muttering, "And just who are you, huh?"

Junie hops up and down. "My best friend, Lola. Like I said.

We're getting the tree today. Daddy promised. Are you helping?"

"That is why I am here," Finn says. "Somebody has to make sure your dad doesn't pick out the ugliest one in the lot."

I roll my eyes. "Ivy gets to pick. We're just here to haul it."

Ivy leans her hip against the counter. "Hey, I had an idea and wanted to run by you, Remy."

"Here we go," Finn mutters, but he looks interested.

Ivy lifts her chin, undeterred. "What if we set up mini photo shoot sessions at the farm? A local photographer can do holiday portraits by the trees. Families, couples, even Christmas card shots. People would book time slots, and it would bring more business out here. I have a few people I could reach out to. A portion of the money can go to the tree farm."

Junie gasps like Ivy just invented Christmas. "Can we do that? Please, Daddy?"

I glance at Finn. His brows are raised, but he is nodding slowly. "Actually, that is not a bad idea. The more people on the property, the more trees sold. Plus, it makes the place look good online."

Ivy grins. "Exactly. Can I set it up?"

"Yeah," I say, a little stunned at how easily she thought of it. "That's a great idea."

"Perfect," she says, clapping her hands once. "I will have her start next Saturday."

"Wait," Finn says, straightening. "You already lined this up, didn't you?"

She just smiles, all smug and sweet, and glances away guiltily.

I shake my head, but I am smiling, too. She is good for us. Good for this farm., I correct myself.

But I still can't help thinking about how damn good she

looked naked. I don't think I'll ever be able to get that out of my mind.

* * *

By midmorning, we are bundled in coats and scarves as we trudge across the fields to where the trees stand tall in neat rows. The air smells of pine and frost. Junie runs ahead, Lola bounding beside her, both of them weaving between the trees as if they are on some grand adventure.

"This one!" Junie calls, pointing to a stout spruce. Two minutes later, she changes her mind. "No, this one!"

Finn throws me a look. "We are going to be here until next week."

Ivy crouches next to Junie, brushing snow off a branch. "Take your time. The right tree will pick us."

My daughter beams at her like she just solved the mystery of the universe. My chest tightens at the sight.

Finally, Junie finds it. A small pine, oddly shaped, with sturdy branches. It has to be one of the ugliest trees I've ever seen. She plants her mittened hands on her hips and says with all of her five-year-old authority. "This one. It is ours."

Finn says, "I mean...technically, they *are* all yours."

I crouch and test the trunk. "Good choice, kiddo."

I smile because I always chose the Charlie Brown Christmas trees, too. The ones nobody wanted. I always felt like they deserved the best Christmas. My mom would always say, "Don't you want the full, pretty one over there?" But, no. I always wanted the scraggly ones, much to her and my Uncle Carl's dismay. Finn could have cared less. He was ready to go sled down the big hill behind the barn and get his energy out. I always loved the tradition of picking out the very best Christmas tree.

Ivy nods and grins, knowing damn well this is one of the worst trees, and that it probably wouldn't have been sold.

With Finn's help, I saw it down and haul it back across the field. Ivy and Junie cheer like we just won a championship. We get it ready in the barn and, just as I suspected, it is in fact the ugliest tree on the tree farm.

Back at the farmhouse, we drag the tree inside. The living room fills with the sharp, fresh scent of pine. Finn sets up the stand while I steady the trunk. When it's upright, Junie claps her hands, bouncing on her toes.

"It's our first tree! Time to decorate!" she says excitedly.

I string the lights, watching them all in the warm glow. Ivy kneels with Junie, showing her how to hook the ribbon across the branches. Finn pretends to be annoyed but hums along with the Christmas music Ivy puts on.

Boxes of ornaments appear that Ivy looks like she had ready for this. Junie digs through them, pulling out glass balls and wooden stars. She hangs every ornament on the same two branches until Ivy gently shows her how to spread them out. Finn laughs as tinsel gets tangled in her hair.

It feels unreal, standing here with them, like I stepped into someone else's memory. A family gathered around a tree. Laughter bouncing off the walls. Not silence. Not weight pressing me down.

I lean back and take it all in. Ivy's cheeks are pink from the cold, her smile brighter than the lights we just hung. Junie's laughter rings out, pure joy. Finn shakes his head, but he cannot hide the grin tugging at his mouth.

This is what life should be. Not working until my body aches. Not dragging through days just trying to survive. It is this. Making memories. Being present. Enjoying my daughter. Laughing with my brother. Watching Ivy weave herself into every corner of our lives until I cannot imagine the house without her.

She makes everything better and brighter. I don't know what we did to deserve Ivy, but I'm grateful she's here.

She looks over, and her eyes catch mine, and she nods in appreciation at the tree. I look away, as I can't stop grinning.

And for the first time in a long time, I let myself believe I deserve this.

# Chapter 10
# Ivy

"Okay, so are we just not going to talk about how he went and got your dog and your stuff and pulled a whole Mary Ann to your Wanda?" Willa asks as she pours the foam into a Christmas tree shape on my latte.

I roll my eyes playfully at The Chicks song reference. "It wasn't like that," I insist. But great song.

"Oh, we're talking about it, Rowan says as she nudges my shoulder and slides onto the stool next to me.

Junie's at school, and I borrowed Remy's truck to run some errands and stopped at the bookstore to check in with my sisters.

"There's nothing to talk about, you guys. It's just a job," I say as Willa slides my latte over to me.

"Thanks," I say and take in the design on the foam and smile.

"Spill it," she demands.

"It's been almost a week since he went and got your things from Derek's, and I am just imagining how that went down," Rowan murmurs. "Remy was probably so hot."

"Hey, don't call him hot. And did you know Remy used to

be a criminal defense attorney?" I ask them, changing the subject.

Willa nods. "I knew he practiced some sort of law, but I didn't know what kind."

"I knew he left a big career behind to take over the tree farm when his uncle died," Rowan says as she twirls her tea bag in her mug.

"I was just surprised," I murmur. "He doesn't seem like the lawyer type."

"You know, he's not Derek," Willa gives me an all-knowing big sister look.

"I didn't say he was," I say, pretending not to know what she's hinting at.

"Just because Derek is a lawyer and Remy was a lawyer, doesn't mean anything," she continues.

"He does have that hot daddy thing going for him, "Rowan mutters. "If you're into that sorta thing."

I say nothing, taking a big sip of my latte, so I don't have to respond.

Oh, I'm into it, all right. But I'm not sharing that with them just yet. They'll try their hardest to get us together and meddle. Because that is what this town is good for. And god help them if they knew that Remy saw me naked with our shower mishap. I've been using the shower in his bathroom ever since, and let me tell you, the water pressure is the best. And it smells like him in there, and I like it.

The front door opens, and my mom comes in. "Well, hey there. All my girls in one spot. What's going on? What did I miss?" she asks as she shrugs off her coat and hangs it on the back of a bar stool.

"Not much, just catching up," Rowan shrugs.

"What's going on at your shop today?" My mom asks as she

glances over at the doorway between the shops that's been cut and taped up for now.

"It's coming together," Rowan says. "I need to finalize the plans for the grand opening, but I don't have dates yet because we're held up with the permits."

"It's going to be perfect," I try to reassure her.

"Yes, everything will work out," Mom says as she beams at all of us.

"And Ivy has Lola and her things back, and she was just telling us how much she loves working with Remy," Willa grins.

I kick her leg from where she's standing at the edge of the counter, which makes her duck out of the way and grin even bigger.

"I do like working with Junie and Remy," I tell them. "And it was nice of him to take me to get my things back."

"Very nice..." Rowan says with a wicked grin.

Which I ignore.

"Did Derek give you any trouble?" My mom asks, tilting her head at me as if she already knows the answer.

"Surprisingly, no," I admit.

My sisters exchange a knowing look.

"What did you do?" I demand. "I *know* you did something."

My mom smiles, and Rowan looks away guiltily. Willa stands to pour my mom a cup of coffee.

"Tell me now."

"Okay, well...I might have put Derek on ice for you," Willa shrugs.

Which means she put his name in a jar of water and froze it. Something that she likes to do when someone is bothering her or someone in our family. Oh, great.

"Well, that seemed to work. He has left me alone. Thanks for that. I guess," I tell her. "And what about you two?"

"I decline to answer on the grounds that it may incriminate me," Rowan says with a serious face.

My mom laughs and shrugs. "Same."

"Put it this way, times might get hard for Kristin and Derek," my mom says as she sips her coffee.

And this is why I love my family. They have my back, even if it's in the most unconventional ways.

They always have my back.

It's pizza night at the house, and I have the list of groceries that Remy requested. Tonight he says it's just us, Junie, his mom and Finn. We're going to watch a Christmas movie and make reindeer poop. Every time I brought up reindeer poop, Junie laughed so hard. It's basically muddy buddies, also known as puppy chow. But she loves when we make everything silly and fun.

I take my time at the Wisteria Cove General Store, pausing in an aisle when I hear Remy's name and glancing down to listen as two women talk.

"He's Wisteria Cove's most eligible bachelor," one of them says. I think her name is Vanessa, but I'm not sure. I've seen her at Rowan's yoga classes when I've filled in for her. I remember her as being kind of snarky and having mean girl energy.

"He really is. I heard he used to be a big hotshot Boston lawyer. He gave it all up to work on a tree farm. He's like a real-life Hallmark movie come to life," the other woman says, her back to me so I can't see who she is.

Both women seem to notice me and turn. "Oh, hey, Ivy," the woman—Marilyn—says sweetly. Too sweetly. "How are you? I heard you were a nanny for sweet little Junie."

I shrug. "Yeah, she's a great kid. How are you guys? Been keeping up with yoga?"

"Oh, you know it. And Pilates. Gotta keep up. Can't let the pounds creep up, if you know what I mean," Vanessa says as she gives me a look.

*Bitch.*Yeah, I'm curvy. But I'm also strong. I can do ninety minutes of yoga without breaking a sweat, while Vanessa here flops onto her mat in Child's pose every five minutes like she's dying. And I caught that snide comment loud and clear."What do you mean by that?" I say, voice low but sharp, locking eyes with her.Vanessa shrugs, flicking her nails. "What? Don't take it personally, Ivy. But maybe you'd feel better if you did yoga more often with us or added Pilates. Could do you some good."Her tone drips with condescension, like I'm some project she's trying to fix.I roll my eyes, grab my cart, and head to the checkout. "I'd take your Pilates advice more seriously if you could finish a class without collapsing. Have a nice day, *ladies.*"I don't have time for her mean-girl bullshit. Not today.I get to go home to hot Remy and his adorable kid, Junie. And by the way Remy looks at me, even after he saw me naked in the shower, I don't have the impression he had a problem with my curves. In fact, it looked like he appreciated them.

* * *

Junie's grin could light up the entire Bennett farmhouse. "Candy Land again!" she declares, slapping the colorful board down on the coffee table like she's about to win the Olympics.

"Kid, you always beat us," Finn groans, dropping onto the floor beside her.

She waggles her eyebrows at him with the smug confidence only a five-year-old can pull off. "That's because I'm the best."

Remy sits on the couch behind her, arms crossed, trying and failing to hide the smile tugging at his mouth. He looks tired, but there's something softer in his face tonight. Like the sharp edges have been sanded down a little and he's happier than when I first got here. I've figured out that pizza night does that to him. He loves making pizza, playing games, and watching movies. I think quality time might be his love language.

Donna breezes in and sits down on the couch beside me. "Candy Land again? Lord help us all. This child is ruthless."

"She cheats," Finn says, ruffling Junie's hair.

"I don't cheat!" Junie protests. "I'm just lucky. You're jealous."

"Jealous? Of losing to a kindergartner? Never," Finn says, though he looks nervous as Junie shuffles the cards.

I pull a green gingerbread pawn and set it at the start. "All right, champ. Show us what you've got."

Fifteen minutes later, Junie's got us all beat again, crowing in victory while Finn groans dramatically, and Donna watches us all like this is the best entertainment she's had all week. I have to admit, it's hard not to laugh when Junie pumps both fists in the air and shouts, "Three for three!"

"All right, Candy Queen," Remy says, hauling himself off the couch. "Enough winning. Pizza's ready."

The words are magic. I swear I've never smelled anything so good in my life. Remy Bennett, grumpy Christmas tree farmer extraordinaire, makes pizza from scratch every Friday night, and right now I'm living for it. The entire house smells of melted cheese and roasted garlic, a scent that will make your stomach growl even if you've already eaten. And a secret that I saw him do is drizzle Mike's hot honey over it when it is fresh out of the oven. It's got that perfect sweet and savory taste that I crave.

We pile into the kitchen. Remy's pulling another pizza from

the oven, steam curling up as he sets it on the counter. He glances at me, just for a second, and I swear he hesitates before reaching for the pizza cutter. Like he wants to see if I'm impressed.

I am. I grin at him and say, "Need help?"

He shakes his head and smiles. And I don't say anything, but Remy smiling is a big difference from his grumbly faces when I first got here.

We eat at the big farmhouse table. Donna sits at one end, Junie beside her, Finn across, and me... next to Remy. He doesn't say much, but he's different tonight. Gentler. Every time my glass dips low, he fills it. When the pepperoni pizza makes its way around the table, he pushes the plate toward me first.

"Try this one," he says, voice quiet. "Extra mozzarella."

I take a bite and almost melt in my seat. "This is unfair. You could open a pizza place and put every restaurant within an hour's radius out of business."

Junie giggles. "Daddy's Pizza Palace!"

Remy shakes his head, cheeks faintly pink.

"Marco would be devastated if he knew your pizza was this good." I tell him and watch his eyes light up at the compliment.

But when I reach for another slice, he hides a smile full of pride.

Donna, of course, notices everything. She leans her chin on her hand, eyes dancing, and when Remy glances her way, she winks at him. He rolls his eyes and clears his throat, taking a bite of his crust like he can pretend she didn't just call him out without saying a word.

The house looks different tonight, too. I didn't notice at first, but now mistletoe hangs everywhere. Over the kitchen doorway. Above the back door. Even dangling from the light fixture in the living room.

"Real subtle," Remy mutters, glancing up at the sprig dangling above us.

Donna's smile is pure mischief. "Tradition, sweetheart. Anyone caught under the mistletoe has to kiss."

Junie gasps. "That's the rule!"

I press a hand to my chest, eyes wide. "Oh no. Finn, guess I better call Rowan over."

Finn nearly chokes on his soda. "Hey. Not fair."

Donna cackles, and even Remy lets out a laugh, low and rough, that makes my stomach flutter. And luckily the teasing gets us out of kissing under the mistletoe, which without an audience, I wouldn't mind kissing Remy. He could kiss me anywhere.

The teasing doesn't stop through the rest of dinner. Remy doesn't say much, but every once in a while, I catch him looking at me like he's wondering what would happen if Junie shoved me under the mistletoe with him again.

And I wonder myself. More than I should. I wonder what it would be like to wrap my arms around his neck and pull him in. Kiss him slowly, feel his arms around me. I wonder what he'd do if I kissed him. I know that kissing Remy in my fantasies is pretty hot. In real life, I might combust.

After we all clean up, we migrate to the living room for Christmas movie night. The tree glows in the corner, colorful lights reflecting in the window. Donna insists on *It's a Wonderful Life*. Junie curls up between her and Finn on the couch, leaving the other side empty.

I settle in, pulling the blanket across my lap. A moment later, Remy drops beside me. Not close enough to touch, but close enough that the heat of his body makes me hyperaware of every breath I take. I feel like I'm back in high school, sitting next to the crush I swore no one would ever know about.

I pull the blanket over and give some to him, and he says nothing, just settles in as if this is something we do daily.

Halfway through the movie, my eyes get heavy. The laughter from the kitchen, the warmth of the fire, the weight of the blanket...all of it pulls me under. The last thing I notice is Remy shifting closer, his arm brushing mine, steady and warm.

When I wake, the room is quiet. The lights are dim; the movie is long over. Junie's gone, probably tucked into bed with Lola at her feet. Donna and Finn are gone too. The only one left is Remy, still sitting right here, letting me use his shoulder like a pillow.

I jerk upright, mortified. "Why didn't you wake me?"

His voice is soft, deeper than usual in the quiet. "You looked like you needed the sleep."

Heat floods my cheeks. "Oh, my gosh. I drooled on you, didn't I?"

He snort-laughs, the sound rough and unguarded. "I have a kid. I've been drooled on."

The way he looks at me then makes my stomach flip. There's no irritation, no guarded walls. Just warmth. Interest. Something I can't quite name but that makes me feel like my chest might burst.

I can't stop myself. I lean in and press a quick kiss to his cheek. His stubble is rough against my lips, and his skin is warm. He freezes, and his eyes close, and he sucks in his breath. His body visibly relaxes, as if he needed that touch.

"Goodnight, Remy," I whisper before I can lose my nerve, and I head to my room, heart hammering.

I close my door and press my back to it, my pulse racing like I just did something far more reckless than kiss Remy on the cheek. My lips still tingle, my hand itching to go back, to touch him again. I get ready quickly and crawl into bed, pulling the blanket up to my chin, but the warmth under my skin has nothing to do with the quilt. Every time I close my eyes, I see the look on his face, feel the way his whole body went still like he'd been waiting for me to do that forever. I bite back a smile into my pillow.

Tonight, I didn't just say goodnight. I started something neither of us can take back. The ball is in his court now. Let's see what he does with it.

# Chapter 11
# Remy

"**D**addy!" Junie comes flying across the yard, cheeks flushed. "It's our turn for a picture."

The farm hums with life. Laughter carries through the rows of pines, high-pitched and breathless as kids dart between the trees with candy canes clutched in sticky hands. Families pose in front of trees for the photographer, and the air smells like pine and kettle corn popcorn from the farm stand.

When I first took over this place, these were the days that I dreamed of.

It's been almost a week since Ivy fell asleep against me on the couch and then kissed me on the cheek. And damn if I haven't wanted to pick her up and kiss the hell out of her every day since. I'm trying my best here, but keeping my distance is getting harder every day.

I stand near the farm stand, scanning the rows of people. The farm feels different this year and looks like something out of a movie. Lights strung between the trees glow soft gold against the gray afternoon sky. Every time I turn, I catch sight of plaid scarves, red cheeks, and smiles that make the hard work

I've poured into this feel worth it. I think my uncle would be proud of what I've done to carry on his legacy with this place.

I glance at the photographer, who waves me over. "Come on then," I tell Junie, taking her small hand in mine.

She's warm from running, bundled in her puffy purple coat, hair escaping her hat in wild curls. She wraps her arms around mine, and I feel that familiar pull in my chest. This kid is my entire world, right here. Everything I'm building and everything I'm doing is for her.

We take our place in front of the barn where the wreaths hang and the photographer has staged a backdrop for photos. Junie wiggles into place, grinning at the camera.

The photographer lifts her hand. "Perfect. Just the two of you? Or do you want—"

"Wait!" Junie cuts her off, her voice ringing clear. She spins, searching the crowd. "Ivy!"

Ivy freezes at the edge of the group, caught like a deer in headlights. She's holding two paper cups of cocoa, one halfway to her lips.

Junie is bouncing, hat sliding over one eye. "You are family. Family gets in the picture."

The word lands in my chest and sits there, warm and heavy. I look at Ivy. She laughs, nervous, already backing up like she is protecting us from a line we did not draw. I feel the old reflex rise, the one that keeps things tidy and safe, and I choose not to use it. "Get in," I say, and my voice comes out softer than I expect. I make room at my side, and Junie wedges herself between us, grinning so hard her cheeks bunch. Ivy steps close. I can smell cold air and sugar on her scarf. The shutter clicks. Something eases in my ribs. It still scares me. It also feels right.

The photographer chuckles under her breath. "She's got a point."

My heart does a strange kick. I watch Ivy hesitate, glance at me, then step forward. She sets the cocoa on the fence post and walks toward us, cheeks pink, eyes darting like she's still not sure if she belongs.

She does. God help me, she does. I can fight this, but the truth is everyone loves having Ivy here. She fits in better than I could have imagined. But that's not the problem. The problem is, *will she stay?*

She stands next to Junie, smiling, tucking her hair behind her ear. Junie tugs her in closer, giggling. The photographer lifts the camera.

And before I even think about it, my arm goes around Ivy's shoulders. Natural as breathing. Like my heart knew before my brain. She goes still, just for a second, then leans into it. Warm. Soft. The scent of her hair, vanilla and something floral, curls up around me.

"Okay," the photographer says, snapping away. "That's the shot. Big smiles."

Junie beams, and Ivy laughs, a sound that I love hearing. And me, I just stare straight ahead, my arm locked around her like I might never want to let go.

The camera clicks, one frame after another, but the real moment isn't the photo. It's the weight of Ivy against me, the way she feels like she belongs right here, tucked into the frame of my family.

The photographer lowers her camera. "What a beautiful family. You three look perfect."

Three, not two. *Three.* My heart echoes the word.

Ivy pulls back gently, her eyes catching mine for just a second, wide and startled, like she felt it too. Then Junie grabs her hand and drags her toward the farm stand, chattering about sprinkles for sugar cookies.

I stay rooted where I am, the ghost of her warmth still

pressed to my side. For the first time in a long time, the farm doesn't just feel full of other people's holiday magic.

It feels like it could be mine, too.

The photographer's assistant hands me a sample printout of the picture she just took. I look down, and my chest tightens.

It's me, Junie, and Ivy, all together in front of the barn. Junie grins as if she just won the lottery. Ivy smiling, her cheeks flushed. My arm firm around her shoulders, like it's holding her where she belongs.

The word that lodges in my throat is *family*. Something I have desperately wanted of my own, my whole life.

"Remy."

I turn and find my mother watching me. Donna, the one person who can read me better than anyone in the world. She plucks the print from my hand before I can react.

"Oh my," she says, her smile widening. "Now if that isn't a Christmas card."

"Ma," I warn.

She ignores me, tilting the photo toward the light. "Look at you. The broody Christmas tree farmer looking so happy. And Ivy looks radiant. Junie looks like she just pulled off the best scheme of her life. This is...well, this is perfect."

"Don't start," I mutter. "And Junie gets this from you."

Donna raises a brow. "Start what? I haven't said a word about the fact that my son hasn't looked this happy in years. Or that Ivy fits at your side like she's meant to be here. Or that Junie might be on to something with all that mistletoe she's been scattering around your house."

I rub the back of my neck. "She's the nanny, Ma. Nothing more."

Donna's smile softens, and that's almost worse than when she's teasing. "Sweetheart, I'm a romance author. I know it when I see a story unfolding. And believe me, this" —she taps the photo— "is a story that's unfolding."

I shake my head, but I can still feel Ivy's warmth pressed into me, her hair brushing my shoulder.

Donna slips the picture into her bag as if it's evidence. "I'll get this framed and make copies. Junie will love it."

"Don't—" I start, but she's already walking toward the farm stand, humming like Christmas came early.

I stand there, with the sound of laughter in the distance and the smell of pine wrapping around me. Families wander past with their trees, kids giggling. And in the middle of it, I catch sight of Ivy, laughing as Junie tugs her mitten, both of them glowing in the fading afternoon light as they talk to someone in the farm stand.

My mother's meddling might drive me crazy. But when I think about the way Ivy fits against me like she belongs, I don't know what I think anymore. I feel like I'm watching a movie of my life play out and there's nothing I can do to stop it. I just have to sit back and watch as my life unfolds. And for once, it feels like it's unfolding in a way that doesn't hurt. But then I think of how it could hurt, and I'm back to shutting down again.

* * *

A week after the photography session, we are in town. The whole town turns out every year for the tree-lighting ceremony in downtown Wisteria Cove. Main Street glows with festive lights strung across storefronts, wreaths hanging from every lamppost. The air smells of salt from the harbor. This evening it's gotten so cold that it bites the nose, but it feels good because everyone's bundled together, shoulder to shoulder, waiting for the countdown.

I stand near the front with Junie perched on my shoulders. She waves her mittened hands at her friends from school, calling out names, giggling so hard I can feel it rattle down into my chest with how happy she is. This right here is why I wanted to move her back to Wisteria Cove, so that she could experience all of these traditions and have a great childhood here like I did. Sure, it was just my Mom, Finn, and me. But we had Pete, and friends. That almost made up for not having a dad.

This is why when Sloane first told me she was unexpectedly pregnant, I knew that I was made to be a dad. That this was something that was going to change our lives. And it changed mine in the best of ways. I love getting to show Junie everything and have our own family traditions. I knew what kind of dad I was going to be. The kind who stuck around and made sure she felt loved every single day.

Beside me, my mom chats with neighbors, her cheeks flushed from the cold. She's got her arm looped through Pete's, steadying him. It makes my chest pull tight.

At Ivy's insistence, I'm wearing the new scarf she bought me. I have to admit, I like it.

Pete looks smaller tonight. A little more tired. His face is pale under the glow of the lights, his shoulders not as straight as they used to be. He smiles when folks come up to shake his hand, or clap him gently on the back, but there's a weariness in him now that wasn't there last Christmas.

The realization that this is his last Christmas kicks me square in the chest. He told us this fall that doctors diagnosed him with stage four lung cancer, and he didn't have much time. So, I think it was an unspoken agreement amongst all of us that we were going to make sure that Pete felt loved for the rest of his days, us making the most of them with him.

I've been bracing for this, telling myself we'll have plenty of time. But time feels like it's slipping through our fingers. Pete's been like a father to me and Finn our whole lives. My dad left when Ma was pregnant with Finn. I don't even remember his face, and I don't want to. But I do remember Pete, steady and sure, showing me how to hammer a nail, how to tie the perfect fishing knot, how to drive an old truck without stripping the gears.

He's always been there. And now he looks frail. Mortal. And that doesn't seem right. The thought rips something sharp in my chest, making my heart squeeze and my nose run with emotion.

My mom and Pete have never been a couple, but they've always been best friends. Companions. This fall he moved into her house with her so that she could take care of him. She's been helping him get his things in order, and I know that is weighing on her, too. Finn and I are trying to help as much as possible. He's our family.

Ivy must notice it, too. She's standing on my other side, hands tucked into her coat pockets, her breath white in the air. When Pete chuckles weakly at something Donna says, Ivy glances at me, and her eyes soften. No words are needed. She just gives me a look as if she understands. She slides her arm through mine and gives the smallest squeeze. Quick. Gentle. Solidarity.

*He means so much to all of us.*

For a moment, the crowd noise fades, and it's just us, standing together under the lights with Junie giggling above me and Pete smiling thinly beside Ma. The weight of what's coming presses down, but Ivy's touch steadies me. Reminds me I'm not carrying it alone. We're all going to have a crater in our hearts when Pete passes away. Life is brutally unfair.

The mayor, Sammy Briggs, steps up to the microphone and

starts the countdown. *Ten, nine, eight...* The crowd joins in, voices echoing down the street.

When we hit *one*, the tree bursts to life. Strings of white and gold blink on, ornaments glittering, the star at the top shining against the night sky. The crowd cheers. Junie gasps, clapping her little hands.

Pete's smile widens, his eyes bright despite the shadows under them. He leans close to Donna and murmurs something that makes her laugh, a sound that cracks my heart and mends it at the same time.

The ceremony rolls into the cookie swap, tables set up with tins and trays from every family in town. Kids dart between the tables, sugar-high and giddy.

Ivy steps forward to the table where we'd set a big red container in her hands. "All right," she says, grinning, "Junie, and I made my famous hot cocoa peppermint cookies." She pops the lid, and the smell hits instantly, filling the air with chocolate, mint, and marshmallow. She passes them around, and the first bite is chewy perfection. Rich chocolate, the cool bite of peppermint, gooey marshmallow bits melted right into the dough.

Ivy watches me as I try the cookie and smiles with relief when I nod and smile, "These are really good."

"Of course they are, Dad. We made them," Junie says as if this is already a known fact.

"These are sinful," Donna declares, snatching a second.

"Best ones yet," Pete agrees, his voice hoarse from coughing, but warm.

Junie shoves half of one into her mouth and declares, "Ivy wins!"

Even I can't help the small smile tugging at my mouth as I take another bite. Sweet, perfect. Just like her.

For a while, it's easy to pretend everything's fine. The lights glow, the cookies disappear, Junie's laughter rings out across the square. But when I glance at Pete, leaning heavier on Ma than usual, I feel the ache come back.

Time is short. I know it. And tonight, with Ivy's arm brushing mine and her cookies warming the cold from the inside out, I promise myself that we'll get through this. Together.

# Chapter 12
# Ivy

The water is cooling, and I sink lower into Remy's big freestanding soaker tub until it laps at my collarbone, soaking up every minute of this bath. His primary bathroom feels too big, too quiet, the steam curling against the frosted window.

I try to let it soothe me, but his words echo anyway.

*She's just the nanny.*

I hadn't meant to overhear Remy and his mom's conversation after we took photos. Donna had him cornered after the photo shoot, holding up that picture like evidence, and I'd overheard from the farm stand. It shouldn't matter, and I shouldn't still be so bothered by his words. They were the truth. He's right, and that's all I am. Temporary, convenient, filling a gap until he doesn't need me anymore. But the words sting sharper than I expect. I tell myself not to feel it, not to care, but it sits heavy in my chest, anyway.

I drain the tub, wrap myself in one of his thick towels, and pad across the tile. My hair drips down my shoulders, leaving damp streaks on the cotton.

A gentle knock rattles the bedroom door. "Hey," Remy's

voice calls, low, steady. Before I think better of it, I crack the door. Just a peek.

He's there in the hallway, coat half-zipped, beanie pulled low. His eyes widen when he sees me, his gaze flicking down to where the towel knots tight at my chest, then snapping back up. Not crude, not lingering, but enough to make the air stretch thin between us. And a reminder that Remy is a man. And he is so freaking good looking.

Not that I forgot. I think about this daily.

"Sorry," I whisper, my voice catching. "I just got out of the bath."

He clears his throat, softer now. "Did you see we're supposed to get dumped on tonight? Huge snowstorm coming. I'm going to check on things before it hits."

For a moment, we just stand there. The faint rush of the wind outside. The dripping of water from my hair. His eyes on me, softer than I've ever seen them.

"Okay," I manage. My fingers clutch the edge of the towel tighter.

He nods, lingering a heartbeat too long, then steps back. "I'll be back soon if you need anything. Tate's meeting me over at the barn."

When he turns, I press the door closed, leaning against it with my heart pounding. His words still echo in my head, but the look he just gave me whispers something different.

I might *just* be the nanny. But he looks at me like he wants me to be more. And I feel the tension between us. It can't be just me, right? He's different now.

I towel off quickly and tug on my cozy flannel pajamas before slipping down the hall. The house feels hushed and quiet, which seems to come just before a storm. Fitting. I push open Junie's door and peek in.

She's a little heap of blankets, her hair spilling across the pillow in curls, cheeks flushed pink with sleep. Lola lies curled at her feet, tail thumping once against the floral purple comforter when she notices me. I step in and smooth a hand over Junie's hair. She sighs, clutching her narwhal tighter. Lola gives a soft huff, then drops her head back down, satisfied the world is safe, and she's at home with her new girl to watch over. I stroke her soft ears and press a kiss to her head, as well. I'm glad Junie has this. Lola is a good comfort.

My chest tightens. They already feel stitched into me in ways I hadn't planned, in ways I know I shouldn't let myself think about wanting more.

*I am just the nanny.*

Back in the kitchen, I fill the kettle and wait until it whistles. I pour steaming water over a homemade mix of chamomile Rowan made me; the scent rises gentle and floral. The mug warms my palms as I curl into the armchair by the big front window.

Outside, the first flakes of snow drift down, catching in the light above the porch. Soft and slow at first, then thicker, heavier snow that promises the world will look different by morning. And that makes me think about how unrecognizable my life is right now from just a month ago.

I sip the tea and watch it fall; the heat sinking through me while the storm builds.

How am I supposed to get through this season without falling deeper for them? Even my dog fell head over heels for his kid. I'm second best to her now, and I'm okay with that. Junie needed her. I'm falling hard. For Junie, with her excitement and bigger laugh, who calls me her family without hesitation. For Remy, who holds everything tight and pretends he doesn't feel, but then fills my glass before I ask, or lets me sleep on his shoulder without moving. He's everyone's rock and solid, safe place. It makes me wonder what his safe place is? Who is there for him?

I already know the answer. I can't stop myself. Not when I'm feeling like this. Like I finally belong somewhere. Not when the sight of snow falling outside this window feels like the start of something I've wanted for longer than I'll ever admit.

The tea cools in my hands. The snow keeps falling. And I sit there in the quiet, letting myself hope, even if I probably shouldn't. Because people we love leave us and sometimes die. Just like we're watching this play out with Pete. It's like losing my dad all over again. A few years ago, my dad and Tate's dad went out on a commercial fishing run and never came back. Not only was their boat never recovered, but neither were they. And that shattered my mom and my sisters. And Tate. I watched how he lost his dad, and then his mother faded away. People we love leave or die. And that hurts worse than being lonely. Sometimes I wonder if I'm just meant to be alone. But when I look at Remy and Junie, I know that isn't true. I just don't know if I can risk my heart shattering again.

* * *

"It's a snow day!" Junie's shriek down the hall outside my door yanks me out of sleep before the sun even shines through the curtains.

The next thing I know, my door bursts open, and Lola launches herself onto the bed. Forty pounds of excited cattle dog lands square on my stomach, and then there's a cold, wet tongue dragging across my face.

"Ugh, Lola!" I laugh, trying to fend her off. "I get it, I get it. Your new, tiny human is excited. Message received."

Junie bounces right up behind her, curls wild and cheeks already flushed with the thrill of no school. She's still in her pajamas, feet thumping against the floor as she scrambles up beside me.

"Look!" she says, tugging at the curtain. She yanks it open, and sure enough, the whole world outside is blanketed in white. Snow covers the fields, the porch, the fences, glittering under the pale gray morning sky.

"It's beautiful," I whisper, sitting up, Lola wedged happily between us.

Junie turns to me with wide eyes. "What can we check off of our list today?"

"What were you thinking?" I ask, brushing her curls back.

"We need snow angels, a snow fort, and a snowball fight. All today."

"All today?" I pretend to gasp. "That's a lot of snow business to handle. Think we can handle all of that?"

She giggles and nods, and Lola barks like she's in on the plan, too.

I finally swing my legs out of bed, tugging the blanket around my shoulders. The smell of coffee hits me as soon as we make it into the kitchen. A note sits propped against the pot, scrawled in Remy's messy handwriting:

*Out clearing snow. Stay warm. Coffee's ready.*

When I went to bed he was out clearing, and I get up and he's already gone. I wonder if he's avoiding me. But then he goes and leaves me little notes and coffee. Hmmm.

I pour a mug, wrapping both hands around it, the warmth soaking through my fingers. Junie climbs onto a chair, chattering about the snow fort and how big it should be, Lola circling the table like she's already mapping out where the battle lines will fall in the great snowball fight of the year.

Through the window I catch sight of Remy's side-by-side moving across the field by the barn, a trail cut through the drifts with a snowplow attached to it.

Something pulls tight in my chest. He thinks of everything, even down to the full coffee pot waiting here for me. And as Junie leans against my arm, already planning the day, I realize this little family feels more like home than anything has in years.

I sip my coffee and smile. "All right, Junebug. Snow angels, a fort, and a snowball fight. Let's do it."

Junie squeals, Lola barks again, and for a moment the whole kitchen feels lit from the inside out.

I hold up a hand. "But first, we do breakfast. I'm going to make oatmeal, then we'll bundle up and go on our adventure."

"I'll help," she says, dragging out the pan from the cabinet and setting it on the counter. We work together and get the oatmeal going, and she drags out all of her snow gear from the closet. Lola runs outside to do her business, and I see her run to the field where Remy is. He stops, gets out and reaches down to pet her and scratch her ears, then gets back into the side-by-side. She runs around the field and then she comes back. She loves it here. I don't even know if I can take her from Junie at this point. They have made such a close bond.

After I get her to eat a little, we bundle up and go outside. I borrow some of Remy's snow gear that is way too big for me, but I make it work.

The snow is deeper than I expected, already past my boots as Junie and I flop down side by side to make angels. She kicks her legs and sweeps her arms, giggling so hard she can't keep the lines straight. Lola darts around us, barking, her paws sinking into the drifts.

When we stand, Junie declares our angels perfect, even though mine looks lopsided. She points to the side yard. "That's where the fort goes."

We build walls of packed snow, piling them high until our gloves are soaked and our cheeks are numb. Junie pops her head over the top of the fort. "This is the best day ever."

"It really is," I say as I pack in more snow. I love seeing the joy and wonder through her eyes and being present for all of this. It's really a true joy to have this holiday season with her.

That's when the rumble of the side-by-side cuts through the quiet. Remy pulls up, climbs out, brushing snow off his coat.

"Daddy!" Junie squeals. "Get him!"

Before I can react, she pelts him square in the chest with a snowball, and her laugh rings out so loud.

I can't help myself. I pack one fast and toss it. It smacks against his arm with a satisfying thud.

He freezes, eyebrows lifting.

I hold my breath, waiting for his response. Sometimes he can be so serious, even though he's been defrosting.

"Oh, you two want a war?" He says with that sexy smirk of his that hits me right in my lady parts. Whew.

Junie shrieks and ducks behind the fort. I yelp, already scrambling to scoop another snowball. He charges toward us, boots crunching, and the battle explodes. Snow flies in every direction. Junie shrieks with glee as he peppers the fort with perfect throws, and I laugh so hard I can barely aim.

"Run!" I shout, grabbing Junie's mitten and dragging her across the yard, Lola barking wildly as if she's cheering. She circles us as if she's rounding us up.

Remy doesn't let us get far. He lobs one that bursts against my shoulder, then another that explodes at my boots. I squeal and stumble, laughing so hard my sides ache. He throws a few at Junie, making her squeal and duck to hide further across the yard.

Then he turns his focus on me.

"Oh no," I say, backing up, hands raised. "Truce. Truce!"

"Too late." His grin is wicked. He lunges, and I try to dodge, but the snow gives way under my feet. I go down in a puff of white, and he follows, bracing himself but still landing half on top of me.

The world tilts. My breath catches. He's heavy, solid, his coat cold against my body, his face so close I can see every fleck of green in his silver eyes. His hands sink into the snow beside my head, and for a moment, neither of us moves.

Then it happens. With the smallest tilt forward, his lips brush mine. Barely there, but enough to send heat roaring through me. Enough to make me forget the snow, the cold, the entire world. My pulse stutters, his lips feeling like they were meant to be on mine.

And then, thwack. A snowball explodes against the back of his head.

Junie howls with laughter as she runs across the yard. "Got you, Daddy!"

He groans, rolling off me, brushing snow from his hair. I'm breathless, my heart slamming against my ribs. He glances at me, and I see it in his eyes, the same fire that's burning through me. He watches my lips like he doesn't want to stop, either.

We scramble up, both of us shaking our heads like it didn't happen, like it was just a game. But my lips still tingle. My body still hums. Heat pools in my lower belly at how his hard body felt atop mine.

Junie dances in the snow, triumphant, while Remy scoops her up, spinning her around until she squeals. I watch them, trying to steady myself, trying to remember I'm supposed to be just the nanny.

But there's no mistaking what I felt in that half-second under him. And there's no mistaking that he felt it, too.

* * *

Snow continues to fall outside in thick, slow flakes, blanketing the yard and making the world glow white. Inside, the fire crackles and fills the room with that cozy wood-smoke smell I secretly love.

Junie is curled on the floor with a blanket and a bowl of popcorn, laughing at the animated Christmas movie she picked. Remy and I are next to each other on the couch.

I can't focus on the movie. Not when he keeps inching closer. Not when his knee brushes mine every time he shifts.

When I cannot take it anymore, I grin to myself and swing my legs into his lap, pretending it is casual. His hand stops where it rests on his thigh, and his gaze snaps to me.

"What's with the kiss, beast?" I whisper softly, leaning over, just loud enough for him to hear but not Junie.

His throat works as if he is swallowing back words. "Ivy." His voice whispers roughly, and my name sounds like something I want to hear when we're all alone, preferably naked.

I smirk and wiggle my toes against his calves and whisper, "What? Are we just going to pretend you didn't just kiss me in the snow and now you regret it?"

His jaw tightens. He glances toward Junie, who is completely glued to the movie, then leans closer until I feel the warmth of his breath as he whispers to me. "You think I regret it?"

"I don't know what you thought," I say, tipping my head toward him, "But I've been thinking about it all day."

Heat flashes in his eyes. "I have, too."

That one quiet admission sends my pulse racing. I let my hand trail down his arm, enjoying the way the muscle jumps under my fingers. "Good."

"Good?" His voice drops lower, almost a warning.

"Yes." I keep my eyes on him, daring him to look away. "Because I have been waiting to do it again."

His hand slides down my shin under the blanket. His thumb traces slow circles on my skin, light and unhurried, but it makes me shiver, anyway.

"Keep talking like that," he says near my ear, "and I will make you pay for it later."

My laugh is soft but shaky. "Okay."

His fingers tighten slightly before they relax again. "Later."

The single word curls through me like smoke.

Junie giggles at the movie, completely unaware of the electricity sparking between us on the couch. I drag my gaze back to the screen, pretending I am calm, but my heart is racing. His hand stays on my leg, steady and warm, thumb brushing slow and lazy until I can barely remember what we were watching.

And suddenly it feels too hot for a snow day.

# Chapter 13
# Remy

I can't stop thinking about that kiss. It's been hours, but I can still feel the cold bite of the snow on my face, the way Ivy's mouth tasted like peppermint, and the way my lips moved to hers without a single thought. I kissed her like I had been starving for years. And maybe I have been.

If Junie hadn't been there, I am not sure I would have stopped. In fact, when I kissed her, I completely forgot for a moment that my daughter was there. I felt like I couldn't control it.

I scrub a hand over my face as I close Junie's bedroom door, slightly ajar the way she likes it. She is out cold, curled up with her stuffed narwhal. The house is quiet except for the low hum of the furnace.

I am about to head for the kitchen when Ivy's door creaks open. She steps out, barefoot, wearing one of my flannels over a tank top and pajama pants. Her hair is loose, a little messy, and for a second, I just stand there, staring like an idiot.

"You okay?" she asks softly.

"Yeah." My voice comes out rough. "You?"

She nods and moves toward the living room. "Couldn't sleep."

I follow her as if I don't have a choice. We sit on the couch, a safe distance apart at first, but the space between us feels unbearable.

Then she looks at me like she is reading every thought in my head, and that is all it takes.

I lean in just as she leans into me, and I kiss her. It is nothing like earlier in the snow. This one is hotter, deeper, leaving no room for second-guessing. Her hands fist my shirt, and I pull her closer until she is in my lap.

When I finally break away, I'm breathing hard. "Wait."

Her eyes are wide with surprise. "Wait?"

"We have to talk about this." My voice is unsteady.

She nods, biting her lip, and that almost distracts me again. "Okay. Let's talk faster."

I lean back, laughing, scrubbing my hands over my face, trying to pull my thoughts together. "I have not been with anyone since Sloane. I thought I was fine with that, but then you kissed me—"

"You kissed me," she interrupts, a smile tugging at her lips.

"Fine. I kissed you," I admit. "And it was like something snapped inside me. I wanted you so badly I didn't care that Junie was standing twenty feet away. I wanted to kiss you until you forgot your own name."

She goes quiet, her chest rising and falling as she watches me.

"I don't know what this is," I say finally, my voice low. "But I know I don't want it to stop. I'm lonely, Ivy. I'm tired of pretending everything is fine. And when you're around, I feel like I can breathe again."

Something softens in her expression. She shifts closer until I feel my dick painfully harden with her touching me.

"I'm scared," she admits quietly. "Scared this will mess everything up. But I can't stop thinking about that kiss, either."

Relief rushes through me like a tide. I reach for her hand, holding it tight.

"Then maybe we stop pretending we don't want this," I say. "Call it what it is. We are both grown, consenting adults."

The words taste wrong the second they are out. I hear myself trying to make it sound casual and I hate it. I do want her in my bed, but I also want her coffee mug on my counter and her laugh in my truck. I want the small domestic things that live after the lights go out. I want her in my sweatshirt in the morning. I want her key on my hook. I want her.

She watches me, guarded. I can see the line she needs to draw. If this door is the one she can open, I will take it, but I will not pretend it is only that.

"Whatever you want," I say, voice low. I touch her jaw because I cannot not touch her. "Just know I am not going to treat you like you're something casual. That's not what this is."

Her eyes flick, surprised and hungry. The air tilts. When I kiss her again, it is careful for one breath, and then it is not careful at all.

She bites her lip and grins at that, and that is all the permission I need before I kiss her again, slow and deep this time, tasting her like I have no reason to stop. Because maybe we both deserve this. We deserve to be happy.

Ivy's mouth is soft and hot under mine, and suddenly I cannot get enough. My flannel slips off her shoulders as I pull her closer, and she doesn't hesitate, like she has been waiting for this as long as I have.

The sound she makes when I grip her hips and drag her across my hard cock nearly undoes me.

"Remy," she whispers against my mouth, and it is the sweetest, most dangerous sound in the world.

I kiss her harder. I taste her, breathe her in, let years of quiet want pour into every movement. Her hands slide up into my hair, tugging just enough to make me groan.

"Tell me to stop," I challenge, even as my hands slip under the hem of her tank top, skimming her warm skin.

"Don't you dare stop," she says, breathless.

That's all I need.

I shift, laying her back against the couch cushions and bracing my weight on one arm so I don't crush her. She looks up at me, cheeks flushed, lips swollen, and I swear I have never seen anything more beautiful.

I kiss down her throat, slow at first, then faster when she arches against me. Her fingers grip my shoulders, pulling me closer until there is no space left between us.

"Ivy," I rasp against her skin. "You don't know how badly I want you."

She smiles, wicked and soft all at once. "Then show me."

Her words light me on fire. My hand slides down her side and over the curve of her hip, gripping her thigh to pull her against me. She gasps and moans when she feels my fingers find her center, sounds that nearly ruin me.

I force myself to slow down, even though my body is practically begging her to want me, too. "If we do this, it changes everything."

Her hands frame my face, pulling me down so our foreheads touch. "Good," she whispers in a challenge. "Let it change everything."

I lose control then, and I kiss her like I'm starving, like I've been waiting years to taste her, because I have. Every kiss is deeper, hungrier. Her tank top ends up somewhere on the floor, my T-shirt follows, and the heat between us is undeniable.

When her nails drag down my back, I nearly lose it.

"Ivy." My voice is rough, shaking. "We should go to my room before I completely fuck you every which way on this couch."

She nods, eyes dark with want. "Then take me there."

I scoop her up and carry her down the hall, her legs wrapped around my waist, her mouth on my neck. The whole way, I am half praying Junie stays asleep and half thanking God for giving me this woman.

When I lay her on my bed, she looks at me in a way no one has ever looked at me before, making me feel something no one has ever made me feel.

Wanted.

I strip the rest of her clothes and then mine. The way she's looking at me right now is something I'll never forget.

Her hair spills over my pillow like a halo, her cheeks flushed, her lips swollen from kissing. I have imagined this a hundred times, but nothing could have prepared me for the real thing.

I kiss her, slowly at first, because I want to remember this moment. Her hands slide into my hair and hold me there, kissing me back like she wants me just as much.

I trail my mouth down her jaw and throat, tasting the soft salt of her skin and breathing her in. She smells like soap and something warm and sweet that is only her. I cannot stop touching her, the curve of her hip, the hollow at her waist, the smooth line of her thigh. She is soft everywhere and perfect, and I take my time, learning every inch. I gently pinch, sucking and licking her nipples. Her hands trail from my back to my chest, almost as if she is memorizing every inch of me as I am with her.

My hands rise, slow, and she draws a breath that shakes a little. I cup her gently, thumbs skimming the warm swell, a light tease that has her arching into my palms. Heat runs through me.

I lower my head and let my mouth follow, lingering at the edge where her heartbeat flutters under my lips, tasting the heat there while my hands coax another soft sound from her. She answers me without hesitation, guiding me closer, greedy for more in a way that makes my control slip.

She is not passive for a second. Her hands claim me, bold and sure, sliding over my hips and lower, then up my back in a slow path that pulls a rough sound from my chest. Fingertips first, mapping muscle, then the light scrape of nails that turns the air bright and dark at once. I savor the way she reaches and takes, how we meet in the middle with nothing left to hold back.

When I slip two fingers into her, she gasps and her hands bite into my shoulders. She does not pull away. She rises to meet me, eyes fluttering, breath catching on a sound that goes straight through my chest. The way she opens for me, the way she trusts me to learn her rhythm and keep her there, steadies me and undoes me at the same time. She is heat and velvet under my hand, pulse quick against my fingertips, and every soft plea she gives me makes my control slip another inch. I match her, slow at first, then deeper in the way she asks without words, and the look on her face makes me feel like I am holding something precious and burning and absolutely mine to take care of.

"You're so damn beautiful," I whisper, because I have to say it. She is watching me with those wide, dark eyes, and she deserves to know exactly what she is doing to me.

I take my time, stroking her until she's pulsing under me, her breathing ragged. I want her to feel good. I want to be the one who makes her fall apart. When she finally cries out, trembling, pride and hunger crashes through me at once.

"That's it," I murmur against her throat, holding her through it. "Good girl."

She pulls me down for a kiss, wild and desperate now. Her

hands skim my chest and back like she is mapping me, memorizing me, and I swear I almost lose it right there.

"Tell me what you want," I manage.

"You," she says instantly, breathless. "All of you."

God help me.

I take my time. I want this to be good for her, something she will never forget. I have waited so long for this with her, and now that she is here, in my bed, I am determined not to rush.

I reach in my drawer for a new box of condoms I've had for a while, just in case. Not that I've needed them. I hurry and put one on, her watching my every move, hooded eyes looking like she can't wait another minute for this.

She tips her hips and opens for me, legs easing wider, eyes dark steady on mine. Her breath comes fast, chest lifting, then falling, a small sound catching in her throat when I brush along her and hold there. I have to brace a hand beside her head just to keep from rushing. She watches me with a hungry, certain look that strips me down to the truth.

I take my time, guiding us together, teasing along the place that makes her squirm and clutch at my shoulders. The sight of her focused on the space between us nearly undoes me. My jaw locks. I breathe through it and press forward a little, then pause, feeling the way she welcomes me, the way she relaxes and draws me closer. Another breath. A little more. Slow, careful, deliberate, until there is no space left, and we are all the way there.

I rest my forehead to hers and try to steady the thud in my chest. She is heat and velvet around me, tight and perfect, and the trust in her eyes wrecks me. I force myself to go slow because I want to feel every second of this, every small shift and soft sound. I want her to know I am here for all of it, not just the blaze but the way it builds, the way it lasts.

"You okay?" I ask, searching her face.

She nods, her fingers digging into my shoulders. "Yes. Please don't stop, Remy."

I move, slowly and steadily, watching her expression with every thrust. Her mouth falls open, her lashes fluttering, and she is so beautiful it hurts to look at her.

"Ivy," I rasp. "You feel so good. I never want this to end."

She clenches around me and whimpers, and I bury my face against her neck to hold back a groan. I keep the pace deep and even, wanting to draw it out, to make her come again before I let myself go.

Her back arches, her nails drag down my back, and she calls out my name like she means it. That is all it takes. I give in, moving faster now, chasing my own release until it hits me hard, pulling a rough sound from my throat as I come hard.

I collapse on my side, pulling her with me, both of us breathing hard. She is flushed and glowing, her hair a mess, her lips curved in the softest smile.

"We really just did that," she whispers.

"Yeah," I say, pressing a kiss to her hair. "And I'm not done with you yet."

Her quiet laugh vibrates against my chest, and for the first time in years, I feel completely, bone-deep whole.

I get up, dispose of the condom and turn on the shower, and she joins me; the spray warming us while I take my time kissing her, cleaning her up and washing her hair. She leans into me and groans, and I hold her, memorizing every inch of her body, because she's so beautiful and perfect. Having her in my shower like this is intimacy I've never experienced with anyone else.

The water beats down hot, steam curling around us, fogging the glass. Ivy's hair is wet, plastered to her shoulders, her skin flushed and glistening. She is standing under the spray, looking at me like she cannot believe we are here, like she is waiting for me to make the next move.

I cannot stop staring. "God, you're beautiful," I say before I can stop myself.

She smiles, a little shy, which only makes me want her more. My hand slides over her wet skin, down her side, lingering at the curve of her hip. She is soft and smooth, and I swear I could spend hours just touching her like this.

Her breath hitches when I trail my fingers lower. "Remy..."

"You have no idea," I murmur, stepping closer until her back is against the tile. "I can't stop looking at you."

I kiss her slowly, letting the water run over both of us, and she melts against me. My hands roam, learning her body in the dim light, every dip and curve. Her breasts press against my chest, her thighs slick against mine, and I am shaking from holding back, from trying to make this last.

"You feel perfect," I say against her mouth. "Every inch of you."

She tilts her head back as my mouth trails down her throat, giving me more to taste. The water mixes with the sounds she makes, soft and desperate, and I know I will never get enough of this woman.

I touch her gently at first, wanting to draw it out, wanting to watch her come apart. Her hands brace on my hips, her head falling back against the tile as I work her higher and higher until she gasps, coming apart under my hand.

I hold her through it, kissing her softly, murmuring against her lips, "That's it. So damn gorgeous."

When she blinks up at me, her cheeks flushed, her lips parted, I almost lose it.

"I want you," she whispers.

"Wait here."

I slip out of the shower and grab another condom, silently thankful I bought the bigger box.

I step back into the shower and kiss her again, hard this time, lifting her easily so she wraps her legs around me.

The heat of her body against mine is magnetic, like gravity itself is bending to pull us together, and I can't tell where I end and she begins. When I push into her, I have to close my eyes and breathe through the rush of it.

I move slowly at first, every thrust deep and careful, because I want to feel every second of this, want her to know how much she means to me. The sound of water, her gasps, my ragged breathing, it all mixes until I think I might go crazy from how good it feels.

"You're so beautiful," I tell her again, because I cannot stop saying it.

When she comes again, clenching tight around me, I let go, groaning her name as I follow her over the edge.

I keep holding her after, kissing her forehead, her wet hair sticking to my cheek. She is smiling, soft and sleepy-looking, and it hits me hard—this is it. This is what I have been missing.

"Come on," I whisper, brushing a strand of hair out of her face. "Let's get you dry before I keep you in here all night."

I turn off the water and grab a towel, wrapping it gently around her before she can reach for it herself. She lets me, her cheeks pink, her smile small and shy in a way that makes my chest ache.

"You don't have to—" she starts.

"I want to," I say quietly, meeting her eyes.

I pat her skin dry slowly, careful and tender, memorizing every curve and freckle. She leans into my touch, and I swear my heart beats harder at the trust in that small gesture. When I am done, I grab another towel for myself and then scoop her into my arms, carrying her down the hall.

She laughs softly. "I can walk, you know."

"I know," I say, smiling despite how serious I feel inside. "But I like carrying you."

When we reach my room, I set her on the bed, the towel slipping a little as she sinks into the sheets. She looks up at me with those dark, soft eyes, and I feel like the ground tilts under me.

I get into bed beside her, pulling the blankets over both of us. The air is quiet, heavy with everything we just did. I brush her damp hair back from her face and press a kiss to her temple.

"We should talk," I say finally, my voice low.

She nods, pulling the blanket closer around her. "I know."

I stare at the ceiling for a long moment before I say it. "I told myself I didn't need anyone, that it was easier to just focus on Junie and the farm." I glance at her, my chest tight. "But then you came along. And after tonight...I don't think I can go back to how things were."

Her expression softens, and she reaches out, sliding her hand over mine. "You don't have to go back. I don't want to, either."

Relief hits me so hard I almost laugh, except it comes out as a long, shaky breath.

"I'm scared," I admit. "Scared I'll screw this up. Scared Junie will get attached and then..."

"She's already attached," Ivy says gently. "And I'm attached, too. This isn't one-sided."

Those words land like a stone in my chest and then melt into something warm.

"I like you a lot," I say, because it feels too small for what I feel but it's the truest thing I can get out. "I have for a very long time. So much."

She smiles, soft and sweet, and leans in to kiss me. "Good. Because I like you, too. And I think we deserve to be happy."

Something eases in me then. I pull her closer until her head is on my chest, my hand splayed across her back.

"Go to sleep," I whisper against her hair. "I've got you."

Her breathing evens out after a few minutes, and I just lie there, staring at the ceiling, holding her. For the first time in a long time, I feel like everything might be okay. Like maybe I get to have this with her, Junie, a home that feels full.

I press one more kiss into her hair before I finally let myself drift, still holding her close.

# Chapter 14
# Ivy

The sunlight pouring over us wakes me first. It's warm and soft, slipping through the curtains and spilling across the bed. Remy's arm is heavy and protective around my waist, pinning me to the mattress, and for a moment I just lie there listening to him breathe. He looks younger like this, softer. Relaxed and not as if he has the weight of the world on his shoulders.

When he stirs, his eyes find me instantly, that lazy smile making my stomach flutter. I love that smile. I would do anything for that smile. "Morning," he says, his voice rough from sleep.

"Morning," I whisper back, biting my lip to keep from grinning.

He pulls me closer until my back is to his chest, his lips brushing my shoulder. The touch is enough to make me shiver with excitement to his touch. "You okay?" he murmurs.

I nod, turning to face him, and before I can say anything else, he kisses me. Slow and unhurried, a kiss that makes me forget the world outside even exists. The sheets rustle as I press closer, and just like that we are tangled again, skin on skin, slow and lazy and perfect.

He likes me. I am trying to play it cool, but I am anything but cool. Last night was incredible. Literally the best night of my life. I've liked Remy for so long. And now it's *real*.

"Daddy," Junie calls through the bedroom door. "Where's Ivy?"

He slides out of bed and picks up his shorts and pulls them on, giving me a slow smirk while he does it. "I'm coming, Junie. Ivy has the morning off."

"But she's not in her bed," she calls through the door sounding sad. "Did she leave us?"

My heart breaks hearing that, and I give Remy a horrified look.

"No, baby, she's just using my bathroom in here getting ready. I'll be right out," he tells her through the door.

"Are you guys smooching like Uncle Finn said you would?" she asks, sounding hopeful.

I cover my mouth as a laugh escapes. "Hi, Junie! I'll be out in a minute," I say and give Remy a look like 'oh my gosh.'

Remy slides on sweatpants that look damn good on him and grins at me, shaking his head. God, I love that smile now that I've earned it. And hell, I hope I earn it again later, too. He bends down and kisses me quickly before he leaves.

His body is so hard and toned, and he made me feel so raw and vulnerable. But he also made me feel safe. And that made it worth it. Getting to know this side of Remy that he rarely shares with anyone is like getting a prize.

He opens the door enough to slide out and shuts it behind him, and I hear him talking to Junie in that soft voice he uses with her. And he uses that with me now. Like his guard is down. He's gruff and rough with others but soft with her.

I love that about him.

I quickly get cleaned up in the bathroom and brush my teeth. I fix my wild hair and get dressed in his T-shirt and a pair of my shorts and scan the hall for Junie before heading down the hall.

The smell of coffee already fills the kitchen as I move around barefoot. My cheeks are hot even though I am alone because this feels...domestic. And I like it.

Then he comes up behind me in front of the coffeemaker, sliding a warm hand around my waist. "You look good in my shirt," he says, low in my ear.

I laugh softly. "You're just saying that."

He turns me until my back is against the counter, caging me there with his arms. The kiss he gives me is deep and hungry, enough to make my knees go weak. I clutch his shoulders to keep from sliding to the floor.

When the coffee pot hisses and sputters, we both break apart, breathless and grinning.

I cover my mouth, not realizing how carried away I got kissing him. I forgot about Junie seeing us. "Where's Junie?"

Remy pulls down two mugs from the shelf, his shoulders broad and distracting, and says, "Willa and Tate just picked her up to go into town for donuts. They're bringing some back to hang out for a while. We have at least forty-five minutes to talk... or do other things."

I grin, heat curling low in my stomach. "Oh, really?"

I slide my arms around his waist and press myself against him.

"Other things sound a lot better than talking," I murmur, tilting my head back.

His eyes darken. That look does me in every time.

Remy cups my face and kisses me, slow at first, just tasting, testing. Then it deepens. My fingers curl in his shirt, and he makes a low, quiet sound that sends a shiver straight through me.

"Let's see what you have on underneath this..." he says softly, skimming my belly with his fingertips, making me shiver and moan into his neck.

Before I know it, his hands are on my hips, lifting me like I weigh nothing and setting me on the counter. I gasp when his palms slide over my thighs, spreading them so he can step between them.

The kiss turns hungry, all heat and tongue and months of wanting boiling over. He kisses me like I'm the only thing that even matters in this moment, like he's starving for me. My legs wrap around his hips on instinct, pulling him closer until there's not a breath of space between us.

"God, you taste good," he mutters against my mouth, trailing kisses along my jaw, down my neck.

"Remy—"

And then the front door swings open.

We both freeze and look over, like deer caught in headlights.

Finn strolls in like he owns the place, grinning as he shrugs off his jacket. He's halfway through the kitchen before he actually looks up, then he stops dead, eyes widening as he takes in me sitting on the counter in Remy's shirt, legs wrapped around his brother.

"Well, well, well," he drawls, leaning a hip against the island. "Should I come back later, or...?"

"Finn," Remy growls, stepping back, but his hands are still on my hips, which just makes Finn's grin grow wider.

"You two finally figure out what all that tension was about?" Finn asks, crossing his arms. "Took you long enough."

My cheeks are on fire, but I can't help laughing. "Hi, Finn."

"Hi, Ivy," he says with a smirk. "You look...very...cozy."

Remy glares. "Out."

Finn throws up his hands in mock surrender, still grinning. "Fine, fine. Donuts better be worth this awkwardness when I get back. Text me when Tate and Willa get back. I'll be in the barn."

He grabs his coat and heads for the door, whistling under his breath.

As soon as it shuts behind him, Remy groans and buries his face in my neck. "I'm going to kill him."

I giggle, tugging his shirt to pull him closer. "You won't. But you can definitely pick up where you left off."

His answering growl is low and dangerous, and then he's kissing me again, harder this time, like Finn never existed.

Remy is a beast, and I was right about that. He's even better than I could have imagined now that he stopped pretending to not like me.

The front door clicks shut behind Finn, and the house is quiet again, except for the sound of Remy's breath against my throat.

"We should probably talk about things," I say softly, brushing my fingers through his hair.

He pulls back enough to look at me, still standing between my knees. His hands stay on my hips like he doesn't want to let me go. "Yeah," he says, voice rough.

I slide my hands down his hard chest, anchoring myself, because I know this is the moment we figure out what we're doing.

"This thing between us," he starts, hesitating. "Ivy, I'm not saying I don't want this—God, I do—but I have to be careful."

"Because of Junie," I say gently.

He nods, shoulders tense. "She's been through enough. Her mom..." He trails off, pressing his lips together. "Her mom lets her down a lot. I can't have someone in her life just...walking away. Not again."

The words hit me in the chest. There's a flicker of pain in his eyes that tells me this isn't just about Junie. This is about him, too. He's the man who has had to pick up the pieces, who's had to keep it together when someone else broke not only his little girl's heart, but his, too.

My own heart softens, "Remy," I whisper, reaching up to cup his face. "I'm not going anywhere. This isn't a fling for me. You're not just some guy I'm hooking up with. You and Junie—" My throat catches. "You're so important to me."

He exhales slowly, like I've just taken some of the weight off his shoulders. "You're sure about this?"

"Yes," I say without hesitation. "Are you?"

His mouth curves into the smallest smile, but it's real, deep, like he feels it all the way through. "Yeah," he says, his voice low. "I've been sure for a while. I just didn't know if you wanted me the way I wanted you."

I laugh, shaky with relief. "Remy Bennett, you have no idea."

He grins then, full, unguarded, and makes my stomach flip. He leans in, brushing his lips over mine once, twice, before kissing me like he can finally breathe again.

"This isn't going to be casual," he murmurs against my mouth.

"Good," I whisper back, winding my arms around his neck.

He kisses me again, slow and sure, sealing it like a promise.

I hurry and get dressed in jeans and a hoodie and then we drink coffee together on the couch, snuggled up under a blanket and sneak glances at each other.

Junie runs in not long after. "We got apple fritters!"

"Ivy's here now!" she calls back to Willa and Tate who follow Junie, closing the door.

They kick their boots off, and Willa raises her eyebrows at me and mouths, "What is going on?"

I give her a look and mouth back to her, "I'll tell you later."

Tate looks at us and raises his eyebrows and then smirks.

Okay, so we're not going to get away with not addressing them. I know it, and Remy knows it based on his facial expression.

The back door creaks open and Finn's voice booms through the kitchen. "Juniebug! Tell me you got me a fritter!"

Junie grins like the cat who caught the canary. "Sure did, Uncle Finn. And now you owe me ten bucks."

"Ten?" Finn kicks the door shut with his boot and hangs his jacket, raising a brow. "Whoa, inflation hit hard. Last week it was five."

Junie shrugs, completely unfazed. "Supply and demand. I'm the supplier."

I bite back a laugh as she sets the donut box on the counter and pulls out a napkin with dramatic flair.

Finn leans over her shoulder to examine the donut selection. "And what exactly am I paying for, boss lady?"

"You bet me Dad would never kiss Ivy," Junie says proudly, like she just cracked a case wide open. "And he totally wants to. You can see it all over his face. I bet they kissed this morning when they were in his room with the door..."

"Junie," Remy groans, covering her mouth.

Junie ignores him, shrugs him off, and takes a giant bite of her sprinkle donut. "So. Pay up, Uncle Finn."

Finn looks between me and Remy, grinning like the devil. "Well, now I have to see some evidence. Gotta make sure my ten bucks is legit."

I clear my throat and raise my brows at Remy. "Well? You heard the kid. Is this true? Do you want to smooch me?"

Junie breaks into a fit of giggles, and Finn grins so big he has to brace himself on the counter. Tate and Willa are watching this all with fascination.

Remy just shakes his head and mutters something about meddling, but when his eyes meet mine, they're dark and warm and full of trouble.

"Yeah, Ivy," he says finally, leaning closer. "I definitely want to smooch you."

Junie gasps, and Finn whoops. "That's ten bucks well spent!" as Remy cups my face and kisses me right there in front of everyone.

* * *

Later, when everyone has gone home but Finn and the kitchen still smells like sugar and coffee, Junie bounces on her toes as Remy grabs his coat.

"Come on, kiddo," he says, pulling his hat on. "Come help me at the farm stand."

Junie grabs her coat and darts after him. "Don't forget my ten bucks!" She calls over her shoulder.

The back door shuts, and suddenly it's just me and Finn.

He doesn't say anything right away. Just leans against the counter and gives me a look. The kind of look that says *we're going to talk.*

I think I know what's coming.

"So," he says finally, "you and my brother finally got your heads out of your butts."

My cheeks warm. "Yep."

He nods like he's absorbing the news. "I love you, Ivy. You know that. You've always been like a little sister to me."

My throat tightens a little. "I know."

"But," he says, holding up a finger, "you mess this up, and I will never forgive you. They've been through so much, and they deserve good things."

I laugh so hard I nearly choke on my coffee. "Oh, Finn. You don't have to worry about that."

"Not kidding," he says seriously. Then he softens, leaning his hip against the table. "Look. Sloane really messed them up for a long time. Junie got the worst of it, but Remy..." He shakes his head. "He held it together for her, but it cost him. He doesn't do this stuff lightly. He hasn't been with anyone else. Never took a chance. And he's had plenty of people interested in him. You are special, and he really likes you. So don't run off if it gets messy, okay?"

Something in my chest aches. "I'm not going anywhere," I say quietly.

Finn studies me for a long moment, then nods. "Good. I haven't seen him smile like that in years. And Junie? She was practically skipping on the way to the barn. You're good for them."

My heart swells so much it feels like it might burst.

"And," Finn adds, his grin returning, "I can't wait until our mom hears about this. She's going to lose her mind. Like full-on planning-the-wedding, naming future kids, lose her mind."

I groan, covering my face with my hands. "Oh, no."

"Oh, yes." Finn's grin is wicked. "You think *I'm* bad? Wait until your mom hears this, too. Those two are going to be insanely annoying. Better brace yourself."

"Finn!" I peek at him between my fingers, mortified and laughing.

"Hey, I'm just saying—we have all been rooting for this. Even Junie can see it." He winks.

I shake my head, still smiling. "You're insufferable."

"Yeah, but you love me," he says cheerfully, grabbing another donut from the box.

And annoyingly, I do.

When the back door opens again and Remy and Junie come

stomping in with snow on their boots, Finn straightens like he wasn't just giving me the most heartfelt pep talk of all time.

"Everything good in here?" Remy asks, eyeing the two of us suspiciously.

"Perfect," Finn says with an innocent smile. "Just getting to know my future sister-in-law better."

I nearly spit out my coffee. "Finn!"

Remy narrows his eyes. "What did you say to her?"

"Nothing you wouldn't have," Finn says with a shrug, biting into his donut. "Carry on with your smooching. I'll be over here, third-wheeling like a champ."

Junie giggles, and Remy groans, but when his eyes meet mine, there's something warm there. Like he heard everything I just promised Finn without me saying a word.

And that makes me want to kiss him all over again.

## Chapter 15
# Remy

The tree farm is buzzing and humming with life. Couples, families, and kids run from tree to tree, arguing over which one is "the one." The photographer is back, and families have come in from hours away to take part and pick out the perfect family tree. And Ivy? She's in her element.

She's standing by the big display wreath, talking to a couple about tree care, her hands gesturing animatedly as she explains how to keep their tree fresh until Christmas like I showed her. She's smiling so wide it hurts to look at her—not that I've been able to stop looking, anyway. I've been smiling like a fool, and I'm practically floating around the place.

I hoist a fresh-cut tree onto my shoulder, carrying it toward a customer's truck. Halfway across the lot, I glance back just in time to catch her staring at me. Really staring.

When our eyes meet, she gives me a sexy smirk, and I see the pink in her cheeks.

I grin, bigger than I mean to, and damn, if it doesn't feel good.

By noon, we're starving, so I pull her into the small office and shut the door behind us. The little heater hums as we sit across from each other at the desk, unwrapping sandwiches and brushing pine needles off the paperwork.

Ivy takes one bite of hers, then immediately leans over and snags a chip from my bag.

"Hey," I protest.

She grins around the chip like she's innocent.

"You don't even like this kind," I say. But really, she could have anything she wants.

"I changed my mind. Yours taste better," she says with a shrug, popping another one in her mouth.

I lean back in my chair and just watch her for a beat, the way her hair is messy from the wind, her cheeks still pink from the cold, her lips curved in that smug little smile.

"Oh, yeah?" I ask, voice low.

"Yeah."

I push back from the desk and cross to her side before I think twice.

"Remy," she laughs softly, but she's already grinning when I lean down and kiss her, quick but firm.

She squeaks against my mouth, then laughs, swatting at my chest.

"That was for the chip," I murmur against her lips.

She grabs another chip from the bag, eyes sparking with mischief. "Worth it."

Ivy heads home to take care of Junie, and I get back to work. The day flies by with all of the things we have to get done. But thanks to Ivy helping, I'm able to get home sooner every night now.

By the time the sun sets, and the last tree is tied to the last roof rack, I'm bone tired but still riding on a high of happiness that I get to go home to them.

Inside, Ivy and Junie are settled at the kitchen table with the big wooden advent calendar box Finn built for Junie. They're planning how to paint little numbers on the doors, and Ivy is patiently showing Junie the doors and how to number them.

I stand in the kitchen for a minute, just watching.

Junie is laughing so hard at a joke Ivy told her, she's clutching her sides, and Ivy's right there with her, hair falling into her face as she shakes her head. She's wearing one of my old sweatshirts, sleeves rolled up, and she looks like she's been sitting at that table with us forever. Like she belonged here this whole time.

Something tightens in my chest, a sharp ache that's not painful, just overwhelming.

I want this. Without a doubt in my body, I want this so badly.

I want Ivy in my kitchen, Junie laughing, the three of us making new memories instead of just holding on to what could have been.

But I'm afraid to want this.

Ivy looks up then, catching me staring, and her expression softens. Like she sees right through me and likes what she finds there.

"Come sit with us," she says, patting the empty chair.

I cross the room, sit down next them, and Junie hands me a paintbrush to help paint the numbers.

"Help us, Dad," she says excitedly.

I nod, but I'm not looking at the box.

I'm looking at Ivy, and the way her smile feels like a promise.

* * *

The house is quiet now after a long day.

I push Junie's bedroom door open just enough to peek

inside. She's asleep, tangled in her blankets, Lola curled up at her feet, her tail swooshing across the covers when she sees me peeking in.

I pull the door closed, leaving it open a crack, and head down the hall.

The kitchen light is still on, casting a warm glow over everything. Ivy's standing at the counter, making sandwiches for all our lunches tomorrow, her hair loose and falling around her shoulders.

She looks over her shoulder when she hears me, smiling that soft smile that does me in every time.

"Hey," she says quietly.

"Hey. You don't have to do that. I can make our lunches," I tell her.

I cross the kitchen and lean against the counter beside her. For a second, we just stand there, not speaking, like neither of us wants to break the moment.

"You okay?" she asks.

"Yeah," I say, meaning it. "Better than okay."

I reach out and tuck a piece of hair behind her ear. My fingers brush her cheek, and she tilts her face toward my hand, her breath catching just slightly.

"You were amazing today," I tell her. "With the customers. With Junie."

Her lips curve. "You were pretty great yourself."

Something inside me loosens. I didn't realize how tight I'd been holding everything until this moment with the farm, all the responsibility, the fear of letting someone into my space. I've been protecting this space for so long that letting my guard down hasn't been easy.

I step closer, my hand sliding to the back of her neck.

"It feels like you've always been here," I admit, my voice low. "Like this is how it was supposed to be."

She swallows hard, her eyes shining. "Remy..."

I kiss her then, slow and deep, because there's no way to say what I'm feeling without it.

She rises on her toes, pressing closer, and I can feel the smile against my mouth when I cup her face and kiss her again.

"I'm glad you're here, and I'm sorry I was a dick to you at first," I say when I finally pull back, breathing hard.

"Good," she whispers and reminds me, "because I'm not going anywhere."

That reminder hits me right in the chest. I rest my forehead against hers, just breathing her in, letting it sink in that she's really here, that she wants this. I need the reminders.

"Come sit with me," I say, nodding toward the couch.

We curl up together under the throw blanket, her head on my shoulder, my arm around her. The house is quiet except for the crackling of the fireplace.

For the first time in a long time, I feel like the future might actually look better than the past.

And with Ivy pressed against me, warm and soft, I can't wait to find out what comes next.

* * *

Ivy is in my sweatshirt and soft leggings, bare feet on the tile, brushing her teeth at the sink. Her hair is loose and wild from the shower, damp at the ends, a natural and careless kind of pretty that makes my chest feel tight. She catches my reflection in the window over the sink and smiles with her eyes before she smiles with her mouth. Toothpaste, foam and all. I don't know why that undoes me, but it does.

"Hi," she says around a mouthful, and it comes out like a laugh.

"Hi." I lean on the doorframe with my arms crossed,

pretending I am not staring. "You leave the cap off that tooth-paste again, and we are going to need a serious talk."

She pulls the toothbrush out, rinses, spits, and flicks a little water at me with her fingers. "Or what? You'll punish me?"

I push off the door frame and come up behind her, palms sliding over the front of the counter on either side of her hips. My chest fits against her back. She smells of clean skin and the vanilla stuff she used in the shower. I meet her eyes in the mirror, and for a second both of us go quiet.

"No, because you seem to like punishment," I say, my voice low, not meaning to say anything at all, but there it is. "I like this with you, even when you're a brat."

Her smile softens. "Me, too."

I press a kiss to the curve where her neck meets her shoulder. She shivers, not from cold, and I feel it everywhere. My hands find her waist. Her hands cover mine. In the mirror, my sweatshirt hangs off one shoulder, and I am a goner for the sight of her in my clothes. I let my mouth trace a slow path up the line of her neck to the corner of her jaw. She tilts her head to make room for me, and the small sound she makes is grateful and a little greedy.

"Careful," she whispers. "Junie is asleep."

"I know," I say, but I don't move away. I kiss behind her ear and feel her melt back into me. The mirror catches everything. The way my hands span her hips. The way her eyes go heavy and half-lidded. The way I am not trying to hide a single thing anymore.

She turns in my arms and hooks her fingers into the front of my sweatshirt. The counter nudges into the small of her back. We are close enough that breathing feels like a choice. I tip my forehead to hers and taste the last sweet hint of mint on her breath.

"You are staring," she says softly.

"Yeah," I say. I don't bother to deny it. "Been doing a lot of that lately."

She laughs into my mouth as I kiss her. It starts easy, sweet. Her hands slide up my chest to my neck, and the kiss deepens because I cannot help it, and she does not want me to. Her mouth parts for mine like she has been waiting for this all night.

I kiss her slow. I kiss her like it is the one thing I know how to do right. The counter presses into her back, and she arches into me, and I can feel the heat of her through the cotton. Every part of me goes unsteady.

I pull back an inch and just look at her. Her cheeks are flushed. Her lips are kiss-bitten. She is beautiful in the bright kitchen light, not hiding in shadows, not trying to angle herself into anything else. Just Ivy. I could fall to my knees to thank whatever stubborn grace moved her back into my life.

"Come on," I say. "Bed."

She blinks, playful and shy at once. "You need better pillow talk than that, Bennett."

I slide my hand down her spine, slow, and catch the little gasp that slips out of her with a kiss. I step back and take her hand. "You are sleeping with me."

A flush climbs her throat. "I was going to take the guest room. I did not want to assume. What if Junie sees us?"

"No," I say, voice a little rougher than I intend. I squeeze her fingers. "You are sleeping with me. I don't want to sleep without you. I sleep better than I have in years when you are by my side. I'll lock the door."

Her eyes shine in a way that feels like light hitting water. Something in my chest opens up and fills at the same time, a rush and a settling. She nods once like it is a vow and lets me lead her out of the kitchen, down the dark hallway, past the photos on the wall that mean history and trying and stubborn love.

In my room the lamp throws a gold circle over the bed. The sheets are clean and cool. I shut the door gently, and the small click feels like a promise that the world can wait. Ivy stands at the foot of the bed and looks at me like this is our first night in a place that knows we belong.

She climbs in first and pulls the blankets back for me. We meet in the middle like magnets. She tucks herself under my arm and finds the spot on my chest where her head fits. My hand settles at her waist, then curves low over her hip, palm spanning warm cotton. We lie there listening to each other breathe. I don't know if I have ever felt so awake and so ready to sleep at the same time.

"You run hot," she murmurs.

"You steal the covers," I say.

She snorts. "We'll get a bigger blanket."

"We will," I say, and there it is, the easy *we* that used to scare me. It doesn't now. It feels like walking a field I know in first snow.

She tips her face up, and I meet her halfway. Kissing in bed is different. Slower. Deeper. The kind of kiss that teaches your body what home feels like. I angle her under me a little so I can take my time. Her fingers slide into my hair, and I feel it right down my spine. I make a noise I don't plan to make, and she smiles against my mouth like she understands it already.

"Remy," she says softly, a warning or a prayer, I cannot tell which, and I don't need to. I kiss her again, slower, until the warning bleeds right into the prayer. I love hearing my name on her lips.

We take our time. Hands learn. Mouths map. The room turns quiet and warm except for the rush in my ears and the sound she makes when I trail kisses along her throat. I want to know every way she wants to be touched. I want to memorize every way she touches me back. I want to give her the careful and the hungry and everything in between. I want to earn the look she gives me when I pull back to breathe, and she drags me down again with a laugh that trembles.

We could keep going. God, we could. But the steady thing inside me takes the reins, the part that wants to make this last and last. I ease us back into the pillows and pull the covers up and hold her tight. We keep kissing until the heat settles into something softer. We keep kissing until the urgency fades into gravity. We keep kissing until her hand on my chest goes slow and then slower and then still.

"You make me feel so safe," she whispers into my skin, her voice almost asleep.

I close my eyes. "You make this house feel alive."

We lie there in the gold light and the quiet, and I think about how long it has been since I let myself tell the truth after dark. I don't want to shatter the calm, but the words sit there and ask to be let out.

"Ivy," I say.

She hums, a soft sound that means *I am listening*.

"I used to stay up late just to avoid walking into this room. I would fall asleep on the couch. I would doomscroll. Anything to put off climbing into an empty bed. I hate that part of myself. The part that is afraid of quiet."

Her fingers start to move again, the slow circles over my heart. "That sounds lonely," she says.

"It was," I say, and my voice betrays me. I swallow and keep going because it feels like a thorn I am finally pulling. "I did not want to hear the thoughts that showed up when the house got still, the ones that say *you are failing her*. The ones that say *you're gonna mess it up again*. The ones that sound like echoes of people leaving us."

She does not rush in with comfort. She is deliberate and gentle. "How do things feel right now?" she asks.

I breathe in the smell of her hair and the clean cotton. I listen to the steady beat under my palm where my hand rests over her ribcage. I listen to my heartbeat, not galloping, just strong and even.

"Peaceful," I say. "Hopeful."

Her breath leaves her in a small sound that might be a laugh or a sob. "Good," she says. "Because I want to be here. With you. For all of it."

I have to close my eyes because the ceiling blurs. I pull her closer because words are not big enough for what moves through me. *Thank you* feels thin. I give her my mouth instead, and whatever she hears in it makes her fingers clutch at my T-shirt and hold me like she is the one keeping me steady.

Maybe she is.

# Chapter 16
# Ivy

Donna texted me and asked me to meet her for breakfast, and she picks the place, of course. I don't mind when she says it's my sister's bookstore, because I love going there.

Wisteria Cove smells like salty sea air this morning, and Wisteria Books & Brews smells like cinnamon. The bell chimes over the door as I step inside. The windows are fogged a little from the ovens and the cold winter air. Someone is laughing near the fiction shelves, and an espresso machine hisses in the cafe. I breathe in and out and try to settle my nerves. Breakfast with Donna sounded casual over the phone, but this is *the* Donna Bennett. A woman whose paperbacks live on half the coffee tables in America. That part doesn't intimidate me because I've known her all my life. But what intimidates me is that this is Remy's mother. The man I'm falling deeply in love with, along with his daughter. His mother. That matters to me. What she thinks of me matters.

She is already here at a corner table under the bay window, scarf draped like a banner, hair swept up with a pencil stuck through it, sticky notes dotting the cover of a spiral notebook.

She waves me over as if we have been doing this for years. Well, we have. Just not with me sleeping in her son's bed.

"Sunshine," she says, standing to hug me. She smells of vanilla and fresh paper. "You look beautiful, and you're glowing and radiant."

I've always loved Donna so much, and she's called me sunshine for as long as I can remember.

"That is the nicest thing anyone has ever said to me," I say, laughing, as she pulls me into a second hug just because she can.

Willa pops up from behind the counter holding a tray of scones and wearing a black apron and a smile. "Ivy! Hey! Your usual?"

"Make it fancy. I am trying to impress our favorite author," I tease, which makes Donna press a hand to her chest and sigh.

Willa leans on the table like we are gossiping at a sleepover. "Two cinnamon rolls, one giant bowl of fruit, and a side of bacon. Coffee for Donna and a maple latte for Ivy. I am the boss, so you cannot argue. I know what you both like by now."

"Boss of this entire town," Donna says. "I should have brought you a sash."

Willa laughs and flits away, calling hello to Tate as he ducks in. Rowan breezes past with a tray of scones for the display and squeezes my shoulder as she goes.

"You okay?" Rowan asks, eyes soft.

"I'm good," I say, and I realize that I mean it.

"Excellent. I will be back to interrogate you about a certain tree farmer," she sings, which makes Donna wiggle her eyebrows like she's jumping in line for this, too.

"I'm nervous," I admit when we sit. "I shouldn't be. It's just breakfast."

"It is not just breakfast," Donna says, tapping her notebook. "It is a fresh new start for you as my son's love interest."

I groan and laugh. "Donna..."

The laugh shakes something loose in me. I take off my coat and fold it over my chair. Outside, the harbor is a sheet of gray, and gulls cut the sky like paper kites. Inside, the table feels warm under my palms.

"Thank you for inviting me," I say.

"Thank you for making my son smile again," she says without missing a beat.

Heat rushes to my cheeks. "I like that smile." The words come out honest and simple, and Donna's eyes shine.

"That's the magic," she says.

Before I can ask her what she means by that, Willa arrives with plates and plates and more plates, then the maple latte with a foam heart so perfect I hesitate to ruin it. "Eat," she orders. "And tell me something good."

"Junie has a Christmas program coming up," I say, and all three of us make plans to attend together.

Tate calls goodbye from across the room as he leaves with a bag of scones. Mrs. Callahan from the florist pops in to pin a flyer for the Holiday Bake Sale to the community board. Someone asks Willa about a book club pick. Rowan dips through the new opening between the shops. She helps Willa, and Willa helps her. Having adjoining shops was a genius idea.

Donna waits until I have powdered sugar on my mouth to slide a canvas tote across the table. The bag looks ordinary, but it lands with the weight of a gift.

"For you," she says. "A little light reading."

I peek inside and freeze. The covers are unfamiliar, and yet I recognize the names. Top romance authors. All galleys. All not out yet. Books people wait months for and would sell a kidney to access. Books I used to preorder to the Kindle I had to hide from Derek. God, why didn't I see the red flags with that guy sooner? Sometimes I remember something with him and question all of my choices.

"Are these for me to borrow?" I ask, even though I know the answer. My hands shake in the best way.

"For you to keep," she says, "And if one of them makes your heart flip, no pressure. If you hate them, hand them back to me and blame my poor taste. But I think you will love at least three. Maybe five. I know your favorites."

"I have not read in ages," I say, throat tight. "Not for fun."

Donna tilts her head. "Why not?"

Willa looks over like she wants to answer for me, but she stays quiet and slides a plate of bacon over.

"Derek," I say. The name tastes like stale gum. "He didn't like that I read books and said that romance novels were unrealistic. That they gave women dumb expectations."

Donna's mouth falls open. "Expectations of what?"

I laugh, a quick burst. "If I had a book in my bag, he would say, you know that stuff never happens in real life. I got a secret Kindle and kept it in my purse, so he couldn't see what I was reading and judge me."

My mom, Lilith, arrives and carries the scent of the harbor in on her coat. She kisses my cheek, then hugs Donna, then peeks into the tote.

"Presents," she smiles. "Good. She needs them."

"We were talking about Ivy's ex," Donna says gently, then catches herself. "Sorry, darling. Should I not say his name out loud?"

My mom's smile is bright. "Derek could not measure up to the bare minimum. There. I have said my truth for the day."

Donna looks floored and a little delighted. "I agree after what I'm hearing."

My mom shrugs and steals a piece of bacon. "Romance is the best," she says, as if we are stating the weather. "If we don't believe in romance, what are we even doing?"

Donna points with her fork. "Put that on a T-shirt."

Willa reappears with a pot of coffee and tops us off. "We can hang the T-shirt in the front window," she says. "Next to the display for Donna's new book."

"Speaking of," Donna says, then pretends to hide under the table. "I have a new one due to the editor next week, and I am a monster until launch day on the current one. Please forgive me in advance for texting you all at two in the morning to ask if the ending makes you sob in a good way."

"It does," Willa says. "I read the last pages last night and then cried myself to sleep because we have to wait so long for your next one."

I am smiling so hard my cheeks hurt. I love spending time with all of them. The tote sits against my calf like a bag of gifts. I let myself imagine a night where I climb into bed and open a book, and no one makes a face about it. The thought lights me up from the inside. No way would Remy ever make fun of romance books. His mom is a romance author. And for that, Remy has never made fun of me for anything. I don't think I've ever seen him make fun of anyone for something they love. Except maybe Finn. Those two give each other hell like brothers daily, and it's kind of funny.

"Books are so important, honey. Anyone who makes fun of someone for reading is ignorant. I know my sons would never," Donna says with a pointed look.

"I've missed this," I say. "Not just reading. Being back here."

Donna reaches across and covers my hand. Her fingers are warm and steady. "You get to have all of it," she says. "Love in your life and love on the page. Anyone who tells you differently doesn't know how good it can be."

My mom nods. "Your heart knows what it wants. It always has. It picked Wisteria Cove. It picked your sisters. And now it has picked a man who finally puts you and your feelings first."

"He reads to Junie at night," I say, and I don't try to swallow the emotion in it. "He voices all the characters. She lives for it and then she falls asleep on his shoulder."

Donna dabs at her eyes with a napkin. "I am fine. Carry on."

A couple from the school board waves on their way out. Mr. Gardner from the hardware store stops to tell Donna he saved her space for book night. Rowan slides a small glass bottle onto our table with handwritten tags. Joy, she has written. For courage and for opening. She does not explain. She does not need to. Rowan just mixes things and knows things.

I tuck the bottle into the tote between the galleys. The weight changes. It feels like a future I can hold in my hands.

"Tell me what you love to read," Donna says, pencil ready. "Tropes, witches, cowboys, fake dating, secret identities. Give me your heart, and I will give you six titles to match."

I laugh and do as I am told. I tell her about books that felt like doorways when I was fourteen. I tell her about a college library where I hid in the romance aisle because every spine looked like a promise. Willa adds a recommendation so fast she has to run and grab the last copy off the shelf before someone else does. My mom adds in a couple of her favorites, then orders more bacon for the table.

When Donna talks about her new book, she lights up in a way that makes everyone at the next table lean closer. The heroine runs a flower cart by the pier, and the hero is a widower who keeps every love letter his wife ever wrote, then learns how to write new ones to a future he never thought he could have. I am done for by the time she hits the midpoint.

"Put me on the pre-order list," I say. "Take all my money. I need it."

"You are on the dedication page," she says, deadpan, then breaks into a grin at my face. "Kidding. But you can be in the next acknowledgments if you promise to bring me donuts the morning after launch."

"Deal," I say, and we shake like we are closing a real estate contract.

After a while, the plates look like stories. Smears of jam, coffee rings, crumbs that glitter with sugar. The morning has shifted to later. People come and go. Everyone says hello to us at the corner table. Every hello holds a little vote of confidence. It is simple, and it is beautiful.

Donna buys one cinnamon roll to go for Pete, then tucks a small notebook into the tote on top of the galleys. "For your thoughts," she says. "On books or on life. They are the same thing most days."

"Thank you," I say, and her love hits me in the chest.

We stand at the same time. Before I can reach for my coat, Donna pulls me into a hug that feels like coming home. My mom wraps an arm around both of us and kisses my cheek. We all say our goodbyes, and I head out with a full heart. My cup is full.

Outside, the harbor wind lifts my scarf, and the sun finds a seam in the clouds. The tote is heavy. I hold it close and head toward the truck parked up the street. I can see the tree farm in my mind as I walk, the way the rows look like music and the way Remy smiles when he sees me. I think about tonight, and the bed, and a book waiting on the nightstand. I think about how it will feel to read for an hour while Remy catches up on paperwork at the kitchen counter and Junie sneak-watches an animated show with her headphones on, both of us glancing up at each other to share the good parts.

Romance *is* the best, Donna said. If we don't believe in it, what are we even doing?

I tuck the tote higher on my shoulder and believe it with my whole life.

# Chapter 17
## Remy

Junie bounces on the couch, clutching her overnight bag like it's a golden ticket. Lola is planted at her feet, tail thumping against the floor every time Junie moves to look out the window to watch for Lilith. She's nervous about whether she gets to go with her favorite tiny person or not. It's become clear to everyone that Junie is Lola's chosen person, and I'm okay with it. More than okay with it. I love that they have each other.

"Lilith said we're making moon water tonight!" Junie crows. "And dream catchers! With real gem beads!"

I smile even though my chest feels tight. I love that Junie has so many people here that love and support her. "Sounds like you're gonna have the best night ever, bug."

"She said we can mix potions, too." Junie's voice drops to a whisper, conspiratorial. "Real witch potions."

I glance at Ivy, who's leaning against the kitchen doorway, watching the whole thing with that soft smile she tries to hide. The sight of her standing there, hair loose, wearing one of those slouchy sweaters that make me think of fireplaces and kissing her, almost makes me lose my mind.

Almost. I'm focused because I've got something planned. And I'm nervous if she's going to love it or not.

"You about ready?" I ask Ivy.

Her brow arches. "Ready for what?"

I swallow, trying to keep my voice casual. "Be ready to go at six. Both of you," I nod at Junie. "Lilith's coming for you at six. Then we have plans after."

"What about Lola?" Ivy asks.

"We'll find out if she likes cats," I say, crouching to scratch Lola's ears. "She goes everywhere Junie goes, right? Lilith said she'd love to have her granddog over for a sleepover, too."

Junie nods solemnly, as if this is a sacred truth. "She loves you, Ivy, but you're second place now. Sorry."

Ivy laughs, low and warm, and the sound wraps around me and makes my chest tight in a good way. "That's okay, bug."

By the time six o'clock hits, Junie is zipped into her coat, hair in pigtails, ready to go. Lilith pulls into the drive with her old Honda Pilot, and Junie takes off like she's headed for summer camp. Lola gallops after her. Ivy stands on the porch, watching with fond eyes.

When the car disappears with both of them waving, she looks at me. "So now what?"

I tug on my coat, heart pounding. "Now we wait."

"For what?"

The answer comes with the crunch of snow on the drive. A soft jingle of bells. Ivy's mouth parts as the horse-drawn sleigh glides into view, lanterns swinging gently at the corners. The white sleigh is decorated for Christmas with greenery and red bows.

"Oh my gosh," she whispers.

I grab the two big quilts off the couch and drape one over her shoulders. "We're getting picked up," I say, proud of myself for keeping this a secret.

Ten minutes later, after petting the horses and talking to the driver, we're bundled under the quilts, side by side, as the sleigh glides across the property. The horses snort clouds into the snowy night air, their hooves crunching rhythmically. The whole place is lit up with strings of lights on every fence line, the barn glowing warm, wreaths hanging from the paddock gates.

A light snow falls, lazy flakes catching in Ivy's hair. She tilts her face toward the sky, smiling.

"This is…" she trails off, breath visible in the air.

"Yeah." I can barely talk around the lump in my throat.

The driver pulls to a stop near the tree line, giving us a moment to walk. I help her down, keeping her hand in mine, not ready to let go.

"What's your favorite job been?" I ask as we walk through the quiet.

She laughs softly. "Favorite?" She thinks for a moment. "I don't know if I've ever had a favorite. I never stay anywhere for too long."

"Why?" I ask curiously.

Her shoulders lift. "If I don't stay too long…get too close… then people can't leave me. Or die." The last word is a whisper.

I stop walking, turn toward her. Her eyes are shiny in the moonlight, and my chest aches. "Ivy—"

She says the last part so quietly I almost miss it.

"My dad," she says. "And Tate's dad. When they all went missing, we all had to figure out how to keep breathing without them. And it was so hard. It broke something inside me. He was my dad."

The words hit me like a punch to the chest. My breath catches, sharp and heavy.

I just stand there, taking it in.

God. I hadn't seen it before. I thought I was the one who needed to keep my distance. The one carrying the damage. But she's been carrying it, too. All this time, I kept telling myself I was protecting my daughter. Protecting Ivy. Protecting myself. But I was just afraid. Afraid that if I let her in, she'd leave like my ex did and take pieces of me with her. But here Ivy is, cracked open in front of me, admitting that she's just as scared of love as I am. But she has lost and persevered and still retained that big, beautiful, trusting heart.

We're both standing in the same place, afraid to reach out. Afraid to lose.

She is looking at the ground, not at me, her hands fisted at her sides like she is holding herself together with everything she has left.

"Come here," I say, quiet. I don't want to tower over her when she is giving me something this vulnerable.

She hesitates for just a heartbeat, then steps forward, and I pull her against me. I hold her as tight as I can without crushing her.

"I am so sorry," I say into her hair. "I am so damn sorry you went through that."

Her breath shakes, and I can feel the tremor through my arms where they circle her.

When she pulls back, her eyes are wet, and I wipe her cheeks with my thumbs, slow and careful.

"You are the strongest person I know," I say. "You kept going when everything felt impossible. And look at you now. You are building something beautiful. A life. A family. You amaze me, Ivy."

Her chest rises and falls like she is finally letting herself exhale. "It still hurts. Sometimes it feels like it just happened yesterday."

"I know," I say. My voice feels rough. "I cannot take that

pain away, but I can carry it with you. You don't have to hold it alone anymore. You have us."

Her eyes find mine, searching, and I make sure she sees all of it. That I am here. That I am not going anywhere.

She nods, just once, and I press my forehead to hers and breathe with her until we both feel steadier.

"Remy?" she whispers.

"Yeah?"

"Thank you for not running when I get like this."

I give her a soft smile. "I'm not a runner."

Her lips curve the slightest bit. "I know."

"Good," I say, and kiss her. Slow. Deep. Her fingers curl in my shirt, and I feel the last of the weight leave her shoulders.

I squeeze her hand. "I worry about losing people. About Junie... about you." My voice goes low. "I can't—" I shake my head. "I can't go through that again."

Her throat works as she swallows. "We both fear losing someone we love. We're a mess."

I nod and squeeze her hand a little and pull her in closer. I stop and pull her in toward me.

The snow swirls between us, quiet and soft, like the world is holding its breath. She looks at me like I've just handed her something fragile and holy.

"Remy," she says, and my name sounds like a promise. Like a vow she has already made in her heart.

I look straight into her eyes, and it feels like the rest of the world falls away. "Yeah?"

Her breath comes quick and uneven, and I can see it between us, curling in the cool night air. "I'm falling in love with you," she says.

For a moment, I just let the words wash over me, warming every part of me that used to feel frozen. My heart pounds so hard I feel it in my throat.

I step in closer, close enough to catch every flicker in her eyes. "I think I've been in love with you for so long," I say, my voice low and certain.

Her lips part, but no sound comes out. Then she lets out a startled laugh, tears bright in her eyes.

"You're serious," she whispers, like she wants to be sure.

I reach for her hand, threading my fingers through hers. "I have never been more serious about anything in my life."

"So am I," she says, her voice barely there. "I want to see where this goes with us."

Something inside me unlocks, like I have been holding my breath for years and finally let it go.

The world is so quiet I can hear the distant jingle of the horses, the soft hush of snow landing on the trees. I reach up and tuck a strand of her hair behind her ear, slow, careful, like she might vanish if I rush.

She shivers, but I know it isn't from the cold.

I cup her cheek and let my thumb brush her skin. "Then stay," I whisper. "Stay with me. Let's build something together."

Her breath catches, and then she smiles, soft and full of something that feels like forever.

"Ivy." My voice feels raw. "I want every day to be mistletoe and magic. I want everything with you."

Her answer is a whisper that slams straight through me. "Me, too."

I don't hesitate. I cup her jaw and cover her mouth with mine, slow at first, like I've got all the time in the world, then deeper when she rises on her toes and presses into me. Snowflakes melt against her skin, against my own, and the rest of the night vanishes until there's only this, her breath, her soft gasp, the taste of her smile.

When I finally break away, our foreheads touch, both of us breathing hard.

"Okay," she says, laughing breathlessly. "That was worth getting frostbite for."

I grin, dizzy with it, and wrap the quilt around both of us, pulling her against my chest. "Then let's make sure you don't."

We stand there for a long time, wrapped up in each other and the falling snow, while the horses wait patiently, as if they know something just shifted forever.

* * *

The next day after we close up shop for the day, the harbor smells of salt and fish when we pull up, and Pete's already waiting on his bench. He's bundled in blankets, cap pulled low, grinning like we're the only thing he's been waiting on all day.

"Thought you'd stand me up," he rasps.

"Not a chance," I tell him, clapping him gently on the shoulder. "You ready for the Dairy Witch?"

"Been ready since breakfast."

Junie practically dances ahead of us, Lola trotting at her side. The bell over the Dairy Witch door jingles, and Pete points at the menu like a man on a mission.

"Ritzy AF is the only ice cream worth eating," he says.

Ivy bites her lip, scanning the flavors. "I can't decide."

Pete snorts. "Then get the Ritzy AF. Trust me."

So we do. Junie picks cookie dough with rainbow sprinkles and proudly licks the first drip before it hits her coat. We carry everything back to Pete's bench, the dark sky a watercolor wash of grays and blues over the water.

Pete takes a bite, sighs like it's the first good thing that's happened in months. "Promise me something."

"Anything," Ivy says softly.

"Get ice cream every year on my birthday," he tells us. His voice is steady, but there's something behind it, something that makes my throat tighten. "Celebrate life. Every single day. Don't take anything or each other for granted. Not for one damn second."

Ivy reaches over and squeezes his hand. "Promise."

I reach over and squeeze his shoulder gently, reassuring him.

Donna's quiet, a single tear sliding down her cheek as she takes another bite of ice cream, her chest rising like she's holding back more.

Junie shrieks suddenly and takes off after a seagull, Lola hot on her heels. "Junie!" I'm already running, catching her before she gets too close to the dock's edge. She giggles breathlessly, arms thrown around my neck as I carry her back.

We finish the last bites in companionable silence. When Pete looks tired, we walk him and my mom to the bookstore so they can warm up. The fire is already crackling in the hearth when we settle in, mugs of cocoa in our hands, Junie on the rug, reading aloud in her wobbly little-kid voice. Pete dozes off in the armchair for a while, his blanket sliding to his lap, until Donna gently wakes him and helps him out to the car.

The ride home is quiet. Ivy reaches over and laces her fingers through mine, her thumb stroking once, twice, like a secret promise. It hurts seeing Pete go downhill.

In the rearview mirror, Junie's head lolls against her booster seat, Lola curled against her like a furry shadow.

I glance back at them, then at Ivy. The streetlights glow against her profile, and I realize with a sudden, fierce clarity that I have everything I need right here. We're going to be okay.

By the time we pull into the drive, Junie is out cold. I carry her inside, careful not to wake her, and tuck her into bed with Lola curled up at her feet. Ivy meets me on the couch, already in her pajamas, looking as if the day emotionally exhausted her as well.

"She didn't even stir," she whispers.

"She had a big day." I lean against the porch railing, taking in the stretch of quiet fields under the stars. The world feels softer tonight, like Pete's words are still hanging there with the frost.

Ivy steps closer, wrapping her arms around herself. "He's right, you know. About not taking things for granted."

"Yeah," I say. "He is."

The night is quiet except for the crackling of the fire. I wrap an arm around her shoulders, pulling her in close.

"I don't want to waste a second," I say quietly. "Not with you. Not with us."

She lifts her head just enough to look at me, her eyes shining in the firelight. "Then we don't hold back. Not anymore."

I nod, my throat tight. "We go all in. Whatever comes, we face it together."

Her fingers curl into my shirt, like she is anchoring herself to me. "Together," she echoes.

The fire pops and the night settles around us, but I feel lighter, stronger, like something inside me has finally clicked into place. I pull her even closer and let myself breathe her in, let myself believe this can last.

For the first time in years, I am not just surviving. I am ready to live. With her.

# Chapter 18
# Ivy

My mom's kitchen smells like cinnamon and rosemary...like home. She's always got something simmering in her big pot on the stove or fresh bread baking in the oven. Rarely did we ever go out to eat while growing up here, because nobody can cook as good as our mom. She puts love and intention into every bowl and bread she makes for us, and you can just taste both. Rowan and Willa are perched at the island with mugs of tea, and I'm cross-legged on one of the barstools, feeling lighter than I have in years. I keep glancing at my phone, thinking about texting Remy to see what he's doing. I miss him.

Junie's on the rug with Lola sprawled beside her, one paw gently draped over Cobweb, who purrs so loudly it's practically a motor. Junie giggles every time the kitten bats at Lola's tail, and Lola just sighs like she was born to babysit a tiny human and a cat cousin.

"See?" Willa says, nodding toward them. "I told you Cobweb would win her over."

"She's a good girl," I say, smiling as Lola rolls onto her back so Junie can rub her belly. "Honestly, I think she'd follow Junie to the moon if she could."

My mom sets a plate of cookies on the island, hands a napkin of them to Junie, and sits, brushing flour from her hands. "All this love in my house," she teases, her eyes sparkling. "Tate and Willa making eyes at each other every time they breathe, and now Remy and Ivy...who knew?"

My face goes hot, but Willa grins like a cat. "Oh, everyone knows," she says. "You two have that look."

"What look?" I protest, but I can feel the smile tugging at my lips.

"The look," Rowan says knowingly. "Like you're half annoyed and half dying to climb him like a tree every time he walks into the room."

I bury my face in my hands, my face going hot. "You're all ridiculous."

My mom laughs. "You're glowing, sweetheart. It's a good thing. Must be all those romance novels you've been reading."

The truth is that I haven't even had time to read any of them. I've been too busy living out my own romance novel, and I'm not complaining.

"So," Rowan says, taking a sip of tea. "Speaking of couples, I'm going on a date this weekend."

All of us turn to stare at her.

"What?" Willa gapes. "With who?"

"His name's Jonah," Rowan shrugs, trying to look nonchalant, but her cheeks are pink. "He's new in town. Works down on the boats."

"Wait, wait, wait," I say, leaning forward. "Are you serious?"

Rowan nods.

*Wow.*

"Oh, boy." Willa grins and sucks in a breath. "Does Finn know?"

Rowan shrugs, too casually. "Why would he care?"

I can't help but wonder that myself. Because Finn will absolutely care. Finn's face flashes in my mind, solid, steady with his broad shoulders and quiet watchfulness. Finn who is wildly in love with my sister and has been for years. Finn, who is also her best friend. Picturing him hurt makes me feel so upset for him.

"You should tell him," Lilith says gently, like she just read my thoughts. "See what he has to say about that date."

Rowan rolls her eyes. "It's just a date, Mom."

"Uh-huh," Willa teases. "I wonder if Finn will think that's just a date."

"I don't think this is going to go over well, that's all I'm saying," I tell her, not liking how this is going to play out.

Junie looks up from the floor and says, "Uncle Finn won't like that, Rowan. He says you're his endgame. I don't know what that means, but I don't think he's going to like you going on a date."

"He said that?" Rowan asks Junie, and she nods solemnly.

She purses her lips and says, "Hmmm."

But I don't miss the thoughts passing over her face that she's not sharing with the class. Something is up with Rowan.

I settle back against the stool, warmth spreading through me. This is what I always wanted. Sisters, laughter, love that fills up a whole room. And maybe, just maybe, a future where we all get to have the love we all deserve.

* * *

The house is quiet when we get home, except for the low crackle of the fire. Remy's on the couch, boots off, stretched out with a book in one hand and an open bottle of beer on the table next to him.

"You're back early," he says, setting the book aside as I kick off my shoes. Junie runs to give him a hug. She bounces off with Lola on her heels to go play before she has to get ready for bed.

"Mm," I hum, crossing the room and sinking onto the couch beside him.

His arm goes around me like it's the most natural thing in the world. "Have fun?"

"So, Rowan had news."

He raises an eyebrow. "Good news or bad news?"

I grin. "Depends who you ask. She's going on a date this weekend."

That gets his attention. "With who?"

"Jonah. New guy in town. Works on the boats."

He makes a surprised sound, rubbing his jaw. "Finn know?"

"That's exactly what we asked." I curl my legs under me, watching his face. "She said no, but I think maybe he should."

Remy leans his head back against the couch, smiling faintly. "I think Finn already knows more than he lets on."

"You do?"

"Mm-hmm." His arm tightens around me. "He notices everything about Rowan. He's just too damn stubborn to do anything about it."

I laugh softly. "Sounds like someone else I know."

He tips his head to look at me, and there's a flash of heat in his eyes that makes my stomach flip. "Yeah, well. Worked out for me, didn't it?"

I nudge him with my knee. "It did."

For a while we just sit there, the fire throwing shadows across the room, Junie's sounds of playing drifting from down the hall. Remy's thumb traces idle circles over my arm, and the quiet between us feels safe, full.

"You think Finn and Rowan would be good together?" I ask after a bit.

"I think Finn needs someone who'll love him for who he is,"

he says. "And Rowan might be the only other person stubborn enough to pull that off."

I smile, picturing it, and rest my head on his shoulder. "Then I guess we'll just have to wait and see."

He presses a kiss to the top of my hair. "Guess we will."

Remy gets Junie to bed and tucked in and joins me on the couch as we sit in front of the fire, wrapped up in each other.

And just like that, the world feels right.

* * *

Tate's helping a customer tie a tree to the top of their SUV while I'm stocking cocoa cups at the stand. Across the lot, Remy is lifting another tree like it weighs nothing.

I hear it before I see her, a familiar woman's laugh, flirty and just loud enough to carry.

"Well, hello, handsome," Vanessa drawls, leaning against the truck while Remy secures the twine. "What Hallmark movie are you in? Because I'd watch it."

I nearly choke on my breath but manage to laugh, the sound sharper than I mean for it to be. Tate glances over at me, smirking like he knows exactly what just lit me up.

Remy doesn't even look at her. He double-checks the knots, steps back, and gives the customer a polite nod. "You're all set. Drive safe." Then he's already turning to help the next person, calm and professional as ever, like the comment never happened.

Only Vanessa reaches out and grabs his arm to stop him. Remy glances down at his arm and up at her and pulls his arm back. "Wait, I wanted to see if you wanted to get dinner some time."

"Not only would my girlfriend have an issue with that, but I would, too. Please don't touch me," he tells her, politely and firmly.

I stroll over and say, "Everything okay here?"

Vanessa's eyes narrow on me. Remy doesn't miss this, either.

Remy ignores her and bends down and kisses me thoroughly. There's no mistake that Vanessa is taking it all in, and she's not happy about it.

She turns on her heels and stomps away, huffing.

"Well," I say softly. "That was interesting."

Remy just smirks and pulls me in tighter.

My pulse is still pounding when the last car rolls out, and the lot grows quiet again. Tate heads to the barn to grab more twine for tomorrow, leaving us alone.

I'm sweeping pine needles, a never-ending job, I've found, when I feel him behind me, close enough that his body heat cuts through the cold.

"You done?" His voice is low, rough, and it goes straight through me.

"Almost," I say, leaning the broom against the wall.

Before I can blink, he's kissing me, hard, walking me backward into the barn. My spine bumps the doorframe, and I grab at his jacket, stunned and breathless.

He breaks just enough to murmur against my mouth, "I saw you jealous, Ivy."

I swallow hard. "I didn't like Vanessa flirting with you."

His mouth curves, but his eyes have gone dark. "How do you think I felt watching you date Douchey Derek all those years?"

My breath catches. "I didn't think you noticed."

His jaw tightens, and his voice is a growl. "I noticed."

He kisses me again, slower this time, but deeper, like he's trying to erase every memory of anyone else. I melt against him, fingers tangling in his hair.

We make it as far as his office before he flips the latch, shuts the door, and lifts me onto the desk like I weigh nothing. The room is small, lit by a rustic overhead light, smelling of hay and pine.

"You have any idea what you do to me?" he mutters, mouth tracing down my neck.

"Show me," I whisper.

That's all it takes. His flannel is off in seconds, then his jeans, my sweater, and the cold air feels like fire where our skin meets. He kisses me until I'm dizzy, until I can't think about anything except getting closer.

He pushes my jeans down, his hands firm on my thighs as he steps between them, and then he's inside me in one deep, perfect thrust that knocks the air out of my lungs.

"Remy—"

He groans my name and starts to move, slow at first, then faster when I grip his shoulders and beg him not to stop. The desk creaks under us, papers sliding to the floor, but I don't care. All I can feel is him, filling me, grounding me, setting me on fire all at once.

When I come, it's sharp and sweet, my whole body shuddering around him. He follows with a low, broken sound, holding me so tight I can feel his heart racing against mine.

We stay tangled together, breathing hard, the office silent except for the faint hum of the heater and the sound of us coming back down.

Finally, he pulls back just enough to look me in the eye, thumb brushing my cheek.

"That clear enough for you?" he asks, voice still rough.

I grin, flushed and wrecked in the best way. "Crystal."

"I haven't been with anyone in years," Remy says quietly. "I know you're on birth control; I've seen the packets."

I nod, "And I got tested when I found out Derek was cheating. I've only been with you since. I'm clear."

He kisses me again, slow and sweet this time, sealing something I think we've both been waiting on for years.

Remy finally steps back, still close enough that his breath brushes my lips. My sweater is hanging half off the desk, his flannel is crumpled on the floor, and there are a few pine needles on the back of my jeans from the desk.

"Well," I whisper, catching my breath. "That was..."

He grins, smug and gorgeous. "Productive?"

I swat his chest, laughing as I hop down from the desk, legs still shaky. "You're a hard worker."

He bends to grab his flannel, shrugging it back on, but not before I get another long look at that chest that should be illegal.

"You think Tate heard us?" I ask, pulling my sweater over my head.

His grin widens. "If he did, he's probably out there taking his sweet time, so he doesn't have to walk in on us."

I groan, covering my face with my hands. "He's never going to let me live this down."

"Good," Remy says, stepping closer and hooking a finger under my chin until I look up at him. "I want everyone to know exactly how crazy I am about you."

Heat blooms in my chest, soft and sweet this time. "You are ridiculous."

"Yeah," he says, leaning in to steal one last, slow kiss. "Ridiculous for you."

When we finally leave the office and step outside the barn, the air is colder, the stars sharp against the dark sky. Tate is leaning against the fence with his arms crossed and a look that says he knows everything.

"Everything good in there?" he calls, one brow arched.

"Inventory check," Remy says smoothly, grabbing my hand and tugging me toward the truck.

Tate just smirks. "Sure. Inventory."

I bury my face in my scarf, trying not to laugh, and Remy squeezes my fingers.

"Date night tomorrow," he murmurs as he helps me into the truck. "No customers, no interruptions. Just you and me."

"Promise?"

His answering smile is slow and devastating to my lady parts. "Promise."

# Chapter 19
# Remy

I slip out of bed, careful not to wake Ivy, and pad to the kitchen. The coffee pot gurgles, filling the air with the warm coffee smell I love. I pour a mug and sit at the counter, taking my first slow sip.

This is my favorite time of day. The sun isn't up; the world is still fast asleep. No customers yet, no chores, no questions. Just me and the sound of the heater kicking on and keeping us warm on this cold winter day.

I let my eyes wander around the room, taking it all in. Every morning, I notice something new these days. Ivy is always quietly fixing things up, making the house homier without making a big deal about it. It's like it's her love language to make this house a home for all of us, and one of my favorite things is seeing what she's done.

Today, it hits me all at once. There are framed photos everywhere now. On the mantle, on the entryway table, even by the kitchen sink. Me and Junie grinning in front of the tree lot. Me and Finn with fishing poles on the dock. My mom holding baby Junie, her face soft and proud. There's even one of me, Tate, and

Finn when we were barely out of high school, arms slung around each other and grinning like idiots.

She must have gotten these from my mom. My heart warms at the kind gesture of doing this.

Then my throat tightens when I see the one of me and my uncle, taken years before he passed. He's got his hand on my shoulder, both of us covered in dirt from working at the tree farm all day.

I whisper into the quiet, "I hope I've made you proud."

It hits me right in the chest that Ivy thought to put that photo out where I could see it. She knows how much he means to me.

But then my gaze moves across the wall, and I notice something else. There are no pictures of Ivy. Not one in any of them. Not in the kitchen, not on the mantle, not even tucked by the coffeemaker.

My stomach knots. What if she doesn't see herself staying here after all? What if she left herself out of those photos on purpose because she doesn't want to take up space?

The thought makes my blood run cold.

I grip the mug a little tighter and force a slow breath. No. I tell myself not to think like that. Not after everything we have been through. Not after the nights we've shared and the way she looks at me like I'm hers. We talked about this, and we were on the same page. I thought so, anyway.

She is meant to be here. Surely, she has to feel that, too.

I finish my coffee and rinse the mug in the sink. The sky outside is starting to lighten with the sun trying to break through. Time to get to work.

Before I leave, I stop by Junie's room. She is curled up under her blanket, hair a mess, breathing deep. I press a kiss to her head and whisper, "Love you, bug."

Then I go back to my room and pause in the doorway. Ivy is

still asleep, dark red hair spread over my pillow like a halo. The sight of her there makes my chest ache in the best way.

I sit on the edge of the bed and lean down to kiss her temple. She stirs, sighs softly, and settles again.

"My girls," I whisper, the words slipping out before I can stop them.

I grab my coat and head out into the crisp morning air. My boots crunch on the frost as I cross the yard, my mind already turning over the thought that won't let me go.

She belongs in those pictures.

And I am going to make damn sure she knows it.

* * *

The house is quiet when I come in from the barn that night, only the soft glow of the lamp over the couch lighting the room. Ivy's curled up under one of the quilts, reading. She looks up when she hears my boots and smiles that small smile that always hits me low in the gut.

All day I replayed this conversation we're about to have in my head, and I braced myself for the worst. Even though I know that's not how it is with Ivy. It would always be the worst with Sloane. I had to brace myself for everything. But with Ivy, she makes everything easy and for that I am grateful.

"Hey," she says softly, setting the book aside next to her.

"Hey." I hang my jacket on the hook and sit beside her, my knee brushing hers under the quilt. For a second I just sit there, staring at the pictures on the wall.

"You did all this," I say finally, my voice rough. "The photos."

Her smile widens, shy but proud. "Yeah. It felt...right. I wanted Junie to see pictures of her family and feel loved here."

I nod, throat tight. "I love it. Every single one. But..." I hesitate, dragging a hand over the back of my neck. "You're not in any of them."

Her brow furrows with confusion. "What?"

"There's pictures of me, of Junie, Finn, Mom, even Tate," I say quietly. "But none of you. Not anywhere."

"Oh." She blinks, surprised. "I just...I didn't think to put myself in them. It felt like it should be about you and Junie."

I take a deep breath, steadying myself. "Ivy, you belong in this house. You belong with us. And I guess...I just need to know if you're going to stay."

Her eyes go wide, her book forgotten in her lap. "What do you mean? Why would you ask that?"

I watch her and make myself say it. "I want to know where you see this going." I hold her gaze even when my throat tightens. "You have moved a lot. Jobs. Places. And I..." My voice frays. I steady it. "I cannot go through losing someone again. Junie cannot, either. She has had enough people leave."

Her lips part like I have knocked the wind out of her. "Remy. This is not just a job. I cannot imagine leaving unless you wanted me to. I thought we talked about this."

Something in my chest loosens. That hard knot from this morning eases. I nod, but I don't let it end there. "We did. I just need to hear it again sometimes." I reach for her hand. "And I need to say it back. I want you here. Not just because of how good you are to Junie. I want you because you are you. This is your home with us if you want it. Not just for the season. For good."

She scoots closer until her knees press against mine. Her eyes shine, careful and hopeful all at once. "I feel like I have been searching for my place forever. Maybe it was here all along. With you and Junie."

I exhale and cup her face and kiss her, slow and sure, relief making the room tilt. When I pull back, I rest my forehead against hers. "I know forever is a hard word," I say quietly. "It's hard for me, too. But I love you. And I can't picture this place without you in it." I swallow and let the last piece out. "I don't want to."

She closes her eyes, then opens them and lets me see what's there. "I love you," she says. "I want this. I want you. I want us."

I press her hand to my chest so she can feel the way it kicks. "Then we do it together," I say. "When it gets hard, we say so. When the old fear shows up, we talk about it."

She nods, a small, shaky laugh breaking loose, and tucks herself closer like she is choosing the spot that already fits. The knot inside me is gone. In its place is the steady weight of something I want to spend the rest of my life keeping.

I press my forehead against hers. "Then we're taking pictures of you tomorrow," I murmur. "And putting them on every damn wall in this house."

* * *

The school gym smells like old cafeteria food and construction paper, with the little stage strung with twinkle lights and dangling paper snowflakes. The whole town must be here. Donna's in the front row with Pete, a tissue already clutched in her hand. Lilith waves us over to save seats, Tate and Willa tucked in beside her. Even Finn and Rowan are here, bickering softly but sitting close enough that their shoulders touch.

Junie bounces nervously backstage, her new Christmas dress sparkling under the lights. Ivy crouches in front of her, braiding her hair one last time while Lola sits obediently at her feet.

"You look perfect, Juniebug," Ivy whispers, kissing the top of her head.

Junie grins and runs to join her class. I snap a picture just as she turns around and waves, and the whole row of us laughs and waves back.

When the music starts, the kids sing with all the enthusiasm of five-year-olds, Junie the loudest of all. My chest swells so hard it almost hurts. I sneak a glance at Ivy, who's smiling so big she's practically glowing.

Pete claps so hard at the end I'm surprised he doesn't throw out his shoulder, and Donna's wiping at her eyes like she just watched Junie graduate from college.

Afterward, we all spill into the cold night air, our breath puffing in little clouds. "Dinner?" Tate calls, and everyone agrees.

The Wisteria Cove diner is packed but we cram into two big booths, eating burgers and passing plates of fries and onion rings back and forth, laughing until my cheeks ache. Junie is still buzzing from the performance, proudly showing everyone the glitter star the teacher pinned to her dress.

That night, when we finally make it home and Junie is tucked in, I catch Ivy by the hand and spin her once in the kitchen, just to hear her laugh again.

"Remy," she says, smiling up at me.

I pull her close and kiss her, slow and deep. "You make me so damn happy," I murmur against her lips.

And I realize it's true. Life can't get any better than this.

The night felt perfect. We're at the bookstore after dinner at the diner winding down. The bookstore is closed, but we're all just hanging out inside, even though the closed sign is on the door. The fire is low, the lights twinkling, everyone lingering with cocoa and half-empty dessert plates. Willa is curled up with Tate near the fireplace, Rowan is perched on the counter teasing Finn, and Ivy is humming quietly as she stacks mugs by the sink. Junie is on the floor coloring, still wearing her glitter star from the program.

Then the bell over the door jingles.

The whole room goes still. I turn around to see who came in that's making everyone go silent.

Sloane steps inside, snow dusting her coat, hair perfect as always.

My body reacts before my head does. A tight pull under my ribs. Jaw locking. The small, useless urge to check the exits. Because Sloane is the shape of an old bruise on all of our hearts and my muscles still flinch when she is near, ready and waiting to protect Junie and myself from her hurt. I remember the late nights that never ended, apologies that did not hold, and of a door that closed and stayed closed.

I glance past her without meaning to, a reflex that is all spine and instinct. Where are Junie and Ivy? I clock them, and they are fine. For now. Until Sloane breaks promises and hearts like she always does.

Her eyes flick over the place like she is taking inventory.

Her perfume hits, clean and expensive, and the past tries to slide its hook between my ribs. She represents a life I buried on purpose.

This is not what Junie needs right now. Not what I need. I need boundaries that don't bend. I need my daughter to feel the ground stay under her feet. I need Ivy to know there is no contest here, no door cracked for old ghosts.

My mom mutters dryly under her breath, just loud enough for everyone to hear, "Guess the spell didn't work."

Ivy blinks, polite and confused. "Oh—hi. Sorry, we're closed and just having a family party. Can I help you with something?"

Sloane's gaze sweeps the room until it lands on me. "I'm looking for my husband," she says coolly, "And my daughter."

My chest locks tight. "Ex-husband." My voice is flat, hard. "And you are supposed to call first."

Junie hasn't even noticed yet, too busy showing Pete her

picture she colored. But then she looks up, sees Sloane, and goes still. She glances at me, shrinking back toward the rug. She looks very uncomfortable.

Sloane's eyes flash, and she doesn't even acknowledge Junie. "Why isn't she happy to see me? What did you tell her about me? You did this, Remy."

"That's enough," I say, standing. "We're not doing this here."

I take her outside, the winter air biting hard against my face, and shut the door behind us.

"Why are you here?" I demand, my voice low but sharp. "You haven't come around for a year and a half, and now you just pop in like nothing? Do you have any idea what that does to Junie?"

Her chin lifts. "I don't care. That's my kid. Not that woman's." She jerks her head toward the window where Ivy is visible inside, gathering Junie close.

I say nothing because I have learned with Sloane, who is the master of manipulation and argument, that anything I say will be twisted. So, seeing Ivy is what set her off. She wants to make herself out to look like the victim and not the person who abandoned her child for the past year and a half. She hasn't seen Junie since she was four. She's five and a half now. That is ridiculous.

My jaw clenches so hard it hurts. "You need to leave."

"I have rights," she spits.

"Yeah? And you don't exercise them," I fire back.

Her lips curl. "I can take you to court."

"Do it." My voice is steady, deadly quiet. "Go ahead. I'll fight you so hard, Sloane. I'll win. And you know it."

Her face pales, because she knows that I'm right, but I don't stop. "I have never kept her from you. You kept her from you. You made this choice every single time you didn't show up.

Thirteen times you did that to her. Do you know what it was like to see her cry and be sad afterward every single time?"

She swallows hard and looks away, but I can see the anger simmering under her skin. "I have been busy with a huge trial."

"Get out of here," I tell her, stepping back toward the door. "You don't get to blow up her life just because you feel like it. Like it's a hobby for you."

She hesitates, then turns on her heel and stalks to her car. "I'm staying in town. I will see my daughter."

I stand there long after her taillights disappear down the road, my boots planted in the snow. The night is so quiet I can hear my breath, harsh and uneven. My fists are clenched so hard my knuckles ache.

Every time she shows up or doesn't show up, she digs into old wounds, rips them wide open, and then leaves us to clean up the mess. And she doesn't even care. She never has.

I tip my head back and stare at the sky. Snow drifts down lazy and soft, landing on my eyelashes, melting before I can blink it away. I feel like I am vibrating under my skin, fury and heartbreak and exhaustion all tangled together.

It would almost be easier if she were cruel outright. If she said she did not want Junie and stayed gone. But she comes in just often enough to remind us she exists, to remind Junie that she once had a mother who chose something else over her. And that's just not something a five-year-old understands.

My chest aches with the old familiar knot of helplessness pulling tight. I hate this. I hate that I am still standing out here trying to calm down so I don't scare my own daughter. I hate that Sloane has this power to shake us.

I drag both hands over my face and let out a sharp breath, watching it cloud in the air. Ivy and Junie are in there, waiting. They deserve better than me standing out here stewing like this.

By the time I open the door and step back into the bookstore, my hands are still trembling. My pulse is still hammering in my ears.

Inside, the warmth hits me, along with the low hum of voices. Ivy is on the rug with Junie, speaking softly, her hand rubbing Junie's back as the kitten curls in her lap. Tate is leaning against the counter, arms crossed, giving me a look that asks if I am okay but does not push. Rowan has her arms wrapped around herself, watching me carefully.

Ivy looks up, and the concern in her eyes nearly knocks the breath out of me.

"You okay?" she asks quietly.

No, I think. Not even close. But I nod once and hang my jacket, forcing my fingers to work.

Junie looks over at me, hesitant. "Daddy?"

I crouch down beside her and smooth a hand over her hair. "Everything's okay, bug. You did nothing wrong."

She nods but stays close to Ivy, and my heart twists. I press a kiss to her head and stand, catching Ivy's gaze again.

I press a kiss to her head and stand, catching Ivy's gaze again. There's so much in her eyes, understanding, worry, something fiercer too, and it hits me square in the chest that I'm not doing this alone for once. For once, I have a partner who wants to do this with me. Take on anything, good or bad, and be with me.

For a second, all I can think about is how fragile this feels, how one unannounced visit can shake the ground under our feet. I hate it. It also isn't lost on me how Junie shrank into Ivy's side instead of running into her mother's arms. And I hate that I have to be the one to hold the line between chaos and the quiet life we're building.

But Ivy doesn't look away. She holds my gaze like she's saying she's in this with me, no matter how messy it gets.

I nod once, the decision solidifying in my chest. Whatever

comes next with Sloane, court, whatever storm might roll through, I'm ready to fight for this. For Junie. For Ivy. For all of us.

And when Ivy reaches for my hand, just the brush of her fingers is enough to remind me of what's waiting for me when I do.

# Chapter 20
# Ivy

The heaviness of last night still lingers.

I pour Junie a mug of milk and slide it across the table. She loves to drink out of a mug, like we do at breakfast. She calls it her 'coffee.'

"Want to help me make pancakes?"

She nods and hops down from the chair. By the time we're cracking eggs, she's talking again and telling me about what she wants Santa to bring her for Christmas. A Barbie house with a dog that looks like Lola and a Barbie that looks like her.

Christmas is in a week, and I've gotten almost everything ready for her. Wrapped, hidden and ready to see her face on Christmas morning and all of her treasures. I love making holidays special for her. And I love that Remy doesn't mind me doing all of this. I love it so much.

When the first pancake hits the plate, I crouch to her level. "You okay after last night?"

Junie bites her lip. "She was mad at me."

I brush her hair back gently. "You didn't do anything wrong. Sometimes grown-ups say things when they're upset, but that doesn't mean they're mad at you or that they don't love you."

Her eyes fill, and I hug her until she's ready to let go.

After breakfast, we pull on boots and coats and head outside. The air is bright with morning light, the snow sparkling where it hasn't been disturbed yet. That's my favorite part—right after it snows. When everything feels perfect and peaceful. Junie runs ahead, giggling when the neighbor goats come trotting to the fence. Their owners went south to visit family, and Remy's keeping an eye on them for a few weeks over here in the pasture.

He sees us from over at the barn and heads over to us, kissing me and grabbing Junie and lifting her up.

"Mouse tried to climb the gate yesterday!" she calls.

Remy chuckles, crouching to scratch Mouse's nose through the slats. "Better not today. We just fixed this latch."

I lean against the fence, watching him. His shoulders are still tense under his jacket, but when he glances back at me, something eases in his face. He stands, brushing his hands on his jeans, and crosses to me.

"You okay?" he asks quietly.

I nod, sliding my gloved hand into his. "I'm more worried about you."

His thumb strokes over the back of my glove. "I hate that she did that in front of everyone."

"You protected Junie," I say softly. "That's what matters. And you don't have to protect me from the hard stuff. I'm in it with you, Remy."

His jaw works, like he's swallowing something he can't quite say out loud. Then he leans in and presses a quick kiss to my forehead. "Good. Because I need you."

Before I can answer, a truck crunches down the drive. Tate hops out, a box of donuts from the diner in one hand.

"Peace offering," he says, holding it up. "Figured you could use reinforcements."

Junie cheers and runs to meet him. A few minutes later, Willa's car rolls in behind him, and she climbs out with a tray of coffee.

"Don't look so surprised," she teases. "Mom texted. Said we might need some backup out here."

It is so busy, as I imagined it would be the closer we got to Christmas. And having everyone around is definitely easing the tension of Sloane showing up yesterday unannounced. She sucks for that. She could have called and spent special time with Junie. Instead, she made it all about her, and she never even hugged or said hello to her kid. I don't get it.

Before long, we're all in the barn, passing out donuts and cups, the goats nosing around like they're part of the conversation. Rowan texts that she and Finn are coming for ornament-making tonight, and the air feels lighter with every laugh.

By the time we get back inside, Junie is practically bouncing. We spread paper over the table and pull out glitter, paint, and plain wooden ornaments. The whole kitchen turns into a sparkling disaster, but Junie is beaming, and even Remy relaxes enough to sit and paint one.

"You're actually pretty good at this," I tease when I see his careful work on a little wooden star.

He smirks. "Don't tell anyone. It'll ruin my image."

Later, after Junie is bathed and tucked into bed, I find Remy by the fire, staring at the ornament tree like he's memorizing every messy, glittery piece.

"Hey," I say softly, sitting beside him.

"Hey." His arm slides around my waist, pulling me closer.

We sit in silence for a while, just listening to the crackle of the fire. Then he says, "Last night scared me."

I turn to look at him. "Me too."

"I kept thinking... what if she tries to come back and mess it all up? What if I lose what we're building?" His voice is low, rough.

I cover his hand with mine. "Can I talk to Sloane? I have an idea. Maybe after the holidays. Give her a chance to cool down. Make her realize that I'm not her enemy. If she wants a relationship with Junie, we can all get on the same page."

He exhales slowly, as if that was the last thing he expected me to ask. Then he kisses me, softly at first, then deeper when I slide my hands up his chest. "I don't need you to, but if you want to, I won't stop you. I know you love Junie and are looking out for her."

"I love you, too," I remind him.

"I love you so much." When he finally pulls back, he rests his forehead against mine. "You make this house feel like a home."

"And you make me feel like I belong."

His mouth curves into the slowest, sweetest smile I've ever seen, and right then I know, whatever storms come, we're weathering them together.

* * *

The gift shop hums with customers picking out trees and last-minute gifts. The heater ticks. Wind brushes the windows. I fold a stack of tree farm sweatshirts and listen for Junie's little hum while she colors. But I don't hear it anymore. She was right here ten minutes ago, sitting in the sunny patch by the window with her sketch pad and a cup of cocoa I watered down so it wouldn't be so hot. Lola was snoring under the counter. Everything was normal.

"Bug?" I call, half distracted, still smoothing the sleeves so they line up. "You ready for lunch?"

Silence answers me. Not the I-am-hiding silence. A flat, empty kind. What the heck.

I straighten, and fear pricks up my spine, worry filling me. "Junie?" I check the corner behind the card rack where she likes to hide, then the tiny reading nook we set up with beanbags and a basket of winter books. Her sketchbook is there, crayon mid-stroke, like she stood up and forgot to put it down. The cocoa sits untouched, a thin skin on top.

My heart skips and then pounds hard enough to make my fingers tremble. I circle the counter. "Junie, sweetie. Come out. You are scaring me."

Nothing.

I yank open the office door. Empty. I check the little bathroom. Empty. The back hall. Empty. I lean over the counter and look under it, because sometimes she curls up with Lola like a puppy. No sign of Lola, either.

"Remy!" I shout, my voice higher than I want it to be.

He is out by the bailing machine with Tate, but he hears me. I know it because he drops the strap in his hands and is already moving. Tate looks up, alarm flashing across his face, and starts toward the shop.

"What is it?" Remy asks, breath fogging as he hits the door.

"I can't find her," I say, and the words scrape my throat on the way out. "She was here. She was coloring. I looked everywhere. She is not here."

For one beat his face empties. The kind of empty that looks like a cliff edge. Then he is past me, checking the office, the bathroom, the back hall. I follow, listing places she could be, things she could be doing, cures to panic that don't work on anything real.

He comes back to the counter, eyes too bright. "How could you lose her?"

"She was right here." My voice is thin. I taste metal. I hate that I let myself lose sign of her for even a minute.

He stalks to the door and bellows her name across the lot. The sound rolls over the whole property and hits me in the chest like a shove. Tate is already in motion, jogging toward the tree rows. I grab my coat and run after Remy.

He turns and yells, "You were never supposed to work the tree farm. You are the nanny!"

I feel gutted with his words. Shredded. But I push it aside and just worry about Junie. I need to find her. I need to know that she's okay.

Snow dusts the ground, thin and glittering, packed down in tracks from the rush this morning. There are too many prints. Too many directions. People have been everywhere looking at trees today. So many people have been in and out of here. My breath comes short and white.

"Junie!" I call, my voice breaking. "Bug, where are you?"

We do a quick sweep of the obvious. The cocoa stand, the wreath table, the truck bed where she sometimes climbs with permission. Nothing. Remy hits the barn at a run and flicks on every light. The goats lift their heads, curious. The tack room is empty. The office is empty. The hay loft is empty. He is breathing like he has been sprinting for miles.

"Pete," I say, half pleading as I reach the back corner. He is in his chair with a blanket over his knees, eyes sharp with worry. "Have you seen her?"

"No," he says, and his face is full of worry, which I hate. "I'll call Donna and Lilith."

Remy pushes past me again. "I can't believe this!" He yells, his face full of worry.

"I'm so sorry, Remy," I say, and the truth of it makes me shake.

He turns on me, and his eyes are wild. "Sorry doesn't make her come back right now. She could be anywhere."

The words crack through me. I feel them, clean and cruel, like stepping on glass. I open my mouth, and nothing comes out at first. My vision swims. My cheeks burn.

"I turned to fold the shirts," I finally manage. "She was right there. I looked up and she was gone. I am sorry. I am so sorry."

He flinches like the word *sorry* is gasoline on a fire. "Folding shirts wasn't your job, Ivy."

I nod, because if I argue I will fall apart. And he's not wrong. I did this. I lost her. This is my fault. I grab for anything steady. "We will find her."

Word spreads fast. Finn's truck fishtails into the lot, door flying open before the engine is off. He takes one look at my face and does not waste a breath on questions. He heads for the creek at a dead sprint. Rowan and Willa pull in a minute later, still in coats, flashlights in hand even though it is daylight. Tate loops around the fence line and calls out that he will check the road to the old dock. Donna and Lilith arrive, bundled, grim, focused.

"Call the neighbors," Donna says to no one in particular, already scanning the tree rows with a mother's courage. "Tell them to check sheds and porches."

I keep moving. I check behind every stack of pallets, under every table, between every row. I call until my voice frays.

Time becomes mud. It is only an hour, they tell me later, but in my body, it stretches long and thin until it feels like it will snap. I run the same paths twice, three times, because what if I missed her hat under a branch, what if I did not call loud enough, what if she answered and I did not hear?

At the edge of the field, I stop and bend at the waist, palms on my knees, gagging on air. Panic rises hard and oily in my throat. I swallow it down. I keep moving.

"Junie," I try again, softer now, pleading. "Bug, it is Ivy. You are not in trouble. Please answer me."

Wind tugs at my hat. Somewhere a crow complains. The property groans and cracks like old wood in the cold. I hear a shout and rocket upright, heart in my mouth, but it is Rowan calling to Willa to check the old chicken coop. Not Junie. Not yet.

I run to the creek path, because I cannot stop thinking about it. Remy beat me there. I hear him before I see him. His boots pound. His voice breaks on her name. He is down the bank, scanning the frozen shallows like his eyes can force her to appear.

"Anything?" I croak.

He shakes his head, fierce and quickly, jaw tight enough to break. He climbs toward me, grabs the low branch of a pine, and misses. His palm hits the trunk. He stares at his own hand like he does not recognize it, then wipes it on his jeans, breath ragged.

"We will find her," I say again, because I have to or I'll crumble. I reach for him without thinking. He jerks away as if my touch burns.

"Keep searching," he says, and his voice is not his. It is shredded. It is a stranger wearing his shape.

I run. I check the equipment shed with Tate. I check the old apple tree grove with Donna and Lilith. I check the road with Willa and Rowan. Finn cuts across the back acreage like a bloodhound, eyes scanning, calling in a steady cadence that keeps me moving. Pete sits in the barn doorway with his blanket and his cane and his jaw set in a line I have never seen. We are all threads in a net, thrown wide and wide again, praying to catch one little fish in a sea of winter.

The hour hits some invisible mark and shifts. The light is different. The air feels colder. Panic tilts to something colder and thinner, a wire stretched too tight. I am shaking so hard I can hear my teeth click.

Then tires on gravel. A car that does not belong. I turn, and my stomach drops.

Sloane steps out of her car.

Of course. Of course, she would come *right* now.

She steps out in a neat coat and boots with clean tread, hair perfect, eyes already narrowed, like she arrived armed. She takes in the chaos. The running. The faces. The silence when we spot her. She zeroes in on Remy, who is cutting back across the lot with snow on his lashes and a look that could cut stone.

"What's going on?" she demands.

He keeps moving. "Not now, Sloane."

"I asked what is going on," she says, sharper. "Where is my daughter?"

He stops. The air changes. I have felt storms roll in faster than this, but not by much.

"We're looking for her," he says.

"You lost my kid?" she accuses him. "You were supposed to watch her. How is this going to look in court?"

I've never wanted to throttle someone more in my life.

"Sloane, I am out here every damn day raising her while you are off doing whatever the hell you want," I roar. "You have no right to come here and act like you care more than I do. If you cared, you would have been here for the last eighteen months."

Sloane crosses her arms, chin high, voice sharp enough to cut. "You clearly cannot handle being a parent."

That burns through me like gasoline. The audacity of her coming here and saying this to me when my daughter is *missing*.

"I don't need you," I snarl. "I don't need anybody. Not even you." My eyes flick to Ivy, who is frozen near the porch, tears glinting. "I can take care of my own kid. This was all a mistake. I should have taken care of her myself."

The words hang there, ugly and sharp, and Ivy's face crumples. She turns away, wiping her cheek with the back of her hand, and I feel something inside me break. Sloane looks at Ivy, confused and back at me and shakes her head angrily.

And then I hear Finn shouting my name.

I spin around, heart lurching. He's jogging across the lot,

snow kicking up under his boots, Junie in his arms, Lola trotting next to him.

"She's here!" he calls.

My legs move before my brain catches up. I meet him halfway, and Junie launches herself into my chest. I fold her up against me so tight I'm surprised she can breathe, burying my face in her hat. The smell of hay and snow and little-kid shampoo nearly takes me down.

"Don't cry, Daddy," she whispers, clutching my neck with both mittened hands. "I'm here. I just got stuck. Uncle Finn came to get me."

My chest heaves with relief.

Her voice cracks. "I was so scared, Daddy. I cried for you to come. Where's Ivy?"

My throat closes, and a broken sound tears out of me. "I'm here, bug. I'm here now. You're safe. I will keep you safe."

I kiss the top of her head, her cheeks, her nose, rocking her without meaning to. Finn is still talking, something about finding her in the back goat pen, the latch half-closed so she couldn't push it open, but all I can do is hold her.

I can't believe I didn't think to look in the goat pen. I should have known she would go there. God, why did I let this happen? I should have had her with me. I should have been watching her.

Ivy is standing on the porch, one hand pressed to her mouth, silent tears running down her face. Sloane still looks like she's ready to explode, but I don't even look at her. I watch her look at Junie, get in her car and start to drive away. Again, not even bothering to speak to her daughter and make sure she's okay. But I stopped trying to figure out why Sloane does what she does a long time ago. Nothing makes sense.

"She's fine," Finn says gently, clapping a hand on my shoulder. "Just cold and scared."

I nod once, still rocking Junie, my chest shaking with left-over fear. "Thank you," I manage, and Finn just nods back, stepping away to give me space.

Junie pulls back just enough to look at me. "Can we go inside now? It's cold. I didn't get lunch."

"Yeah," I whisper, kissing her again. "Yeah, we can go inside."

I carry her toward the house, my arms locked around her like I might lose her again if I let go. Behind me, I hear Ivy's soft sob as she turns and disappears inside.

The relief is so sharp it feels like pain. My little girl is safe. She's in my arms. And yet the damage is done. I saw Ivy's face. I know what I just did to her. I was so scared, and I took it out on everyone. Because that's my default. I need to do everything on my own. Because I am the only one who is supposed to keep it all together.

And as I step into the warm glow of the house, the weight of it lands on me like a boulder, I might have my daughter, but I think I broke everything else.

"Ivy, we need to talk," I say as Ivy turns and walks down the hall.

"Ivy," I say, but it's too late.

I hear her hugging Junie and saying something softly to her and Junie protesting, "No, Ivy. I'm sorry. I won't ever go to the goat pen, again."

"It's not your fault, honey. It's okay. I'm just so glad that you're safe," Ivy says softly, her voice wavering with emotion.

God, I messed this up. I don't deserve Ivy. And she definitely didn't deserve the bullshit I said to her. I would give anything to take it back. That anger had no place directed at Ivy, and I messed this up.

A few minutes later, Ivy is back with a duffel bag in her hand. Lilith is waiting by her car in the driveway.

Junie sees her and starts sobbing, reaching out. "Ivy! Don't go!"

"I have to, bug," Ivy whispers, her own tears running down her face as she hugs her tight. "I love you so much. Keep Lola safe for me, okay? I know Lola loves you just as much as I do."

I say nothing because I don't deserve to say anything. Ivy is right to leave. Hell, I'd leave me if I could. I am a giant asshole. I don't deserve to be loved by Ivy. And I'm also mad that she's leaving.

I stand there frozen as Lilith helps her into the car. The engine starts. The taillights glow red. Then they're gone, and the yard is quiet except for my daughter's hiccupping cries.

I turn in a slow circle, taking in the mess. Customers are standing near their trucks, whispering. Rowan and Willa look like they want to murder me. Donna is glaring like she doesn't even recognize me.

And Ivy is gone because of me. I did this.

I drag both hands down my face and sink onto the porch step, my stomach twisted into knots. I have been through gunfights and bar fights and storms that tore fences out of the ground, but nothing has ever hurt like this.

I drove her away. And I hate myself for it.

* * *

Later that night, the house is too quiet. Too empty.

Junie is finally asleep in her room, curled against her stuffed narwhal like she's afraid to let it go. I stand in the doorway, watching her little chest rise and fall, and every time I blink I see Ivy's face when I told her I didn't need her.

Even the dog is watching me with worried eyes. It isn't lost on me that she left her here for Junie. She always puts Junie first and loves her deeply. Something I took for granted when I yelled at her.

God, what the hell is wrong with me? She loved Junie enough to leave her dog here for her. She loves us. I am the problem here. It was a simple mistake. I know that now. But in the moment, I felt like I was losing it. Losing Junie. And I said terrible things that I never should have said. After everything that Ivy has done for us.

I step into the hall and shut the door a crack, then walk back to the kitchen. The counter is spotless, but there's a single crayon sitting by the sink. Red. The tip is worn down to a nub. Junie left it here this morning.

My throat burns, and my eyes sting from emotion, and I hate that I ruined it. Sabotaged it. Shut it all down before it could shut me down. And here I am, still shut down.

I grab a beer from the fridge and sink into the chair at the table, elbows on my knees, staring at the floor. The silence presses in on me until I can hear my own heart thump with anger.

The door creaks and then shuts. Finn steps into the kitchen, takes one look at me, and shakes his head.

"You really screwed up," he says flatly.

I let out a humorless laugh. "Thanks for the update."

"No," Finn says, his voice sharper. "You don't get to sit here and sulk like you didn't just blow up your whole life. I have seen you mad, Rem, but I have never seen you like that. You lit into Ivy like she was the enemy. She loves that kid, and she loves you. And you practically shoved her out the door."

I grip the neck of the bottle so hard my knuckles ache. "I know."

"Then what the hell were you thinking?"

I drag a hand through my hair. "I wasn't thinking. I was panicking. I thought—" My voice cracks, and I have to stop, take a long breath. "I thought I'd lost her. And all I could see was that empty shop and her gone, and my brain just...snapped. I went after the first person in front of me."

"And that was Ivy."

I nod with defeat.

Finn leans on the counter, arms crossed. "Sloane deserves every bit of your anger that you have for her. But not Ivy. She's done nothing but love you and your kid. You know that."

The words feel like gravel in my throat. "I know," I admit. "I love Ivy. More than I have ever loved anyone but Junie. And now she's devastated, and things might be too far gone to fix."

Finn is quiet for a long moment. "Then you'd better figure out how to fix this. She's not just gonna come walking back through that door, Rem. You hurt her bad. You messed this up big time. I'm so fucking pissed at you. I don't know how you could do that to her. You lost control."

"I know." I groan as I drop my head into my hands. "I saw her face, and I'll never forget it."

That look on her face when I lashed out with those horrible things I said. I don't even want to think about it again.

"You need to do something big for her. Show her that you messed up and it won't happen again. Show her how much she means to you."

He leaves me there in the kitchen, alone with the weight sitting on my chest like a cinder block.

When the house is quiet again, I get up and walk to my room. Her sweater is still on the chair by the bed, one of those soft ones she wears when she's making cocoa or reading with Junie. I pick it up and press it to my face, breathing in the faint scent of her shampoo, and it just about knocks me to my knees.

I sit there on the edge of the bed with that sweater in my hands, and all I can think is that I have to make this right.

I don't care how. I'll grovel or beg. I will fight harder than I ever have for anything.

Because if I lose Ivy for good, I lose the family I have been dreaming of since the day Junie was born.

And this cannot be the end of our story.

# Chapter 22
# Ivy

My hands are shaking so badly I can barely pull the seat belt across me. My mom doesn't say anything as she drives, her profile calm and steady as she lets me cry in the passenger seat. My breath comes in short, uneven bursts, each one scraping against my throat.

I keep seeing Junie's body pressed to Remy's. I keep hearing Remy's voice, cold and sharp, telling me he didn't need me, and this was my fault.

God, I thought we were a team. I love him, and I love Junie so much. I thought he knew how much I love them and would never intentionally do anything that would put Junie in jeopardy. And I thought he loved me. But when he said that part about me being the nanny and that was what I was supposed to do and not work at the farm and be distracted, he was right. And I should have focused. I should have kept her safe. I messed up. That part he's not wrong about.

But I won't be treated like that. I won't live again the way I did with Derek. I thought Remy was different. But did the mask slip? Did he show me who he really is?

The thoughts wash over me, but deep down I know it's not

true. That's not Remy...that's not who he is. He is good, and he wouldn't do this. This was simply a horrible situation where he lost it, and he needs to apologize.

I just don't know if that's going to be enough.

Something that hit me when we lost Junie was whether or not I'm good enough to be there for her and take care of her. What's going to keep me from possibly doing something like this again? Maybe this was a sign that it's time to leave. Move on. Get out before I get even closer to anyone.

Because I broke my own rules. I got too close. I caught major feelings. And I thought he did, too.

I need space. I need time to figure out what I want. Because one thing that I know for sure is that I will never stay in a place where I'm not wanted ever again. I won't just be someone's option. I want to be their choice. Their everything. Maybe I am a hopeless romantic and believe in all of these romance books I read—so what? That's what I believe. And I will find that kind of love. I thought I already had. But does love treat others that way when times get hard? Does love freak out when something hard happens?

Yes. Yes, it does, I think to myself. Because that is what real life and love looks like. I know that. I don't want a fake or boring love. I want the passion, the realness, and the making up. I want Remy to make up with me. And not just with a simple *I'm sorry*. I want him to show me. Fight for me. He's going to have to show me that if he wants me back. Period.

I wrap my arms around myself and press my forehead to the cold window, watching the snow swirl in the headlights. Mom reaches over and gives my knee a squeeze. It's not much, but it keeps me from flying apart completely.

When we pull up to her house, the porch light is glowing warm against the dark. Willa and Rowan are waiting just inside, coats still on, two mugs of tea steaming on the counter.

The minute I step inside, Willa wraps me in a hug.

"He told me he didn't need me," I choke out. "In front of everyone. Like I was nothing."

"Oh, honey." Willa pulls me closer. "That man was hurting and scared. But that was messed up."

"Yeah, it was," Rowan says from the doorway, arms crossed. "Want me to punch him?"

That almost makes me laugh, but the sound turns into another sob.

"Sit down," Mom says gently. She steers me to the couch and tucks one of her quilts around my shoulders like I'm eight years old again. And I let her, because I'm just so freaking sad.

The three of them stay with me while I cry it out, Rowan sitting cross-legged on the floor, Willa rubbing circles on my back, Mom quiet but solid at my side.

When my sobs finally slow to hiccups, Mom says, "He was just scared, Ivy. That doesn't excuse what he said. But fear makes people lash out in stupid ways. I've seen that man take on a lot without blinking, but nothing scares a parent more than losing their child."

"I know he was scared," I whisper, staring at my hands. "So was I. But he made me feel like I didn't belong there. Like I was just...in the way."

"You're not in the way," Willa says fiercely. "You are part of that family now, whether he can see straight or not at all right now through what he's going through. He loves you."

Rowan leans her chin on her hand. "You know what this is, right? The part in every Hallmark movie where the hero screws up right before he realizes he's in love."

"You've been talking to Donna. This isn't a movie," I say, voice sharp. "And I thought he already realized he loved me. Maybe I was just the nanny. Just the person who watched his kid."

"Right," Rowan clips sarcastically. "You guys can work this out. Give him a minute to figure this all out. You just have to let him crawl first. Make him grovel. Maybe beg a little."

Willa snorts and tosses a pillow at her. "You might be wrong, Rowan. Maybe Remy isn't it for Ivy."

"I am right," Rowan says. "I'm saying this isn't over. He loves her. You think he's just gonna sit at that farm and sulk? Please. That man is probably losing his mind with regret right now."

I bite my lip, because the image of Remy pacing the kitchen, wearing a groove in the floor, hits me square in the chest.

Willa still looks mad on my behalf, "I would hex him, but I do like Remy. But he's an ass for how he treated you today."

"Drink your tea," Mom says softly. "Tonight you rest. Tomorrow, you can decide what comes next. Everyone just needs to cool down and have a little space."

* * *

Later, after I've tucked myself into my old room, I sit on the edge of the bed staring at the quilt, lost in thought. Everything here is neat and quiet. Familiar. And yet it feels empty. I miss Remy and Junie. I hope she's snuggled up with Lola, and she's making her feel better.

I won't get to fall asleep with Remy holding me and wake up to his arms around me. I don't know if I'll ever get to do any of these things ever again. This might really just be over for us. It doesn't feel that way, but then again, I know that life can change on a dime. People leave, die, and we don't get a say. Maybe I've been right at pushing people away and keeping my heart safe. Safe felt...okay...safe felt boring. And lonely. Remy felt like a chance. He felt exciting and great.

Sometimes the punches just keep punching. And we have

to take them. And this is why I barely trust my heart with anyone. And I'm kicking myself for trusting it with Remy. Because this hurts.

I think about the photos I hung up around the house. How I didn't put a single one of myself on the walls. Was Remy right? Was some part of me still holding back, still ready to run when it got hard? Did I subconsciously lie to him and to myself? God, I am an idiot for even trying with him.

Tears well again, but I brush them away. I don't want to run. Not really. I want to stay.

The thought is terrifying and plain as day. I want them.

But does he want me?

A knock sounds softly on the door. Mom slips in carrying two mugs of her herbal tea that helps with sleep every time like a charm. Tea is the answer to most everything with mom. Had a bad day at school? Tea. A boy broke your heart? Tea. Always tea.

"Couldn't sleep?" she asks. "I saw you didn't eat much, so I made you a sandwich."

I shake my head. "Just too upset to eat anything."

She sits on the bed beside me, handing me a mug. "Ivy, I know this feels awful right now. But sometimes the worst nights are the ones that teach us who we really are and what we want."

"What if what I want doesn't want me?" My voice cracks on the words.

She squeezes my hand. "From where I'm standing, that man would burn down the world for you to make this right. He just hasn't figured out how yet."

My throat aches. "What if I can't forgive him?"

"Then you can't. Forgiveness isn't something you owe anyone. But don't make that decision tonight. Sleep first. See how the sun feels in the morning."

* * *

I don't sleep much. When I do, I dream of Junie sitting in the goat pen crying for me, her little mittened hands reaching out. I wake with a start, tears streaming down my face, heart hammering, and grab a pen and paper.

I write her a note before I lose my nerve:

*Bug, I love you. You were so brave yesterday. I'm proud of you. I'll see you soon. Everything will be okay.*

I don't know if any of that is true. I don't want to get her hopes up. But I can't imagine how confusing all of this is to her right now. Remy wanted me to leave. He made it clear he was angry, and that was my fault. I did what he asked. And now Junie is paying for this the most, and I hate this.

I fold it carefully and set it out to give to Donna to bring to her.

* * *

In the morning, Willa and Rowan are waiting at the kitchen table with coffee and slices of quiche.

"You look like you didn't sleep at all," Rowan says.

"Thanks," I mutter, sitting down.

Willa nudges the plate toward me. "Eat something. You're no good to anyone if you fall over."

I take a bite but barely taste it. "I keep hearing her cry. I keep thinking about the look on her face when I left."

"Then go see her," Willa says simply.

"It's not that easy."

Rowan shrugs. "Doesn't have to be easy. You can do it even if it's hard. What's he going to do? Keep you from seeing his kid? He messed up, not Junie. She shouldn't have to be punished because her dad's being a dumbass."

"Or you could just talk to him," Mom suggests.

I stare at my coffee. "I still don't know what to say to him."

"Good," Rowan says. "Make him do the talking. He shouldn't have been a dickhead."

Willa smiles softly. "Give him a chance to fix it, Ivy. For you and for Junie. Last night I wasn't so sure that this was going to work out. But I did some thinking and talked to Tate. For what it's worth, Tate says Remy's a wreck right now."

* * *

That night, after the house is quiet, I sit at the window with a blanket around my shoulders and watch the snow fall. It doesn't look like the tree farm and how it's become home.

And I realize that, for the first time in my life, I *want* to go home.

Not to my mom's house, but to the tree farm where Remy and Junie are. Wherever Remy and Junie are, that's where I want to be. Where my place at the table is waiting, whether I believe I deserve it or not.

I press my face into the blanket and cry quietly until there are no tears left, homesick for a place that I'm not sure is really home.

# Chapter 23
# Remy

The barn feels damp and cold, like it's holding a grudge against me, too. As it should, I deserve it. I took out everything I've been holding in for years on the people around me that I love, and I hate myself for doing that. I was so terrified when Junie went missing. Then Sloane showing up in the middle of it made me just lose it.

The air smells like hay and sawdust and bad decisions, a reminder of just how badly I screwed things up. My chest feels tight, like I haven't taken a full breath since Ivy left.

Finn leans against a post with his arms crossed like a damn judge. Tate sits on a stool, dragging his pocketknife over a whetstone, slow and steady, like he's preparing for war. Lola lies at my feet, staring at me like she wants to put me in the woodchipper. Even her damn dog hates me right now. She has no idea what to do with herself when Junie gets on the bus every day. The bus driver has to get her off the bus and bring her back to me because she wants to go with Junie so badly every morning.

I don't know how I'm going to make it right for Junie with Ivy and Lola. If Ivy can't forgive me and leaves us for good, taking her dog, we are going to be devastated even more than we already are right now.

"You better fix this, man," Tate says, pointing the knife at me before sharpening it again. "You messed up bad. Like, historically bad. People in town are gonna be talking about this until the end of time. You messed with a beloved Maren."

"I know." My voice is low, rough. I drag my hand through my hair and stare at the ground, because looking at either of them feels like standing in front of a firing squad.

"No, you don't know," Tate says, standing now. His chair scrapes against the concrete, and the sound grates down my spine. "You can't treat her like that. Ivy's good. She's sunshine, and somehow, she makes your grumpy ass look tolerable."

A few customers walk by and side-eye me. One couple openly glares, then goes to their truck empty-handed. I am sure word has spread around town, and people are mad. They seemed to love seeing Ivy and I together, and now I've let everyone down by my stupid freak-out.

He's right, and every word is a punch to the ribs. I have to fix this. I need to make it right, and I need to make it big. Ivy deserves nothing but the best.

Finn nods once, cool and steady. "She is good. And you hurt her. You better figure out how to make it right, or no telling what will happen to you around here."

That makes me look up, my temper flashing hot even though I've got no right to be angry. "You think I don't hate myself right now?" My voice comes out sharper than I meant. "I haven't slept since she left. I keep seeing her face when she realized what I said and—" My throat feels tight. I shake my head. "I'm trying to figure out how to win her back before she decides I'm not worth the trouble."

That is the truth. I was scared. But that does not excuse

what I did. Fear is not a reason to raise my voice at her or push her away. I know better. I watched Derek treat her like she didn't matter and swore I would never put that look on her face. Then I did. I told her this was her home. I told her she belonged with me and Junie.

Ivy has the same fears I do. She knows what it is to be left and made small. I did not protect her from that. She walked out trying to hold on to her dignity while I hid behind my past hurt.

I need to own it. No explanations. No justifying. I need to say I was wrong, that I hurt her, that I won't do it again. I need to show her I can be the man who steadies, not the man who makes her brace. And if she needs space, I will give it, but I will not hide behind my past. I will meet her where I should have been standing in the first place.

Finn opens his mouth to respond, but the sound of squealing brakes cuts him off. We all turn toward the open barn doors.

Rowan's old truck pulls in and parks abruptly, like she's pissed. Royally pissed.

The three of us go still. The door slams hard enough to echo, and the sound goes straight through my chest. Fuck.

She climbs out, a baseball bat slung over her shoulder, and stalks toward the barn.

Tate whistles low. "I'm legit worried for you right now."

Finn smirks like he's been waiting for this all morning. He rubs his hands together and steps back.

*Shit.*

I square my shoulders and brace for impact. My stomach twists — I've never been on the receiving end of Rowan Maren's temper before, but I've heard stories, and it is not a fun place to stand. Sure, that was back when she was a teenager, and she and Finn got into it. They were always getting into it back then. And she's definitely angry right now as she stalks toward me.

She steps inside, boots crunching on the straw. "Remington Bennett, you broke my little sister's heart."

"Rowan—" I start to object. But it does no good.

"No." She jabs the bat in my direction, and my gut says she wouldn't hesitate to swing it if I say the wrong thing. "Do I need to break your kneecaps, or are you planning to fix this, you dumbass?"

Knowing what I did to Ivy hits me harder than the bat ever could.

Tate coughs into his fist, trying not to laugh. Finn is grinning outright now, like he's got front-row seats to the best show in town.

"I'm going to fix it," I say quickly. The words come out desperate, but hell, that's what I am. "We were just planning what to do to make it up to her. Trying to figure out how to make her forgive me and trust me again."

Rowan studies me for a long second. I hold her gaze, letting her see every ounce of regret and fear in me, because there's no point hiding it anymore.

Finally, she nods. "Good. Because I didn't feel like violence today, anyway." She lets the bat drop to her side, and despite myself, I flinch.

She glares at me, "Fix this."

She turns on her heel and heads for the door, tossing over her shoulder, "Don't screw this up, Remy. She deserves better than what you gave her. Don't be like Douchey Derek."

The barn is silent until the truck door slams again, and her truck growls to life.

Tate exhales slowly and looks at Finn. "Bro. You picked the unhinged one."

Finn smiles as if he just won a prize at the fair. "I know."

Despite myself, I laugh, short, bitter, but real. I scrub a hand over my face. "Fine. Plan time. I'm not letting her get away from me."

Tate grins, satisfied. "Good. Because if you don't win her back, Rowan's gonna come back swinging. And I can't wait to see that. But don't worry, I'll make sure your funeral is nice."

* * *

The house is too quiet when I get home. Junie's at my mom's for a sleepover, which means I don't have her to keep me busy and not think about Ivy not being here right now.

I send her a text because I can't stand it a minute longer.

**I miss you. I'm so sorry, Ivy. Can we talk?**

**Ivy: You hurt me. I don't know if I want to talk yet.**

**How can I fix this?**

**Ivy: I don't know. Please tell Junie I love her, and I'm sorry.**

**I will. I'm going to make this right, Ivy.**

I need to show her how much she means to us. I need her to feel how much I love her and need her. This house is cold and lonely without her. I need her. I want her back here where she belongs.

I toe off my boots by the door and just stand there for a minute, staring at nothing. The fight with Ivy keeps replaying like a bad movie on loop—the way her face went pale, the hurt in her eyes when I yelled at her. I sink my teeth into my bottom lip because it's my own damn fault.

My chest aches, sharp and heavy, and I know if I don't do something, I'll drown in this guilt.

I find myself at the doorway to my office at the front of the house. Calling it an "office" is generous. It's a storage room. The bay windows at the front of the house are hidden behind towers of boxes. Boxes from my old life that contain old law books, files and documents stacked everywhere. You can barely take two steps inside without bumping into something. I don't even know why I kept all of this. There's no way I'd ever go back to practicing law. I know I'm where I'm supposed to be right now.

I lean against the door frame and let out a long breath. This was supposed to be a space where I could start fresh, build something new after Sloane walked out. Instead, it's just a graveyard of the man I used to be. I pictured myself sitting in here working on paperwork. But this room isn't mine. I have other plans for it.

And Ivy...she's the first good thing to walk through my door in a long damn time.

I picture her sitting in here with sunlight streaming through those big windows, plants on tables, maybe one of her candles burning. She'd probably laugh at the state of this room, but I can already see her bringing it back to life. The image hits me hard, right in the ribs. I picture photos on the walls of her, Junie, and me doing life together.

My throat feels tight, but for the first time all day, I feel steady. I know what I need to do.

I pull my phone from my pocket and text Tate and Finn.

**Me: Bring the trailer. Need your help.**

**Tate: For what?**

**Me: Clearing out the office. Tonight.**

Three dots pop up.

**Finn: ...You're serious.**

**Me: Dead serious.**

**Finn: You're so dramatic.**

I slide the phone back into my pocket and take one more look at the disaster of a room. It's going to take hours, maybe all night, to get it cleaned out. But when Ivy comes back, this is going to be hers. A space that says she belongs here.

I press my hand against the door frame, grounding myself.

"I'm going to fix this," I say out loud, the words hanging heavy in the quiet house. And for the first time since she left, I almost believe it.

* * *

The bed of my truck is full of cans of paint, brushes, rollers, drop cloths, the works. It smells like possibility. Like a fresh start.

I back into the driveway just as Mom's car pulls up on the other side and parks. Junie hops out first, hair flying everywhere, then bolts for the porch, Lola fast on her heels.

"Dad!" she calls, bouncing on the top step like she's excited to see me. "Is Ivy back, yet?"

I close my eyes. "Not yet, bug."

I grab two cans of paint from the bed and meet them halfway. Mom gets out of the driver's seat, that pencil perched behind her ear, that sharp, knowing look in her eye like she's curious what I'm up to.

"Did you have fun at Nana's?"

"She let me eat two cupcakes before dinner," Junie says proudly.

Mom just shrugs. "You only live once. So, what are you doing to get Ivy back? Finn said you're working on it."

I jerk my head toward the front door. "Come look."

Inside, the house still smells like sawdust from last night. The office is empty now, just clean wood floors and the big bay windows letting in the afternoon light. The room has wall to wall bookcases that sit empty. The whole place feels... lighter. Like a new beginning.

Mom stops in the doorway and takes it in, her expression softening. "My, my," she says slowly. "I see you've been spring cleaning. What are you doing with this room?"

I set the paint down, my throat feeling tight. "I'm building Ivy a library. Finn is building the ladder and adding the hardware so it rolls across the shelves."

Mom's red-lipsticked smile spreads, slow and sure. "Wow. This is a romantic grand gesture. I love it."

Junie gasps and hugs my waist. "Is she coming back?!"

God, I hope so. I crouch down to meet her excited little face. "I'm trying, bug. This is...my way of telling her she belongs here. With us."

Junie throws her arms around my neck, squeezing so hard I have to blink a few times to keep it together.

My mom clears her throat, like she's pretending she's not getting misty-eyed. "Well, if you're building a library, it needs books. Let me speak to Willa at the bookstore and put in an order. We'll get those shelves filled."

"You don't have to do that, Ma." I huff out a laugh, standing again. Then I ask her, quieter and nervously. "Do you think I have a chance?"

My mom arches one perfectly shaped brow. "Remy, I've been writing romance for thirty years. Do you really think I'm going to let the best love story in Wisteria Cove end before it's properly begun?"

Junie giggles, already spinning in a circle in the middle of the empty room. "Can we paint it pink?"

"Not pink," I say, grinning despite myself. "But we'll make it perfect for her. I hold up the paint. You can help."

My mom pats my arm as she heads toward the kitchen. "Good. Because you only get one shot at this. Don't mess it up. Make it big and make it beautiful."

I watch her go, my chest aching but steady. This room isn't

just for Ivy. It's for Junie. For me. For the life we're going to build if I can just get her to forgive me for being the biggest asshole on the planet. I promise I'll spend the rest of my life giving her the entire world if she wants it.

And I swear to myself, as I open the first can of paint, that I won't stop until it's perfect.

# Chapter 24
# Ivy

I have music playing on the speaker in the bookstore's kitchen, the same soft Christmas playlist I always turn on when I need comfort, but even that feels like background noise against the churn in my chest. It's not working to cheer me up, it just makes me sadder and think of all the times I played it for Junie. Every song is attached to a memory with them, now. The kitchen smells of cinnamon, sugar, and butter. I'm working on the third batch of cinnamon rolls I've baked today, but the sweetness just makes me feel hollow.

I slide the tray onto the counter and stare at it, frustrated tears pricking at the corners of my eyes. "That's enough," I mutter, wiping my hands on a towel. I will not bake my way through heartbreak.

Except, of course, that is exactly what I have been doing all day. It helps Willa at her cafe, but I need to start looking forward and planning my future.

I grab a mug of tea and curl into the armchair by the window, tucking my legs underneath me. The mug is hot, almost too hot, but I hold it anyway, letting the warmth bite into my palms. I watch the shadows stretch across the floor as the afternoon light fades, and the chatter of the shop presses in until it's almost too loud.

My mind keeps looping back to the barn. To the sharpness of Remy's voice. The way his shoulders went rigid, the muscle ticking in his jaw, the look in his eyes that gutted me because it felt like he was pushing me away on purpose.

How did we go from kissing like our lives depended on it to *that*? Was I just that easy to throw away?

Anger rises first, quick and hot. He doesn't get to talk to me like that. He doesn't get to make me feel like I am the one who did something wrong for loving him.

But the anger can't hold. Not when my heart won't stop aching.

Because the truth is, I miss him and Junie. So much.

I miss his warm, steady presence in a room. I miss the way his voice gets rough and sexy when he says my name. I miss Junie's giggles and her socks left under the kitchen table.

And I know what I have been too stubborn to say out loud. Remy has ruined me for any other man. He is it for me. He always has been. Deep down, I think I have known that since we walked through the grove that snowy night when he had a horse-drawn sleigh waiting for us.

The front door opens, and Rowan breezes in like she's on a mission.

"You look like you've been haunting this place," she says, propping the bat by the door. "I told him off the other day, by the way. You're welcome."

I blink at her. "You what?"

"Full Rowan special," she says with a grin. "He looked like he might pass out. Tate and Finn were there. It was practically a public trial."

I bury my face in my hands. "Oh, my god. Rowan. Leave it alone. If he wanted to, he would."

She shrugs, flopping into the chair across from me. "What? Someone had to say it. But honestly, Ivy, he's not a bad guy. He works harder than anyone I know. He's a good dad. He's loyal, solid, and he looks at you like you are the best thing that ever happened to him."

I give her a skeptical look. "Whose side are you on?"

"Yours," she says without hesitation. "Which is why I'm telling you not to write him off just because he messed up. Everyone messes up. But that man is out there tearing himself apart right now because he hurt you. You think he's eating? Sleeping? Not a chance. He looks like shit. Just like you."

"Wait, how do you know that? Who said that?" Suddenly, I'm worried and want to make him a casserole and check on him. Because you can't turn love off like that. Even though he doesn't deserve a casserole right now.

The words crack something open inside me. I stare down at my tea, my throat tight. "That's the problem. I love him. I think I always have. And it scares me, Rowan. Because what if he can't let me all the way in? Or love me back like I need him to?"

"Then he loses you," Rowan says matter-of-factly. "But he deserves the chance to try."

Before I can answer, my phone buzzes on the coffee table. My heart leaps into my throat. His name lights up the screen, but there is no text, just a missed call that vanishes before I can touch it.

"Text him," Rowan says gently.

I shake my head and flip the phone over. "Not yet. If he wants me, he has to come to me. I can't be the only one fighting for this."

Rowan smiles faintly and pushes to her feet. "Then let him fight. But if you stay in this kitchen baking for much longer, you're going to lose your mind."

The warm glow of the bookstore lights wraps around me

like a blanket, and the bell jingles overhead, and Willa grins from behind the counter as customers come in the door in search of treats and their next book to read or last-minute Christmas gifts.

"Perfect timing," she calls. "I just unpacked a stack of new hardcovers."

I wander over and trail my fingers over the spines, breathing in the warm, papery smell that always makes my shoulders loosen. For a few blissful minutes, I can almost forget the ache in my chest.

Rowan catches me smiling, coffee in hand. "See? Still some joy left in there."

"I like books," I say with a shrug.

"You like Remy more."

I roll my eyes, but the small smile lingers. "Yeah," I admit quietly. "I do."

It's after midnight when Rowan and I sit at our mom's kitchen table with a jar of moon water between us. The moonlight from the kitchen window spills across the table, silvering the pages of my open notebook.

Rowan brings her glass to her lips and smirks. "Are you sure yours is moon water? Because mine is vodka."

I glance at her glass, then back at her. "That explains a lot."

She grins unapologetically and leans back in her chair.

I look down at my notebook. The pages are covered in sketches and bullet points, a fresh business plan taking shape under my pen. New products, seasonal pop-ups, classes and parties, all mapped out in neat lists. It feels good to write it out, to remind myself that I am building something for myself.

Still, there is a restless, bothered edge under my skin. Every plan I make feels a little empty without him in it.

"What are you working on?" Willa asks as she joins us, sliding in the chair across from me.

I glance down at the notebook and wrap my hands around my glass, staring at the moonlight glinting off the water. "My future."

Rowan nods as if she has been waiting for me to say it. "And what does that include?"

"I want to be a successful business owner like you two. Take a page out of your playbooks. I want to set up a shop called The Good Witch. I want to do birthday parties and events for kids. Something fun that I can do year-round, that will bring people together to have fun."

"Okay, that is fantastic and something you would be so good at," Willa nods in appreciation. "Where will you do them?"

"I was hoping to use your shops until I can rent a space of my own?" I ask hesitantly.

"Of course," Rowan immediately agrees.

"You've always loved kids. I think you'd be great at that," Willa agrees. "We'll do everything we can to support you."

And I'm finally starting to feel hope. Even if I'm finding it on my own.

* * *

I sit by the window after Rowan leaves, the night so quiet I can hear the frogs down by the cove. The stars are scattered like diamonds, and for a long moment, I let myself imagine him sitting beside me, his big hand warm over mine.

My phone sits face down on the table. I flip it over, type out a message, *I miss you.* Then stare at it until my throat aches and my chest feels too tight. And then I delete the words.

Tomorrow. Tomorrow I will see what he does.

And if he fights for me, maybe...just maybe...I'll let him win.

* * *

The morning air is crisp when I step off the front porch of my mom's house, cool enough to make me tug my cardigan tighter around my shoulders. The sun is just coming up over the trees, streaking the cove with gold, and for a second, the beauty of it steals my breath.

I head into town because I need to do something with my restless energy before I spiral back into overthinking. Willa's bookstore is already open, and the bell jingles when I step inside.

She looks up from the counter and waves. "Morning. You're here early."

"Couldn't sleep," I admit, moving toward the shelf of new releases. "Figured I'd get out before I started reorganizing Mom's kitchen cabinets."

Willa gives me a sympathetic smile but doesn't pry, which I love her for. We chat about the new books she just got in, and I leave with one tucked under my arm, feeling just a little lighter.

I'm halfway down Main Street when I hear a familiar voice. "Ivy!"

Junie barrels toward me from the direction of the hardware store, pigtails flying. Finn follows at a slower pace, looking amused and a little winded.

I drop to my knees, and she flies into me like a little rocket. "Hey, bug," I whisper, hugging her tight. "I missed you so much." She smells like apples and winter, and her hat is a little crooked. I fix it with careful fingers and kiss her forehead. "Are you having a big adventure today?" I ask, smiling. "What are you and Finn doing in town?"

"Helping Daddy!" she says proudly. "We're buying more paint for your—"

"Junie." Finn's voice is sharp enough to cut her off. He swoops in, scooping her up like she weighs nothing, and presses a big hand gently over her mouth.

"Paint for what?" I ask, my heart thudding.

Finn's grin is all teeth. "Nothing you need to worry about."

Junie wriggles in his arms, trying to pull his hand away, her little giggles muffled.

"Finn," I say, crossing my arms.

He starts backing away, still grinning like a man who knows better than to get involved. "Come on, Junie, we've got to get back before your dad realizes we took too long."

Junie yells something against his palm, and my stomach does a funny little flip. What is Remy up to? And he's got Junie and Finn in on it, too.

"I'll tell Lola you said hi!" Finn calls over his shoulder as he heads for his truck, still carrying a squirming Junie. "You two can catch up later!"

I stand on the sidewalk, my pulse racing.

Paint. What in the world is Remy doing?

The thought warms me and terrifies me all at once.

Maybe he really is fighting for me, and now I'm curious.

# Chapter 25
# Remy

Boston hits me like a punch to the gut the second I step out of the truck. Finn is finishing up the library today, and I have something to take care of. Unfinished business that needs taken care of.

The air is damp, smelling like wet pavement, exhaust, and old coffee. Horns honk down the street, a siren wails somewhere blocks away, and a man in a suit rushes past me, almost knocking into me with his phone glued to his hand, not looking where he's going. It is loud, frantic, nothing like home.

I stand there for a second, just breathing it in, letting the weight of it settle over me. The last time I was here, I was still wearing a tie every day. I was still trying to convince myself that this city, this life, was what I wanted.

Turns out, I never really wanted it.

I think about Junie back home, sitting at Mom or Lilith's table and probably eating cake for lunch. I think about Ivy, about the way her laugh sounds, about how her hands felt on my chest the night I kissed her like I'd been starving for years. I miss the way she looks at me like she really sees me. All of me. Even the broken pieces, and she still doesn't care. She just loves me for me. She trusted me, and I broke that trust. Because I let Sloane get in my head again. I let her mess up our world, and I'm going to put a stop to that. I know what I need to do, and I know what Sloane needs to do. We all need this.

I am not here for me. I am here for them.

I pull open the glass door and step inside Sloane's office building. The lobby smells of disinfectant and printer toner, and the buzz of fluorescent lights hums faintly overhead. My boots click against the marble floor. People look at me sideways, men in pressed suits, women with sleek hair and expensive shoes like they can tell I don't belong here anymore.

I wait for the elevator, my reflection in the stainless-steel doors staring back at me. My shoulders look tight, my jaw locked. I roll it out, force myself to breathe, but my pulse is still pounding when a voice cuts through the air behind me.

"Bennett?"

I turn slowly.

Derek stands there clutching his messenger bag like it's a life raft.

If I thought he was smug before, he isn't now. His suit is too tight across the stomach, his skin is pale and shiny, and what's left of his hair is trying and failing to form some kind of comb over. He looks older than the last time I saw him over six weeks ago. Smaller.

What the hell happened to this guy?

"Derek," I say. My voice is flat, but I can feel my blood heating.

He swallows so hard I see his Adam's apple bob. "Uh. Hey. Good to see you."

I raise a brow. "Is it?"

He takes a step back, clutching the briefcase tighter. "I have a big meeting."

I say nothing, just stare at him blankly.

His face goes even paler. "Yeah, so, I better..."

He spins on his heel and takes the stairs two at a time like the devil is chasing him.

I watch him go, jaw tight, and almost laugh. Guess I made my point the last time I warned him to stay the hell away from Ivy. Good. He deserves to sweat a little. But whatever else happened to him...holy shit.

The elevator dings, and I step inside, bracing my forearms against the railing. My reflection watches me in the metal walls as we climb, and for a second, I think about turning around. Walking away.

But then I picture Junie again.

Her face when she asked if her mom was coming to see her, again and again. Always left disappointed and upset.

No. I am not walking away.

When the elevator opens, I make my way down the hallway until I am standing outside Sloane's door. My hands are sweating. I rub them against my jeans and knock.

She calls, "Come in."

Her office smells of coffee and paper. Sunlight streams in through the floor to ceiling windows behind her desk, catching in her dark hair. She looks up, surprise flashing across her face before she smoothes it into a neutral expression.

"Remy," she says calmly. "I wasn't expecting you."

I sit down across her desk, leaning forward, elbows braced on my knees. It's not lost on me she didn't ask if Junie was okay, which is what my first reaction would be. But she never asks if Junie is okay. She doesn't think like that. And no matter how many times I've tried to get her to care and think like that, she just doesn't. My heart feels like it's trying to punch its way out of my chest, but I force my voice steady. "We need to talk."

Her shoulders tense, her hands curling together in her lap. "Is this about Junie?"

"Yes." I drag a hand down my face. "About Junie."

She waits and folds her hands in front of her on her desk, not meeting my eyes, as if she's unsure of where this conversation is going to go.

I take a breath so deep it feels like it scrapes my ribs and just put it out there. "What if you didn't have to worry about Junie anymore?"

Her head snaps up, her eyes wide.

"Not because you don't love her," I say quickly. "But because you love her enough to let her have the mom who shows up every time. Someone who wants to be there for her school plays and birthdays. Someone who doesn't make her sit by the window wondering if she's coming."

Her face crumples. She looks down at the papers on her desk, blinking hard. "What would people think of me?"

And again, it's not lost on me that she isn't worrying about what Junie will think. Only what other people will think.

"They'd think you were the bravest, most unselfish person for doing that," I say, my voice rough. Telling her this and putting into words something that I could never wrap my head around as a father is hard. But they need to be said because I think deep down this is the best for both of them. She needs to let Junie go. She needs to let go of the expectations and hurt that she's only going to continue to cause.

I continue, "They'd think you gave her a chance to grow up without wondering why she isn't enough for you."

A tear slips down her cheek, and she swipes it away fast. "I tried, Remy. I swear to God I tried. I thought I could do it, but every time I think I'm ready, I choke. I freeze. I cannot be who she needs me to be."

The words hurt, but there is something freeing in hearing her say them. And I would much rather have her tell me this now so that we can move forward accordingly so this never has to be a conversation that my five-year-old has with her.

"Then let her have that with someone else," I say gently. "Let her have the chance to be loved by a mom who chooses her every single day."

She turns and looks out the window, another tear slipping down her cheek. She turns back to me and looks relieved and sad at the same time. She nods once, then again, slower. Her fingers twist together. "How does this work? Do you need money?"

I shake my head. "No. I don't need money, Sloane. I just need you to sign the papers. For Junie."

She stares out the window for a long time, the city reflected in her glassy eyes. Finally she nods. "I'll have them drawn up. Come back in an hour?"

Relief hits me so hard I almost sag in the chair. "Yeah. You're doing the right thing."

Her lips tremble. "You're a good dad. I wish I could be like you. Tell her I'm sorry."

I stand slowly. "I know. I'll come back."

* * *

Outside, the air feels sharper, almost clean. I shove my hands into my coat pockets and walk aimlessly until I find myself near an old coffee shop I used to go to back when I worked cases late into the night.

I buy a black coffee and sit outside at a little metal table, watching the city rush around me. The noise is constant with buses rumbling past, people shouting into phones, car horns blaring, but it all feels far away. Like I'm watching a movie and not a part of this.

I take a slow sip of coffee and let myself really think. I used to think this was what I wanted. The city. The suits. The grind. The idea of being someone important in a place that never sleeps.

But sitting here now, I don't miss any of it.

I miss the tree farm with the smell of fresh pine and sawdust. The sound of Junie's laughter echoing through the house. Ivy's hair loose over her shoulders, the soft sound she makes when I pull her close.

I miss coming home to them and asking how their days went. I miss the small things like new pictures Junie drew on the fridge, proudly on display. I miss seeing what new crafts Junie and Ivy have been working on.

Today isn't as much about Ivy, but more about Junie. It's doing what needs to be done so that Junie can be free of being let down continuously. And not have her mom randomly showing up and upsetting her. Junie will probably have a lot of questions someday when she's older and fully understands the situation. But I know in my gut this needs to happen.

I don't know whether Ivy will come back. I don't know if I can fix what I broke between us.

But I am damn sure going to try.

* * *

When I get back to Sloane's office, the papers are ready. She hands them across the desk, her fingers trembling.

"Here," she says quietly.

I look them over, then meet her gaze.

"Can I still check in sometimes?" she asks. "Just email. I won't bother her. I just... want to know how she's doing."

"Yes," I say. "Of course you can."

She nods, takes a deep breath, and stands. "Oh, and Remy?"

I glance back.

"What did you do to Derek? He's terrified of you."

I shrug. "No clue. Don't really know the guy."

For the first time, she smiles just a little, then says. "Take care of her."

"I will."

I tuck the papers under my arm and walk out, my steps lighter than they have been in years.

On the drive home, I crank up the heat and breathe easier than I have in years. The past is finally settled. No more wondering, no more waiting. No more watching my little girl get crushed and then scared when her mom shows up and is angry that she is even there, as if that was somehow Junie's fault. The whole situation is sad. And I have to think about how I'm going to explain it to Junie in a way that makes sense to her at this time.

When I get back to Wisteria Cove, I am going to keep working on that library until it is perfect.

Because the next step is proving to Ivy that I am all in for her, for Junie, for the life we deserve.

And I will not waste this second chance.

* * *

By the time I pull into the drive, the sky is streaked with pink and gold. My headlights sweep over the porch, and I see the boxes stacked there.

I kill the engine and climb out, boots crunching on gravel. There are three big boxes labeled **BOOKS. FRAGILE.** And one thinner box with my name on it.

I haul the boxes inside, the cardboard biting into my palms, and set them down in the middle of the empty office. The room still smells faintly of fresh paint. The bay windows catch the last light, making the whole space look soft and warm.

252

The thin package catches my eye. I crouch, tear the tape open carefully, and pull out the canvas print.

It's the photo from the tree farm with Ivy and Junie, all of us grinning, Junie between us, Ivy smiling and leaning into me. It hits me square in the chest, so hard I have to sit back on my heels.

I love this picture.

I can already see it hanging on the wall, right above a cozy reading chair. I want her to walk in here and feel like she belongs, like she is home.

Headlights sweep across the yard outside, pulling me from my thoughts. A moment later, Willa and Tate come up the porch carrying more boxes.

"Delivery service," Tate calls as they step inside.

"Donna had these shipped straight from her publisher," Willa says, setting her box down. "She called me and said, 'Make sure Remy has these tonight. We're not letting him half-ass this.'"

I huff out a laugh and shake my head. "She never does anything halfway. And I love that she has connections to make this happen."

Willa steps into the office and takes it in, her eyes going wide. "Remy... this is perfect."

"Not yet," I say, glancing around at the empty shelves we built last night. "But it will be. I want her to have everything."

Tate leans against the doorway, grinning. "Hell of a gesture. This is going to blow her away."

"I need it to," I admit. "I need her to see I'm not just saying I'm sorry. I'm proving it."

Willa sets a hand on my arm, her smile warm. "Then let's make it perfect. I'll help you unpack. Tate can put together the chair you bought."

"I was hoping you'd say that."

She glances at me as she kneels to open a box. "You want me to get her out here tomorrow?"

"Yes," I say, my voice low but steady. "If she won't come for me, maybe she'll come for you or for Junie."

Willa's smile turns knowing. "She'll come. She's been miserable without you, you know. It sucks having you two on the outs. Everyone in town knows you're meant to be together. You just have to get it together."

I let out a slow breath. "I'm trying."

"Good," Willa says, handing me a stack of books.

We work until the sky goes dark and the moonlight streams through the bay windows. Willa stacks books by color, Tate curses softly as he fights with the Allen wrench, and I hang the canvas photo on the far wall.

When I step back to look at it, my throat tightens. It already feels like Ivy's room. Like Junie's room. Like *ours*.

When Willa and Tate finally head home, I stay in the office, unpacking until the floor is covered with stacks of books.

I stand in the middle of the room, breathing hard, and whisper it into the quiet house.

"I'm going to fix this."

Then I roll up my sleeves, open another box, and keep going until there's nothing left but the faint smell of paper and the hum of hope in my chest.

# Chapter 26
# Ivy

The bookstore smells like roasted coffee beans and paper, the familiar scent that always calms me. I sit at the counter with my latte, tracing the rim of the mug with my finger. My notebook sits open in front of me, but the words on the page are a mess with half-plans, half rambling thoughts about Remy that I don't dare read too closely.

Willa leans her elbows on the counter across from me, her chin resting on her hand. She has been watching me, letting me stew.

"You're brooding," she says finally.

I glance up. "I am not brooding."

"You are. And it's starting to depress the customers. You're going to scare off the regulars with your bad vibes."

I try to glare, but it just makes her grin. "I'm fine," I say, even though I know how unconvincing I sound.

She arches a brow. "You're not fine. You've been sitting here for an hour pretending to drink the same latte."

I sigh and push the mug away. "What do you want me to say, Willa? That I miss him? And I miss Junie. That I hate that we're not talking? That every time I close my eyes, I see the look on his face that night in the barn?"

"Yes," she says simply. "I want you to say all of that."

My throat burns, and I rub at my chest like I can ease the ache there. "He really hurt me."

"I know," Willa says gently. "But I also know he's been trying to make it right. And maybe it's time you let him. Anyway, we're going out there."

I stare at her. "What?"

"We're going to Remy's."

I blink. "Right now?"

"Yes, right now." She grins, too satisfied with herself. "Come on, Ivy. It's time you two talked. Plus, he has something to show you."

I narrow my eyes. "What are you talking about?"

She just shrugs, all innocent.

"I'll admit I've been curious about what Junie said the other day when she let something slip with Finn."

"You've been miserable, and so has he. Let's fix this."

I hesitate, my fingers gripping the edge of the counter. My heart is hammering so hard I can hear it in my ears.

"I don't know if I'm ready," I say nervously.

"Sure, you are," Willa says. "You just need someone to shove you out the door."

She hops off her stool and grabs her keys.

"Willa," I protest, but she just grins.

"Let's go."

* * *

The drive out to the farm is quiet, but my stomach feels like it's full of butterflies. My palms are damp against my jeans, and I keep staring out the window like the trees might offer me advice.

"You okay?" Willa asks softly.

"I feel like I'm going to throw up," I admit.

"That's how you know it's real," she says, her tone light but warm. "Buckle up, babe. It's time."

As we turn up the long drive to the farm, I see the glow first.

"Oh my God," I whisper. The whole place is lit up. Twinkle lights wrap the fence posts and line the driveway, and little wooden signs are propped along the road every few feet.

The first one says, *We miss you, Ivy.*

The next one says, *Ivy, we have a surprise for you.*

And then, *Ivy, we love you.*

The handwriting is Junie's careful, slightly wobbly letters, painted in bright colors with little hearts and flowers doodled around them.

My hand flies to my mouth. "He had her paint signs?" My voice cracks.

Willa's eyes are suspiciously shiny as she pulls to a stop. "Yeah," she says softly. "He did."

When we pull up, I see him.

Remy is standing on the porch, hands shoved in his pockets, his shoulders tense like he has been standing there for hours waiting for me.

The Jeep's headlights flash over him and then die when Willa cuts the engine.

"Go," she says gently. "He's waiting for you."

My legs feel shaky as I climb out, but somehow, I make it to the porch. He doesn't move toward me, just watches me with those deep, stormy eyes that make my stomach flip.

"Ivy," he says quietly. "I'm sorry."

The words hang in the air between us, heavier than they should be.

"I've missed you so much," he adds, his voice rough.

I nod, my throat tight. "I've missed you, too."

I take a step closer, then another, until I am standing right in front of him.

"You really hurt me, Remy."

He swallows hard. "I know."

"I'm so sorry," I say, the words tumbling out. "I swear I would never let anything intentionally happen to her."

"I know," he says again, his voice steady now. "I was scared. That's not an excuse. I hurt you, and I hate that I did that. I want you, Ivy. We want you. Our family feels complete with you here. I don't want you to ever leave us."

My chest aches so badly I press a hand against it.

"I need to figure out what I'm doing with my life," I whisper.

He nods. "Can you figure it out here? With us? We'll encourage you to chase all of your dreams, and we will support you every step of the way."

I blink hard, tears threatening, and nod.

His face falls with relief.

"I want to show you something," he says.

He steps back and holds the door open. I follow him inside, my heart thudding against my ribs.

The house feels warm and alive. I notice things I hadn't before with framed photos on the mantle, most of them with Junie, but some with me. One of me and Junie in my mom's garden last summer before I really even knew Remy like this, one of all three of us on the porch steps this winter.

My hand goes to my mouth. "Remy..."

"There's more," he says softly.

He leads me into the kitchen. A photo on the kitchen island of the three of us at the tree lighting ceremony, my head thrown back laughing. I didn't even know anyone took that photo of us.

But it's a real life candid photo showing us doing life together, and we look like a family.

"You did this?"

He nods, still watching me.

My chest squeezes so tight I almost can't breathe.

"One more thing," he says, his voice quiet.

He leads me to the front hall where his storage room is. My breath catches when he swings it open.

The room is glowing with soft light. The walls are lined with floor-to-ceiling bookshelves that are navy, full and colorful, a rolling ladder gleaming in the corner. A rug warms the center of the room, and a cozy chair sits by the window. Soft golden lamplight shines on end tables and makes the room cozy and inviting. It's beautiful.

My hand flies to my mouth, and a laugh bubbles out of me, half shocked and half amazed.

"What's so funny?" he asks, looking almost nervous.

"You, beast," I say, still laughing through tears. "You made me a library just like *Beauty and the Beast*."

He rolls his eyes playfully, relief softening his face. "Do I need to keep you locked up here to get you to stay?"

"No." I smile through happy tears. "You don't have to lock me up. I had already planned on staying."

I cross the room and throw my arms around his neck, kissing him like I had been waiting to do it for weeks.

When we finally pull back, he cups my face in his big hands. "What do you think?"

I look around at the shelves, my chest so full it almost hurts. "You did all this so fast."

"Plenty of room to add more," he says. "I'll give you the world, Ivy Maren. If you'll let me."

My gaze catches on the canvas on the wall, the picture from

the tree farm of all three of us. Junie's in front of Remy, his arm around me, and both of us are smiling. It's one of my favorite memories.

I touch it, my throat too tight to speak for a moment.

"I love it," I whisper finally. "I love you."

He kisses me again, softer this time, like a promise.

A little voice pipes up from the hallway. "Can I come in now?"

We turn to see Junie hovering in the doorway, bouncing on her toes.

"Are you all made out?"

"Made up," Remy corrects her with a laugh.

"Whatever," she says with a dramatic eye roll. "I just miss Ivy."

I crouch down and open my arms. She barrels into me, nearly knocking me over, and I hold her tight.

"I made you signs!" she says proudly.

"I saw," I say, grinning through the tears that won't stop. "They were perfect."

"Are you back for good?"

I glance up at Remy, my heart catching. "Yeah," I say softly.

"Forever?" Junie asks, her little voice hopeful.

I look back at Remy. He smiles, warm and certain.

"Forever," I say.

Junie squeezes me tighter.

From the doorway, Tate appears with my overnight bag slung over his shoulder. "Brought your stuff," he says, setting it down.

I look at Remy again, my heart hammering, and he just nods like everything is finally where it's supposed to be.

* * *

Junie pulls back and looks at me with those big, hopeful eyes that undo me every single time. "Can we read a book in here tonight? In the new library?"

My throat gets tight again. "I would love that."

She cheers and races toward the shelves, her little boots thudding on the floor. "Which one do we read first?"

"Whichever you want," Remy says, smiling.

"Even the big ones?"

"Even the big ones."

Junie lets out an excited squeal and starts running her fingers along the spines. She looks so small in here, barely reaching the second shelf, but she moves with the certainty of someone who already knows this space belongs to her.

There's even a shelf in there full of new books for her. I love that Remy thought of everything. He really would give us the world.

I stand and turn to Remy. He's still watching me, his hands in his pockets again like he doesn't know what to do with them.

I step closer and press a hand to his chest, right over his heart. "This is perfect, Remy. You didn't just make me a library. You made me a home."

His eyes soften. "I wanted you to know you belong here. That you always have."

My heart swells until it almost hurts. "You didn't have to do all this."

"I did," he says simply. "Because I needed you to see that I'm serious. I'm not going anywhere, Ivy. Not now, not ever. And if that means building you a floor-to-ceiling library like some fairy-tale beast, then so be it."

I laugh, a little breathless. "You're ridiculous."

"You love it."

"I do," I admit. "I love you more, though."

"Good," he says, and kisses me again, longer this time, until Junie groans loudly from across the room.

"Are you done? I found a book!"

Remy chuckles against my mouth. "Guess we're done for now."

* * *

We end up on the rug in the middle of the library, Junie between us with a massive hardcover open on her lap. She's so animated, reading aloud every other line, her little finger tracing the words as best she can.

Remy leans back on one hand, his thigh pressed against mine, the heat of him grounding me. I sneak a glance at him while Junie is reading, the strong line of his jaw, the way his mouth curves just a little when he watches her.

This man.

He catches me looking and smirks, mouthing, *what?*

*Nothing,* I mouth back, smiling.

He doesn't look away for a long time.

When the story is over, Junie yawns so wide her jaw pops.

"Bedtime," Remy says gently.

"Nooo," Junie protests, flopping dramatically onto the rug. "I want to stay here with Ivy."

I smooth her hair back from her face. "You will, bug. But you still need to sleep."

"Fine," she grumbles, climbing to her feet. She wraps her arms around my waist in a quick squeeze, then looks up at Remy. "Can Ivy tuck me in?"

He glances at me, and my chest goes warm.

"If she wants to," he says.

"I do," I say without hesitation.

Junie takes my hand and pulls me down the hall toward her room. I go through her routine with her and tuck her in under her quilt, and she looks up at me with sleepy eyes as she clutches Arnold, her narwhal.

"Are you really staying forever?" she whispers.

"Forever," I promise.

"Good," she murmurs, already drifting off. "I like when we're all together."

My throat feels tight as I brush a kiss across her hair and slip quietly out of the room.

When I turn back toward the library, Remy is leaning in the doorway with his arms crossed, watching me with an expression that makes my knees feel loose.

"She loves you," he says quietly.

I nod. "I love her, too."

He straightens and comes closer, one step, then another, until my back finds the doorframe and my breath catches.

"You love me, too?" he asks, mouth tipping into that teasing half smile that always gets me.

"You know I do," I whisper.

"Say it anyway."

"I love you, Remington Bennett."

His smile softens. He cups my face like it is something precious, and when he kisses me, it's slow at first, a promise I can feel, then deeper, hotter, until the world narrows to the slide of his mouth and the careful way his hands anchor me. Home settles in my chest like a warm light.

"Come here," he murmurs, and I nod because I don't want to let him go. "I love you, Ivy Maren."

He locks the door. The library is quiet and golden, the lamps casting pools of light across the stacks. He backs me toward the reading nook by the window, hands skimming my waist, my hips, the curve of my back, remembering me again like he can't help it. I tug him closer by the collar, greedy for more, and he laughs under his breath, that deep, pleased sound that makes heat bloom under my skin.

We find each other by touch and memory. I taste winter on his mouth and the hint of coffee, and he tastes like the only place I want to be. Here. With him. My sweater ends up on the arm of the chair. His shirt falls to the floor. He lifts me easily, settling me on the wide window seat, and the glass fogs with our breath. I hook my knees to bracket his hips. His palms span my thighs, warm and sure, and when he drags his mouth along my jaw to that spot beneath my ear, my head tips back on a sigh I cannot swallow.

"Tell me what you want," he whispers, voice rough with it.

"You," I breathe. "Just you."

He gives me exactly that. No rush, no doubt, only the careful build of heat as his hands and his mouth follows, as my fingers map the breadth of his shoulders, the lines of his back, the steady thud of his heart under my palm. I pull him closer, and he comes, meeting me in every place I ask, giving and taking equal measures until I'm shaking with it.

The world outside goes on. In here the only sound is our breathing and the soft creak of the window seat as we move together, slow and then not slow, careful and then not careful at all. He holds my gaze when I unravel, eyes dark and tender, and I say his name on a gasp that feels like a prayer. He follows me, head bowed to my shoulder, a quiet curse against my skin that turns into my name said like a vow.

After, he kisses my forehead and my cheeks and the corner of my mouth like he has time to trace every place I am smiling. Cool winter air radiates off of the window, making our hot bodies feel cooler. I tuck into him, legs still tangled with his, and let my hand rest over his heart.

"This is what home feels like," I say, and it is not a thought, it is a truth. It is the hard weight of his body and the warm glow of the lamps and the way he looks at me like I'm where I belong.

He presses his mouth to my hair. "I love you so much, Ivy," he says, as if I ever could doubt it again.

"I love you, Remy," I answer, and I mean it with all of me.

# Chapter 27
# Remy

I can smell the salty sea air before I see the harbor. The whole town carries that scent tonight, mixed with wood smoke and cocoa and the cold bite of snow that has been threatening all afternoon. Lights lace the eaves of every shop and strand across Main like a net of stars. My favorite part about town is when it looks like this right at Christmas. Finn and Ivy joked that I hate Christmas, and it couldn't be further from the truth. Christmas has always felt magical to me. When I was little, sure I loved presents. But it was always my favorite time of year when my mom would make it so much fun for me and my brother. She would take us sledding for hours, bake our favorite cookies, and we'd eat pizza and watch Christmas movies several times a week. We'd get together with Pete and whoever else needed a place to go at Christmas and we'd make so many memories. Christmas is my favorite.

Willa's bookstore looks like a snow globe that someone shook and forgot to set down. People are already drifting toward the gazebo with paper bag luminaries in their hands, the little flames breathing inside.

I tighten my grip on Ivy's gloved fingers. Junie swings between us, careful with the unlit candle she is determined to carry like a grownup. My heart feels so full. I try to tell myself it is only the cold.

"You look nervous," Ivy says, soft enough that only I hear.

"I am."

She tips her face up to study me. Snow freckles her dark lashes. "He is going to love this."

"I hope so." I tell her. But what I don't say is that I am more afraid of loving her this much and knowing how fragile and short life can be. I have learned how to hold a family together with my own two hands. But what I'm going to have to learn is how to let go of a man who raised me to be the man that I am. I'm afraid of losing Pete. And it's happening sometime, and I hate that I can't fix this, or fix him.

My mom catches sight of us first. She is a red-lipped general in a winter coat, clipboard tucked under her arm like a medal. Pete is at her side, hat on and bundled up, already shaking his head like he cannot believe anyone would bother to throw a night like this in his name. He looks good. Smile lines dug deep, good that comes from being loved and celebrated.

"About time," Mom calls. "My headliner arrives unfashionably on time."

"I am not a headliner," Pete mutters.

"You are the whole show," Donna says, then turns to me and smooths my scarf like I am seven. "You. Smile. Tonight matters," she says, making a joke, but I know it's a reminder that she's nervous, too. We want to celebrate Pete tonight and give him a night where we pour love into him.

Her eyes shine when she says it. I nod. "Yes, ma'am."

Willa waves us over to the cocoa booth. She looks like an advertisement for winter in her moss-green sweater and knitted cap, cheeks pink from the cold. Tate stands behind her, double-fisting marshmallow containers and pretending he is not having fun. He winks at Ivy. He narrows his eyes at me like he is deciding if I have earned the right to hold the woman I am holding. Then he grins and hands Junie a cup with a mountain of whipped cream.

"You two look disgustingly in love," he says.

"We are," Ivy says, not missing a beat. Her smile is small and private and aimed at me. It hits like a hand to the chest.

Finn and Rowan arrive in a swirl of cold air and mischief. Finn claps me on the shoulder hard enough that my teeth click.

Finn mutters, "Behave," and gets a kiss on the cheek by our mom.

The square fills. The high school choir mills in a cluster, blowing steam into their hands and trying to look dignified while Tate hands them candy canes. Lights burn against the cold. Laughter hops from group to group like a warm animal.

My mom steps up onto the gazebo and lifts one hand. Everything settles.

"Friends," she says. Her voice carries as if it has always belonged to ceremonies. "Thank you for coming. Tonight we gather to celebrate a man who is the quiet hinge on which this town swings. He will tell you he is not special. He will tell you he just does what needs doing. I will tell you he is wrong. He is everything and so important to all of us."

A ripple of laughter moves through the square. Pete looks like he might disintegrate and drift away with the snow.

Gladys tells the porch-step story. The one about the storm and the slick ice and her foot going through the third board. How she cursed and Pete appeared like a knight with a toolbox, how he fixed it in ten minutes, then salted her whole walk while she pretended not to cry. People laugh at the punch line and then sniffle five seconds later, which is exactly how Donna planned it.

Willa takes the mic next. She clears her throat and pushes her cap back and says, "He came in last year and asked if I had more large-print romances. I said, 'For whom?' He said, 'For everyone who needs love to be easier to see.' So I ordered a whole shelf. He was right. We sold out in a week." The crowd laughs and claps. Willa's eyes shine. She looks at Pete and says, "Thank you for seeing what people need before they know they should ask."

All these stories don't surprise me at all. I know Pete did so much for everyone in this town.

Tate saunters up. He announces he has prepared a Top Ten List of Things Pete Has Taught Me About Life. Number ten: always measure twice and flirt once. Number nine: oak splinters are a conspiracy. Inside joke. Number eight: coffee should be black enough to scald a lie. The list gets worse and funnier. Number three is not fit for church.

Rowan hollers, "You never listen to him, anyway."

Tate bows. Pete shakes his head and tries not to laugh and fails, coughing and covering his mouth, his eyes shining with emotion.

Lilith steps forward with a paper in her hand and then does not look at it once. Her voice has the steady comfort that I'm surprised she has right now. "When we needed a ride early to an appointment in the city, you were there. When the power went out and we could not keep the herbal tinctures from freezing, you brought your generator and did not leave until the lights were steady. When Ivy came home with a heart in pieces, you looked at her and you looked at me and you said, 'She will be okay.' I believed you."

She finds Ivy with her eyes. Ivy squeezes my fingers.

Rowan follows with a grin that tries to hide the fact that she is swallowing hard. "You listen, and I talk a lot, so that is impressive. You bring so much happiness and joy to this town. We all love you so much."

The crowd is warm and wet-eyed. Breath rises like prayers in the cold air.

Donna tips her head at me. It is my turn.

I step up. The boards under my boots creak. The air feels thin. I look at Pete. I look at Ivy. I look at Junie. The words arrive like they were waiting for me to be brave.

"You made the world feel steady," I say. "When I thought it was falling apart. You gave Junie a grandpa to look up to who is someone she can be proud of. You told me the truth when I needed to hear it. You loved my mom and my brother and me like we were your own. You made space for Ivy and me to believe that love after loss is not only possible, it is an everyday work that is worth doing. I am proud to call you my dad."

I don't realize my voice has gone rough until the last sentence. I clear my throat. It does not help. Pete blinks fast and fails at not crying and presses his hat harder against his chest.

Ivy climbs the steps. She does not take the mic. She just turns to face him, the lights making a halo of her hair.

"You kept our town safe and always made people feel welcome," she says. "You told me that belonging is not a door that opens on its own. It is a thing people hold for each other. Thank you for holding it for me." She laughs a little and wipes her cheek with the back of her glove. "Also, you bullied Willa into buying more romances, which is my favorite thing you have ever done besides loving Donna."

The square laughs and sighs at the same time.

Donna lifts a taper. "Let us light the night."

The first flame is small. It touches a second wick and becomes two, then four, then twenty. Candles tilt toward each other like they are hungry to be kin. The beeswax smell floats up, warm and honeyed. The choir begins a carol, low and sweet. It is an old song that Pete has always loved. Snow begins to fall, gentle and certain. The flakes catch in Ivy's hair. I want to kiss each one before it melts.

Junie stands on her tiptoes and shields her candle from the breeze with her mitten. "The snowflakes look like stars close enough to catch," she whispers.

"Catch one," I say.

She opens her free hand and lets a flake land on her palm and smiles like the world is brand new.

Rowan sniffs loudly on purpose. "I warned you all. Yule Be Crying."

People laugh. A few do cry harder. Finn slings an arm around her shoulders and kisses her temple. Lilith lights Gladys's candle. Willa touches hers to mine. Tate's goes out, and the choir director glares at him until he relights it.

The carol ends. The silence after is peaceful and soul crushing at the same time.

Ivy looks up at me, cheeks pink, eyes laughing. I tuck a knuckle under her chin and kiss her. It is not a long kiss. It is not a show. It is a promise set to candlelight and snow. The town cheers, anyway. Junie groans and then giggles like she has been waiting for this. Pete laughs so hard he hiccups. He wipes his face with the back of his hand. "I am not crying," he declares. "My eyes are thawing."

"Liar," Rowan says, delighted.

Donna presses her shoulder to his. "Hush. Let yourself be loved."

He does. I watch it happen. I watch a man decide to stand in the warm middle of the circle and let us tell him who he is to us.

This is us celebrating and showing up for him while he's still here. Some people have funerals after someone dies, and everyone talks. Not us. We're going to love him well past when he's gone. And he's going to know it, feel it, and remember it for the rest of eternity.

After the candles gutter and people drift toward cocoa and the choir breaks ranks and steals candy canes, after Lilith tucks a scarf tighter around Willa's neck and Tate pretends he is not cold and Finn loads a stack of folding chairs under one arm like a show-off, after Rowan leads an off-key chorus of "We Wish You a Merry Christmas" and nobody bothers to correct the tempo, after Donna announces that the after party is at the bookstore whether or not anyone has RSVPd, we walk there with our hands linked and our girl tired and happy between us.

The library windows glow like a lantern in the snow. That sight will always make my throat feel tight.

Inside, the air is warm and full of paper and pine. The plaque of a lighthouse waits on the counter, a tiny brass rectangle that catches the light. Willa ordered it. Tate drilled the holes this afternoon while pretending not to tear up. The inscription is simple.

For Pete.

I hold the tiny screws while Ivy steadies the plaque, and I turn the driver slow. The metal kisses wood. The engraving shines. My chest does that thing again, the hurt that is not pain.

Junie hovers, swaying with tired pride. "It looks fancy," she says.

"It looks perfect," Ivy says, and rests her head against my shoulder.

People trickle in with wet boots and laughter, as if Donna's decree has the weight of law. Willa brings a tray of gingerbread and a thermos she swears is only hot chocolate and not spiked. Donna and Pete arrive last and stand in the doorway like a couple who have just walked into their own surprise party. I watch his face as he takes in the plaque. He looks like a man beside himself with happiness. I have never been happier to witness this.

Later, after we make it home, I carry Junie to bed. She is heavy with exhaustion from a long week. She wakes enough to mumble, "Merry Christmas, Pete," and is gone again. I stand there and watch her for a minute, because I won't take these moments for granted.

I find Ivy back in the library, barefoot on the rug. She looks up when I step in. Her eyes are soft with a mix of tiredness, contentment, and sadness.

"How is she?" she asks.

"Dreaming about cocoa and candlelight," I say.

I sit behind her and pull her into me, and we lean on the canvas of the three of us like we are leaning on a future we just started painting.

"I love you," she says, simple as a breath.

"I love you," I say back, because the best things are not complicated.

She tilts her head toward the window. "Look."

The snow is falling harder now. The flakes streak through the lamplight like silver threads. Our windows glow like a house that has decided against darkness.

"We are really doing this," she whispers.

"Yeah," I say, tucking my chin into her shoulder and breathing the clean scent of her hair. "Forever."

"We're going to build a beautiful life here," she says softly.

We don't speak for a while. We listen to the small sounds a house makes when it is warm and full.

When I stand to turn off the lamps, Ivy catches my sleeve. "Leave the window light," she says. "For him."

"For Pete?"

She nods.

I leave the window light.

We walk the hall to our room with our shoulders touching. I look back once, because I want the picture in my head. The look on Pete's face tonight when he felt the love of a town that treasures him.

# Chapter 28
# Ivy
### Christmas Day

The house is so quiet I can hear the snow. It touches the windows in soft little ticks, like the day is tapping to come in. I slip out of bed and into a sweater that smells like cedar and the laundry soap Donna swears by. Remy's side of the bed is cool. A faint line of cold air curls under the door from the mudroom. He is already out with Tate, plowing the drive so the town can reach us later. I picture the two of them under the gray-blue sky, headlamps cutting through the drift, Remy's mouth set in that focused way he gets when he is taking care of people. It makes my chest ache in a good way.

I pad to the living room first and plug in the tree. The lights blink on in a wave, warm and steady, and the whole room seems to come alive. I stand a minute and let it sink in. First Christmas morning in this house. First Christmas as a family. The words are still new on my tongue. I don't want to rush a second of this day. Last night Remy and I had fun playing Santa for Junie, getting her stocking ready and putting all of her presents out. I can't wait to see her reaction when she gets up.

The kitchen waits like a station I know by heart. I gather bowls and flour and sugar without looking, set the butter by the stove to soften, light the candle that smells like orange peel and clove. The playlist plays low, an old crooner singing to nobody in particular about coming home for Christmas, and I hum along as I whisk eggs and milk. Two casseroles, because one is never enough. Sausage, eggs, sourdough torn in ragged chunks, cheddar grated in curls that melt just watching me. Then a bacon one with caramelized onions, roasted peppers, spinach, a dusting of cheese on top. I slide both into the oven. The warmth of the oven whooshes out against my legs.

Cinnamon roll dough is ready in a covered bowl from last night. I flour the counter, turn the dough out, press it flat with my palms. It is soft and elastic and alive. Brown sugar, cinnamon, butter. I roll the whole thing tight, cut with dental floss because my mom taught me the trick, and line two pans with spirals that look like little galaxies. They rise while I make icing. Cream cheese, vanilla, a splash of milk, more powdered sugar than any person should admit to using.

I grin to myself. It is Christmas. I can do what I want.

Boots thud on the porch. The door swings open and cold air gusts in, sharp and clean. Remy comes in, cheeks pink from the wind, eyes bright. "Smells amazing in here," Remy says, voice warm even with the cold still in it. He kisses my cheek, then pulls me in for a hug like he cannot decide what to do first. "Merry Christmas."

"Merry Christmas," I tell him as I kiss him. "I need you to try this."

I hand him a bite of casserole to test, "You're the best." He takes a bite and closes his eyes. "Oh, this is magical. Marry me."

"That better not be a real proposal," I say low, with a frown. "I want romantic gestures, Remy."

His eyes sparkle. He winks.

"Is it time?" Junie's voice squeaks from the hallway. She is all pajamas and bedhead and wide eyes, clutching Lola like a stuffed toy. Lola tolerates exactly three seconds of that before she hops to the back of the couch, tail high, queen of this kingdom.

"It is time for stockings," I say, and Junie's feet drum a little tap dance against the floor.

We settle in the living room. Remy pulls the knit stockings down from their hooks. Junie climbs into the space between us on the couch and does not stop bouncing. The tree lights glow on her face. She looks like a storybook illustration of a child on Christmas morning. I reach for her hot chocolate, add a second cloud of whipped cream just because, and hand it over. She beams.

She dumps her stocking in her lap and gasps at every single thing like each one is the first. Fuzzy socks with tiny trees. A pack of glitter pens. Chapstick that smells like peppermint bark. Stickers. A little plush goat that screams when you squeeze it. She squeezes it eight times and cackles every time.

"It is like the goats at the farm," she says. "I am going to name him Sparkle."

Remy hides a smile behind his mug. "Perfect."

I watch her fingers open each little bundle I wrapped, slow when it makes sense to be slow, fast when she cannot help herself. Art supplies, a set of watercolors that travel in a neat tin, a charm bracelet with pinecones and stars. I tucked these small things away all fall, stashing them in drawers and under the bed and once in the flour bin for two days because I ran out of hiding places. It feels like magic watching them land in her hands now.

Remy leans in. "You nailed it," he whispers.

"You think?"

"She is over the moon. And so am I."

Junie's big present sits under the tree, all paper and ribbon and a tag she reads by sounding out each letter. When she tears it open and sees the sled, she screams. Then she hugs the sled, which is an experience I did not realize my life was missing until now.

"There is more," Remy says, and his voice gets funny and soft. He is trying to play it cool, but his eyebrows give him away. He reaches behind the tree and pulls out a giant gift bag and sets it in my lap.

"Remy," I say, already laughing a little. "What is this?"

"Open it."

Inside are a dozen small gifts, each wrapped in brown paper with a tiny piece of twine around it. My heart pounds for no reason at all. I open the first. Gloves. Soft and lined, the kind I picked up in shop in town and put back because I was saving. The second is a pair of earrings I admired at the craft fair when we were both pretending not to fall in love. The third is a thin bracelet, warm brown leather and a tiny brass clasp. My breath catches. The fourth is a stack of journaling notebooks, cream pages and gilded edges, the exact brand I once said in passing felt like writing on something kind. Then books. Four of them. A botanical field guide, a new novel I have been waiting for, a cookbook with hand pies on the cover, and a hardcover I held at Willa's bookstore and sighed over without meaning to let anyone hear.

I set the books in my lap and shake my head. "Did you not already get me enough books with the library?"

"You can never have enough books," he says, mock scandalized.

Junie leans in and peers at the pile like a dragon admiring a hoard. "This is amazing, Ivy. You scored. My dad loves you."

Remy grins and bends to kiss me, unhurried and sure, one hand at my jaw. The room tilts a little. "I do," he says against my mouth, just for me.

I kiss him again. "Good. Because I love you."

He pretends to be shocked, one hand to his heart, then breaks into that rare laugh that starts in his chest and ends in his eyes.

"My turn," I say, and pull a tidy stack of gifts from under the tree that I have been saving for him. Work shirts with the softest inside. Thermal socks that will not quit. A wool beanie in a green that makes his eyes go even darker. A thermos engraved with Bennett Tree Farm. He smiles like it is all too much and exactly right at the same time. The last gift is flat and light. He opens it slowly, careful with the paper even though that makes no sense.

When he sees the photo, he stops moving. It is the three of us, caught at some perfect angle by a kind photographer. Junie on his shoulders, my hand on his arm, both of us laughing at something out of frame. The frame says *Our Family* in little stamped letters. He swallows once, hard, then looks up at me, and I see the exact second something steadies inside him.

"Ivy," he says, and my name sounds like a promise. "I love it."

Junie has been waiting for this part. She shoves two flat envelopes at us with deadly seriousness. "I made these at school. Don't bend them."

Inside are ornaments made from baked clay and paint and glitter. Three stick figures and a dog lined up under a triangle tree. Our Family across the top in glitter that will be everywhere forever.

"They are perfect," I say.

Junie nods like *yes, obviously*. Lola, who has returned to drape herself along the top of the couch like a living stole, flicks her tail at us all in approval.

Remy clears his throat and reaches behind him for something else I did not see. A long, thin box. I give him a look. He grins.

"This is not fair," I say. "I did not know we were doing extra surprises."

"This is not a surprise. This is insurance." He sets the box on my lap. "Open it."

Inside is a letter in his handwriting. The paper shakes a little in my fingers as I unfold it. The first line steals my breath. It is simple and sure. I read the whole thing twice and then set it in my lap and look at him, because I cannot speak for a second. It is not a legal paper. It is not a list. It is a letter about choosing each other every day. About holding the door for love like Pete said. About building a life with both hands and not getting scared and slamming the door when it feels big. About how he wants to spend the rest of his stupid life with me—his words— and how if I say no, he will ask again tomorrow and the next day until I get tired of hearing the question and say yes just to shut him up.

"Remy," I say, and the word breaks. I kiss him until Junie coughs and covers her eyes like she is tired of our nonsense.

"Is it time to open the rest of the presents?" she asks.

"Yes, boss," Remy says, and I slide back to my cushion, breathless and certain in a way that scares me and settles me all at once.

We take our time with the little things. By the time the casseroles come out of the oven, our small family Christmas is complete, and the day is just getting started. I set the pans on the stove to rest, drizzle the cinnamon rolls with more icing than they need, and take a long look at the kitchen, at the tree, at my people. If the day stopped right here, I would still call it perfect.

The door bursts open, which is how the best parts of our life always seem to arrive, and the house fills with cold air and voices. Willa and Tate first, then Finn and Rowan with Lilith right behind, and Donna and Pete last. The living room goes from serene to alive in three seconds. Coats fly to hooks. Scarves land in a heap. Someone's hat lands on Lola and she looks personally offended and then climbs onto the couch to recover her dignity.

"Merry Christmas," Willa sings, and sweeps me into a hug that smells like frost and peppermint.

"You made so much good food," Tate says, peering around me in the direction of the kitchen.

"What can I say; it's Christmas." I grin.

Pete follows with his hat in his hands and a look like he cannot believe his luck. He squeezes my shoulder and tells me it already smells like the best Christmas he has ever had.

I did not plan to cry before brunch. I wipe my eyes and blame the onions.

We pass plates and forks and mugs and napkins, and it is chaos in the sweet way. Remy looks happy and content, more relaxed than I've seen him in weeks. Tate returns to the counter for seconds and steals the corner cinnamon roll that has extra icing like we cannot all see him.

Junie opens the rest of her gifts in the middle of the floor like a sun with planets around her. She holds up each thing for us to admire. New mittens from Willa that match mine. A wooden puzzle of a forest from Lilith and Rowan. A handmade scarf from Donna that has tiny hearts knit into the pattern. Pete presents a little tool belt that fits her and has safe kid tools, and she hugs his knees.

We eat until the house smells like new memories. The sausage casserole disappears first because men named Finn exist. The cinnamon rolls earn praise that makes me blush. They vanish in a way that suggest a crime was committed. Someone starts a game in the corner that involves charades and a paper crown, and Rowan will not stand down from anything. Finn tries to get out of the paper crown and fails. The crown sits on his head at a dignified tilt, and he looks very handsome and surprised about it. Willa takes photos from the ladder in the library doorway and then makes me stand with Remy under the frame that says Our Family and kisses the top of my head while she clicks the shutter because she is documenting history.

I sneak back to the kitchen to refill the coffee kettle and find Remy already there, stacking plates in tidy towers and rinsing forks like the world depends on it. He hums something under his breath, and his hair curls the tiniest bit at his neck from the heat in here. I stand and watch him. It is possible I have never loved anyone more than I love this man rinsing forks on Christmas morning.

"You don't have to do this by yourself," I say, stepping up beside him to take a dish towel.

"You already made half a feast and played Santa," he says. "Let me do the boring part."

"I like the boring part if you are in it."

He sets the plate down and turns. Wet hands touch my waist where the sweater lifts. I shiver and move closer. He smells like coffee, cold air, and a little of the pine that seems to cling to him even on a day off.

"Why do you look at me like that," he asks, soft and curious.

"Because you are mine," I say.

He kisses me like a seal on a promise. Someone wolf whistles in the living room, and Donna yells to get a room and then follows it with a comment about eventually giving her grandbabies, and I laugh into his mouth because I love this family, and I love this man and I am not afraid of wanting things any more.

We load the dishwasher together, moving in a little dance we have not practiced but always know. When he reaches for a stack of bowls and I beat him to it, he smiles like the soup at the center of winter just got richer.

When the last guest finally leans a shoulder into my shoulder and says thank you, when they leave with leftover plates and hugs that take longer than normal, when the house settles and the air still glitters with something I cannot name, I wrap both arms around Remy's waist and press my face into his chest.

He runs a hand down my back. "Thank you for making this house a home. Why don't you go read in your new library? Put your feet up. I'll finish."

I tilt my head back to see his eyes. "I will, after. I want to be with you."

He searches my face for a second that feels like forever. Then he kisses my forehead and nods. "Okay. Then be with me."

We wipe the counters and fold the cloth napkins. We step into the living room together and right a pillow that fell. Lola lifts her head and pretends she was not snoring. Junie sprawls on her stomach with her new books, reading aloud words she is maybe guessing at and still making true. The tree twinkles. The radio plays a quiet song that must have been written before any of us were born.

Later, when the kitchen sighs in that particular after-dinner way, he takes my hand and draws me down the hall. I know where he is going before we turn the corner. The library waits, golden in the winter afternoon. The canvas of the three of us catches the glow and throws it back.

We sink into the oversized chair by the window, our legs tangling in the blanket across our laps. I open one of the new books, the one with the pressed flowers on the cover, and read a page aloud, then read the same page again because he likes the sound of my voice on words. He kisses my wrist every time I turn a page. After a while, we stop reading. We stare at the snow falling and talk about nothing and everything. What to make for dinner if we are ever hungry again. When to take Junie sledding. How many people Rowan will recruit for her New Year's

Day plunge in the cove and how many will regret it immediately. Whether the lights on the tree can stay until February if we pretend the season still needs them. We are soaking up every last ounce of holiday joy.

"I want a hundred more Christmases like this," I say.

"You are going to get them," he says.

I believe in the way Remy looks at me, like the lights came on for the first time, and he never wants them to go dark again.

# Chapter 29
# Remy
## A month later

The house smells like garlic and whatever dessert magic Ivy has going on in the oven. The tree is gone now, packed carefully into boxes and hauled out to the attic of the barn until next year, but the living room still feels magical. Junie is sprawled on the rug with her colored pencils, Lola watching her like a furry best friend chaperone.

Pizza night is still our thing every Friday, rain or snow, and I look forward to it every week. There was a time I would have been in the barn until dark, eating cold leftovers over the sink. Now, I'm standing in a warm kitchen, flour up to my elbows, waiting for my girl to tell me what toppings she wants.

The sauce is simmering when Ivy slides onto a stool at the island with her notebook. I wipe my hands on a towel and raise a brow. "That looks serious."

"It is," she says, smiling, but there's a nervous edge to it. "I've been working on a business plan. I am finally ready to tell you about it."

I turn off the mixer and lean on the counter, curious. "Why haven't you told me yet?"

She chews her lip, then says, "I kind of wanted to prove to myself that I could do this before I said anything out loud."

I flip the towel over my shoulder and grin. "Ivy, this is amazing. Whatever it is, I'm in. Tell me."

She lays the notebook flat and starts talking, flipping pages she's filled with neat handwriting and little sketches. It's an idea for a kids' program with farm tours, seasonal workshops, even summer day camps where they can learn about trees, animals, nature. She's mapped out costs, schedules, even a list of local sponsors she could approach to get it going.

"I've been thinking about this for months," she says. "I figured I'd test the idea this spring with a weekend workshop, see how it goes, and if people like it, I could expand. With your blessing, of course."

I can't stop smiling. "This is brilliant. You'd be amazing at this, Ivy. Kids would love it. Parents would love it. You could do it year-round if you wanted. Use the barn or hell, we can build you a new building just for this. You could host your own retreats, kids' parties, whatever you want."

She goes quiet, blinking like she's trying not to tear up.

"Hey," I say, stepping around the counter to stand between her knees. "Whatever you want, I am here for you."

She smiles, soft and certain, and kisses me. "Thanks."

"Don't thank me yet. You haven't seen my marketing plan."

Her laugh makes my chest feel too full. I tuck her hair behind her ear just because I can, and the oven timer dings before I can kiss her again.

* * *

The front door opens, and cold air and trouble blow in.

"Hey, guys!" Finn calls, stomping snow off his boots. Rowan is right behind him, scarf trailing like she was running here.

They look like they have been up to something, which means they have.

Ivy calls from the kitchen, "You're early."

"Had to be," Rowan says. "We brought a special guest."

I frown, dusting flour off my hands. "What?"

Finn grins like a man who knows he's about to get punched. "Marco."

"Marco?" I repeat, not following.

"As in Marco's Pizza," Rowan says, practically vibrating with glee.

I stare at Finn. "You didn't."

He grins wider.

"You're going to get it," I tell him, trying to be dead serious.

Rowan laughs so hard she has to hold onto the back of a chair. "Finn might have told Marco that his pizza was just as good as yours, and Marco was wildly curious. So...he's joining us for pizza night."

"You're both dead," I inform them.

Finn shrugs. "I regret nothing."

Before I can reply, there's a knock at the door and Marco himself steps in, cheeks red from the cold, carrying a crate of fresh garlic bulbs and a tiramisu cake like some sort of saint.

"Remy!" he booms, his Italian accent warm as summer. "Thank you for having me. I am so excited to watch you cook."

I glance at Finn, who is trying not to laugh, and then shake Marco's hand. "Come on in. But if you tell me my pizza is trash, you're never allowed back."

He just grins. "I would not dare."

* * *

It turns into the best kind of chaos. Marco jumps in like he has been part of pizza night forever, tossing dough in the air to show Junie, who squeals every time it lands without falling. We talk shop, dough fermentation, oven temperature, hydration percentage. He teaches me a new trick for stretching dough without tearing it, and I have to admit, the man knows his craft.

"If you ever get tired of your tree farm," he says, "come partner with me. We will be the best!"

"Tempting," I say, laughing. "But I think I'm where I belong. And you're already the best, Marco."

"Good answer," Ivy calls from the couch, smiling at us.

By the time the pizzas come out, the house smells like heaven. We line them up on the island with pepperoni, margherita, white pizza with roasted garlic and spinach and everyone piles plates high.

Ivy and Rowan sit together, Rowan flipping through Ivy's new books.

"You've got good taste," Rowan says. "Where'd you get these?"

"Willa set them aside for me," Ivy says.

Rowan sighs dramatically. "Lucky. I wish I had time to read. I'm trying to fight to get my permits so I can open. It's been delayed and delayed again."

I look up from slicing pizza. "What's going on with your permits?"

Rowan's mouth twists. "Vanessa and Marilyn are holding them up at the town office."

I frown. "Why?"

Rowan says. "They're trying to open a rival Pilates studio, so they're stalling me so they can launch first."

"But you've got an apothecary. Yoga is just in the evenings and early mornings," Ivy says. "Why do they care?"

"Because Marilyn has a thing for Finn," Rowan says. "And she's mad that we're friends."

"I thought they both had a thing for Remy," Ivy says, then shoots me a sheepish look. "Tell you later," she mouths.

I glance at Finn, who is very focused on his plate. "Oh, yeah?"

His ears turn red. "I don't like Marilyn like that."

"Mm-hmm," Rowan says, smirking. But she does not look happy at all.

"I don't," Finn says again, more forceful this time. "And I definitely don't like that she's messing with your permits. This is personal now."

Rowan looks pleased. "Good. Let's burn them to the ground. Metaphorically."

"Metaphorically," Finn echoes, but there's a gleam in his eye that says he is already plotting something.

I glance at Ivy. She's watching them with interest that tells me she knows something is happening here, whether Rowan and Finn know it yet or not.

After dinner, Marco pulls out the tiramisu, and we eat until we can't move. He insists we all take extra garlic bulbs as a parting gift. When he leaves, he claps me on the shoulder and says, "You have my approval, Remy. You make pizza like you do everything, with heart."

It's a silly thing to feel proud about, but I do.

"Thanks, Marco. You're welcome anytime."

"It's not always I get to be the guest. Thank you."

When the door shuts and the house goes quiet again, Ivy leans into me, warm and soft. "You had fun," she says.

"I did," I admit. "Even if I'm never forgiving Finn."

She grins. "It was worth it. And hey, you impressed Marco. That's basically a Wisteria Cove culinary endorsement."

I laugh and kiss her, because she's right, and because her hair smells like garlic and rosemary and home.

Junie yawns wide and announces that pizza night is the best

night of the week. I carry her to bed while Ivy tidies the kitchen, and when I come back, Rowan and Finn are by the door pulling on their coats, still bickering about Marilyn and Vanessa and what to do about the permits.

"We could stage a protest," Rowan is saying.

Finn snorts. "We could just go talk to Jace at the permit office like sane people."

"Where's the fun in that?" she fires back.

I shake my head and grin, already knowing this is just the beginning of whatever storm those two are about to cause.

Later, when the house is quiet and the dishes are done, I find Ivy curled up on the couch with her notebook again.

"Back to the business plan?" I ask, sinking down beside her.

"Yeah," she says. "But I'm adding something new."

"Oh?"

She turns the notebook toward me, her handwriting looping across the page. "I want to add another summer retreat series for kids. Camps, crafts, maybe even music nights in the barn."

I feel my chest go warm again. "Do it. Whatever you want, Ivy. I'm here for you."

She smiles, slow and sure. "I know."

And I do what I've been wanting to do since she sat down at the island earlier. I kiss her until she laughs against my mouth.

Life feels steady. Good. Like we are building something we can keep.

Tonight, the house is warm, Ivy is in my arms, and there's still a slice of pizza left on the counter with my name on it.

# Epilogue
## Ivy

Three months later

"End of April is my favorite," I say. "Everything looks like a fresh start."

The air smells like rain that is thinking about happening. The sky is a soft gray lid, but the groves are waking up in green. New needle growth is bright on the tips of the firs; the ground is springy, and the robins are busy. I lace my fingers with Remy's as we follow the path along the fence. His thumb brushes my knuckles a few times like a secret code that only we know.

He smiles at the ground first, then at me. "Everything *is* a fresh start."

We check the rows like we always do. He stops to nudge soil around a root that looks exposed. I crouch to pick up a bit of twine and tuck it in my pocket for later. We talk about silly things. How the new barn cats have chosen the old seed sacks as their kingdom. How Junie's class is hatching chicks, and the teacher keeps sending photos that make Remy pretend he does not want six of them. My bet is that by the end of summer we'll have a whole chicken coop to go with the goats that the neighbors never came back for, and Remy doesn't complain about. He secretly loves them.

We turn the bend and step into the small clearing. I stop.

There is a blue and white plaid blanket spread on the soft grass. A basket sits ready. Two glass bottles of lemonade catch what little sun there is and light up like they are full of their own glow.

I look up at him. "What do you have planned, Remy?"

He tries for casual and does not quite get there. "Walk. Lunch. Maybe I try to convince you of something."

I laugh and he takes my hand again and leads me to the blanket. He kneels and opens the basket like a magician who is proud of his hat. Sandwiches wrapped in parchment. A container that smells like dill and mustard.

He hands me a sandwich. "Turkey on sourdough with that mustard you like."

"I take a bite and close my eyes. "This is perfect."

He opens another container. "Potato salad. Your favorite kind. Extra pickles."

I eat a forkful and try not to moan with delight. "You remembered."

"I always remember."

And he does always remember. It's the little things that he never forgets. About how I like my food or things I say I want to try to do. He treats everything like it's important and like it means something.

We eat, and it's quiet but not awkward because it never is. Being with Remy and just being still is something that I appreciate. Birds chatter above us. Somewhere across the grove a branch snaps and then settles. The whole place feels like a secret, even though it is just our little clearing off the main path. I lean on one elbow and watch him chew, watch the relaxed lines of his face, watch the way he looks at the trees like they are old friends who always know what to say.

"What is this all for?" I ask finally. "The blanket. The basket. The perfect sandwich. My favorite salad."

He muzzles a smile. "Can I not surprise you with a picnic?"

"You can, and you did." I nudge the other container with my toe. "What is that one?"

He picks it up and sets it between us. "White cake. Buttercream frosting. Your favorite."

"This is a very serious picnic."

"I am a very serious man."

He cracks the lid, and the scent of sugar fills the air. The frosting is pale and swirled like a cloud. In the center sits something that is not cake. Light flashes before my brain catches up.

A ring.

It's tucked into the hollow he has made in the frosting. It catches the gray day and still gleams.

My heart stumbles. My breath trips over it. "Oh."

His mouth lifts. He keeps his eyes on mine. "Now we come as a package deal. Not only do you get a husband, but you get to be an instant mom. How would you feel about that?"

Tears prick so fast I cannot help it. The answer is already in my chest before he finishes the question. "Yes," I say. "Always yes. In every lifetime, Remington, it is you and me."

Something in his face breaks open. Relief. Joy. A thousand miles of worry eased in one breath. He reaches into the frosting, pinches the ring free, wipes it on a napkin that he absolutely planned for, and takes my left hand. His fingers are steady. The ring slides over my knuckle as if it was waiting to be there all its life.

"Perfect," he says, kissing my knuckles.

"It is," I say, but I am not talking about the ring.

He leans in and kisses me. It is soft and sure and tastes like lemon and sugar. The clearing goes quiet for one long moment. The trees hold their breath with me.

A rustle breaks the spell. We both turn.

Finn and Tate are there, each with a hand around Junie's middle like she is a cartoon character trying to sprint. She wiggles free and cups her hands around her mouth.

"Did she say yes?" she calls, lungs like a trumpet.

"I did, Junie," I laugh, and hold my arms wide.

"Will you be my mom now?" she asks, small and serious.

My breath catches, and my heart squeezes.

"Yes," I say, voice thick, "if you'll have me."

She barrels across the blanket, knees first into my lap, nearly knocking me flat. I wrap her up and tuck her under my chin. She smells like crayons and the cinnamon toast she had for breakfast.

"I get to be your mom," I whisper into her hair.

We talked to her months ago, telling her she probably wouldn't being seeing Sloane again.

She didn't cry. Just sort of...tilted her head and asked if she could have ice cream after dinner.

Junie was never very attached to Sloane. How could she be? Sloane floated in and out, cold one minute and distracted the next. She never hurt Junie, but she never made space for her, either. And kids know. Even when they don't have the words for it. But I am here. Not trying to be her mother, just trying to be someone she could trust.

And now, she's in my arms, asking me for something she's never really had before.

Not a placeholder. Not someone temporary. A mom.

She pulls back just enough to see my face. Relief loosens her mouth, and she sags against me again. "I was glad you said yes. I love you, Ivy."

"I love you more," I say, and kiss her forehead. The ring flashes near her cheek and she gasps.

"It's so pretty."

Finn and Tate pretend to look anywhere but at us while they grin like fools. Finn gives Remy the useless manly nod that means everything. Tate wipes his cheek with the back of his wrist and declares it is dust. A photographer walks up, smiling, and takes quiet shots from the side while Junie crawls off my lap to examine the cake with scientific attention.

"Can I have a bite?" she asks.

"You can have the whole piece," Remy says, and she cheers like someone handed her the moon. "I brought extra, because I had a feeling you'd crash this and join us."

We eat cake with forks straight from the container because nothing about this day requires a plate. The frosting is exactly what he promised. Thick and sweet with the kind of buttercream that melts first and then leaves the flavor behind to visit twice.

Finn takes a few photos with my phone. Tate pretends to direct like a film auteur. The photographer stays kind and invisible and somehow gets photos when I forget he is there. Remy kisses my temple, my cheek, the corner of my mouth. The sky brightens like it approves.

On the walk back we go slow. Junie swings between us and counts the steps to the barn like it is a game that matters. Finn and Tate carry the basket and the blanket and talk about how Willa and Rowan are going to want every single detail as soon as possible. Remy squeezes my hand every few minutes like he needs to verify this is real. I squeeze back like I agree.

I wash my sticky fingers in the kitchen sink and stare at the ring while water runs over my hands. It looks right. It looks like it has been there forever, even though it's brand new.

"You keep looking at it," Remy says, leaning in the doorway with his arms crossed and his smile soft.

"I keep checking to see if this is a dream."

"It's not."

"Good," I say, and reach for him again because I cannot not.

He kisses me until Junie yells from the hallway that we're gross and that she needs help. We break apart and try to look like responsible adults.

"Later," he murmurs. There is a promise in the word.

"Later," I agree.

We make the announcement like people who cannot hold good news inside. We stop at the bookstore first. The bell jingles, and the whole place smells like coffee and books. Lilith is behind the counter labeling jars. Willa and Rowan are perched on stools with coffee cups in their hands and grins on their faces when they see us.

Lilith looks up at me at once and catches the light on my hand. Her mouth goes round in a perfect circle. "Oh," she says, and then she is around the counter, and we are pressed together, and I am crying again because she is crying, and Rowan is already getting out a sheet of paper to plan my wedding flowers.

"You said yes," Rowan says, like she participated in the choosing.

"I said yes."

"Of course you did," she says, wiping at her eyes and pretending she is not.

"I'm so happy for you!" Willa says.

Donna is next, because there is no reality where she hears it third. We drive over and find her at her desk with a pen behind her ear and a stack of pages that smell like ink and plot. She stands when we walk in, eyes flicking from my face to my hand to Remy's face. She presses her hands to her chest.

"Oh, sweetheart," she says, and when she hugs me, she smells like powder and peppermint. "I am so happy I could burst. Look at you. Look at you both."

Pete appears from the kitchen with a dish towel over his shoulder and kisses the top of my head. He hugs Remy and pretends not to cry. He winks at Junie and calls her Miss Mayor, and she bows with gravitas like this is a ceremony he prepared her for. Those two always have inside jokes.

Pete's still struggling, but he has had some good days. He's on a new medication and it is making him comfortable. We're taking every day we have with him as a gift and cherishing them, because that's all you can do. Tomorrow is never promised to anyone.

We head back to the farm because it feels right to bring the day home. The sun finally breaks and slips under the clouds, laying a gold edge on the grove. Lola sits in the window with the superiority of a monarch who approves of this match. Junie runs ahead and then runs back, unable to decide whether to be first into the house or first into my arms.

When the door closes behind us, the quiet is not empty. It is full. Remy leans his back against the wood and pulls me in. His voice goes low. "My wife," he says, trying the word on like a new coat.

"My husband," I say, and try it, too.

We stand there for a minute and let the day pass through us. Every laugh, every hug, every time someone's eyes went bright. The ring that flashes when I tip my hand and disappears when I curl my fingers.

"Tell me what you were thinking," I say. "When you proposed."

"That you would hopefully say yes," he says, deadpan.

I swat his arm and he grins, then sobers. "I was thinking about all the ways I could have asked you and then I decided I wanted it to taste like the life we are building. Simple. Sweet. A little ridiculous. Something we could share with sticky fingers and a laugh."

"That is exactly what it was." I press my mouth to his. "Thank you for choosing me."

"I will keep choosing you," he says. "Every day."

After dinner we sit in the library. Remy pulls the throw over our legs and Junie reads the first chapter of her new book aloud, sounding out the long words, confident on the small ones. She reads me the dedication as if it is a spell.

*For everyone who ever wanted a home.*

I lean into Remy until our shoulders are one line. My left hand rests on his knee. The ring is warm from my skin. It fits. It shines when I lift it. It disappears when I lace my fingers with his. Both are true. Both are right.

"Tomorrow," he says, "we can start planning. Cake flavors, a list of songs. Those little lights you like in the trees."

"Tomorrow," I agree.

I think about the girl who arrived in this town with her heart scuffed and empty. I think about the woman who sits in this room now with a ring on her finger and a family wrapped around her like a quilt. I think about the way he said *package deal* and made it sound like a gift.

"Always yes," I whisper, even though I already said it.

He tips my chin and nods like he knows I needed to say it twice. "Always yes," he echoes.

Because in every lifetime, I'd choose him.

# Bonus Content

Want more Remy and Ivy? Check out this bonus scene for Mistletoe & Magic when you sign up for Erin's newsletter! Scan the QR code to get your bonus scene:

# About the Author

Erin Branscom is a creator of happily-ever-after's, crafting spicy, Hallmark-like romances that make readers fall head over heels for charming small towns. When she's not writing heartwarming stories, Erin can be found anywhere there are dogs, with a cup of coffee in hand, or lost in a good book. As a passionate Scorpio, she brings intensity and heart to everything she does. Dive into her world and discover love, warmth, and a touch of spice in every story.

# Acknowledgments

To my family. I love you all and you are my reason for working hard every day. I'm so thankful for all of you and your support. To all my readers, thank you for always showing up for me and being excited!

**Freedom Valley Series**
Falling Inn Love
Baked Inn Love
All Inn Thyme
Love Inn Books
Forever Inn Love
Snowed Inn

**Bridger Falls**
Forever To Me
Wild As Her
Always You
High Road

**Wisteria Cove**
The Pumpkin Spice Spell
Mistletoe & Magic
Hexes & Honeysuckle

**Standalones**
Fall Too Well
Bagpipes & Buns

You can find all of Erin's books on her website:
**Erinbranscom.com**

# Hexes & Honeysuckle

Chapter One
Rowan

The Rusty Anchor is buzzing tonight, and locals call out and wave as I claim a stool at the bar and wait for Finn. Boots scuff the old plank floors of the bar that's older than dirt, the jukebox plays an upbeat rock song, and the air smells like fried food, ocean salt, and spilled beer.

While I wait, I open my dating app and start scrolling, pretending it's not the saddest hobby known to womankind. It's like shopping for shoes that look great in the picture but turn out to pinch, squeak, or are uncomfortable as hell once you try them on. One guy's holding a fish and giving a thumbs up. Always the fish. Not even an impressive fish. And sometimes we can use the term "fish" metaphorically. Sometimes it's not a fish and I really wish it was a fish. Swipe left. Another one says he's "fluent in sarcasm" and "looking for a partner in crime." Left again. I sigh and wonder if maybe I should just marry my air fryer. At least it's consistent and knows how to heat things up.

I hover my thumb over the next when a warm voice leans in from behind me. "Ohhh, hard pass on that one?"

I glance over my shoulder. Finn Bennett stands there, tall and broad, grin bright enough to light up the bar. He looks fresh, like he just stepped out of the shower and is here to torture the world. The problem with Finn is he doesn't even understand how good-looking he is. He's just Finn. The human equivalent of a golden retriever, who is rugged and lovable. Dark blond hair that curls damp under a backward ball cap. Blue eyes soft and amused. White T-shirt clinging to his hard wall of muscular chest. Worn denim jeans that are probably doing the Lord's work for that perfect ass and scuffed up brown work boots that are also oddly doing things for me. He looks like a walking-talking blue collar hottie calendar model without even trying.

And he's my best friend. The real kind. The kind who has been in my life since we were kids. We grew up together in a way that made him part of my daily rhythm. Coffee together on slow mornings. Fixing things around the shop when I get over-whelmed. Showing up for every birthday, every heartbreak, every small disaster I pretend I can handle alone. He knows me better than anyone.

I shouldn't be thinking he looks hot, but I secretly always have. It's the thought that rises in my chest before I can stop it, warm and dangerous, like a spell I never meant to cast.

He slides onto the stool beside me and scoots closer, putting his elbows on the bar and leaning toward my phone. "That guy's a winner."

I say dryly, "That was you, Finn."

The words leave my mouth, but my heart races. Because his profile, smile, and his broad shoulders filling the frame are so natural, like he took the picture without thinking twice. And it hits me in a way I don't expect. A tiny pinch right under my ribs. Finn is on a dating app and out there meeting people, maybe kissing them, maybe touching them in the ways I pretend I never think about.

I shouldn't care, because we're best friends. But the thought of him laughing with someone else over drinks or waking up tangled in someone else's sheets sends a wash of heat through my chest. I look at him, my throat tight, the joke drying on my tongue.

I say nothing about any of that, but the feeling remains.

"I know." He shrugs, but his mouth fights a smile.

I glance at the time and set my phone down. "Why are you so late? Did you finally meet someone and she's not happy that your best friend's a woman?" *Insert biggest fear here.*

"I had a client run late for an estimate," he says as he raises two fingers at the bar. "Mack, can we get a couple of beers and two of the specials?"

We have dinner together here every Thursday night and always order the special. We catch up and he tells me about his week, and I tell him about mine. It's not like we don't talk every day, but I do look forward to these dinners. I won't call them dates, but they are what they are. Dinner dates between friends. *Friends.*

Mack, who is in his late fifties with a gray beard and shaggy hair, has practically been pouring drinks at The Rusty Anchor since the dawn of the Wisteria Cove sea shanties. He gives us a look that lands somewhere between fond and nosy. "How's my favorite couple?"

I roll my eyes playfully. Not this again. "Knock it off, Mack, or I'll curse your jukebox to only play Taylor Swift on repeat from now until Christmas."

He scoffs, looking offended. "But I *like* Taylor Swift."

I hold up my hands. "Hey, I do too. But we'll see how you like it when *All Too Well*, the ten-minute version, plays on repeat for the next six months straight."

Mack rolls his eyes as he puts our orders in and grabs two frosty glasses from the cooler.

Finn grins and says to Mack, "She *almost* swiped right. So close. Maybe next time."

"Don't encourage him, Finn," I mutter grumpily as I swirl a cardboard coaster in circles with my finger.

Mack snorts and places beers in front of us. "If I had to place a bet, I'd say you'll be married before the end of the year. Send me my invitation and I'll bring the kegs."

I flick a peanut at Mack, and he cackles before wandering off toward the game playing on one of the big TVs on the wall behind the bar. Finn lifts his glass and clinks it against mine like this is some kind of quiet celebration between us.

With us, it is always like there is this invisible pull that drags us right back to the same place. No matter how far life scatters us, we shift toward each other without thinking. No one knows me the way Finn does. He has known every version of me, from the quiet kid hiding behind stacks of library books to the woman trying to build a life that sometimes feels too big for her own hands. Maybe that is why I have never let myself look too closely at what I feel around him. Because it has always been there. Soft, quiet, and dangerous. A little spark under the surface that I pretend not to see between us.

We made this unspoken agreement years ago. Best friends only. Safe territory. No crossing lines that could break what we have. And I have stayed inside that boundary like it is a spell I cast on myself.

But sitting here now, watching the way he looks at me, I feel that pull in my chest again. Stronger than I want to admit. His smile is lazy and warm and something a little wilder, like he knows exactly what he does to me even if I refuse to say it out loud.

And for one breath, I let myself feel it. All of it. The bond, the history, the quiet ache I have spent years pretending I do not carry.

"So," I say, resting my chin on my hand, "how's your dating life, Contractor Ken?"

Finn is a general contractor and basically a genius at fixing or building anything. I joke he has a tool belt around his waist most of the time as a permanent accessory. But the truth is that he's good at what he does. I call him Contractor Ken to give him shit because he looks like he could be a Ken doll. The blue-collar hottie Ken version. I gotta keep my friend humble, and he does the same to me.

"Actually," he says, eyes locked on mine like he is trying to read me, "I have a date tomorrow."

The words land softer than they should, but something tightens in my chest anyway. Finn doesn't date a lot. Not seriously. So, hearing it out loud sends a strange little pinch through me, sharp enough that I feel it in my throat. I tell myself it's fine and I don't care. I try not to think about him getting dressed for someone else or smiling at someone else the way he smiles at me.

"Do you now?" I arch a brow, forcing a teasing tone. "Look at you finally swiping right."

He laughs, warm and easy. I smile back, but there is a quiet ache under it. A small twist of something I don't examine too closely, because if I do, I might have to admit what it really is.

"I'm a catch, Rowan. What can I say?" he says as his eyes meet mine and he winks.

"Well, I actually have a date tomorrow, too." I take a sip of my beer and wipe the foam from my mouth with the back of my hand. Classy.

What I don't say is that I matched with someone who isn't really a serious date at all. But Finn doesn't need to know that.

But every time I try to picture myself on a date with

someone or if there'll be chemistry or anything past the first drink, my brain drifts right back to Finn. To the way he listens to me like I'm the only one in the room. Or to how safe he always makes me feel. To how easy it is to be around him and just be myself.

I had swiped right anyway. Because I should be dating. Because I should be trying. Because I refuse to let myself sit here and wait for someone who isn't mine.

But even now, saying it out loud, I can feel how halfhearted it is. A tiny part of me wonders if I'm doing this to distract myself from the way Finn makes me feel. I ignore that thought and take another drink.

We share a look that's tender and warm between us. I clear the air and say, "Want to compare notes afterwards over lunch the next day?"

"Sure." He leans back as if planning time with me is the most natural thing in the world. Then it hits me that I'm looking forward to lunch with Finn more than looking forward to the date.

"Where are you going on your date?" I ask him curiously, trying to get back to the discussion and not let my mind wander to places it shouldn't.

"I don't know yet." He shrugs. "I'll figure it out."

I scoff. "You have to put some effort into these and plan something, Finn."

He leans in and says, "Where would you like to go if *you* were my date?"

Something stirs in my lower belly when he says this. I swallow and brush it off quickly, trying to be casual. "Maybe Marco's to split a pizza, then take a walk down by the harbor. And get some ice cream at The Dairy Witch. That's what I'd choose."

"Hmm, that's a good idea. Is that where you're going?" he asks with a smirk.

"As a matter of fact, it is," I say. "Are you going to copy my date?"

"Maybe. Sounds pretty great, actually."

Mack brings out our burgers and a mountain of fries on a tray to share with various dips that we like. A cheese cup, garlic aioli sauce, and ketchup. We like variety. We fall into our usual and familiar rhythm that has always been there. Finn tells me about the floors he's restoring at his new house that he bought from our childhood friend, Tate. He bought it last fall and is fixing it up, and he's so excited about it. He asks me for my opinion on everything, but he hardly needs it. He talks about the mudroom, the built-ins he's restoring like other men talk about their favorite sports teams. It's exciting to see Finn's house coming together. It's a big old home on Main Street just down the road from my apothecary shop, Salt & Root.

He's also been helping me with my shop I got up and going last winter, but I haven't been able to get the permit from the mayor's office to run my yoga studio on the top floor. That's the last piece I've been waiting on, and I've been waiting for months for city hall to approve. I took a break for a while from teaching yoga during the winter to get Salt & Root up and going, but now I'm ready to do classes again.

I was teaching classes three nights a week at the community center, but they said that Marilyn and Vanessa have been teaching Pilates classes in my class spots now and there's no room for me to teach mine. Which makes no sense because I get texts, emails, and people stopping by every week asking me when I'm going to resume classes again.

My studio above Salt & Root is completely ready. I have all new mats, blocks, straps, and it's beautiful up there with freshly sanded and stained wood floors. Honestly, a dream space to prac-tice yoga with bright sunlight, plants, and it's so calming up there. Just need that stupid business permit from the city that honestly makes no sense that I even have to have in the first place. Seems like a giant hoax to me. Vanessa and Marilyn both work for city hall and I suspect that they are keeping me from being able to open my studio. For reasons that I don't understand.

"Thanks for reinforcing the shelves in the shop, by the way," I say after the conversation moves from his house to my shop. "Now I don't have to worry about coming into a giant mess of herbs and glass now."

He waves me off. "No problem. I'll build you whatever you need."

My stomach flutters and I chase it with a sip of beer. That is just Finn, and he's always saying things like that. He's my best friend, I remind myself. Best friends help each other. That's all this is.

"Well, you did pretty much do everything in the shop," I say as I lean in and bump his shoulder with mine.

He reaches over, and our forearms touch as he drags a fry through the cheese sauce and eats it. His eyes are happy, with wrinkles at the corners, as he grins at me in return.

We start a roast session on each other over the dating app because I need to laugh about my non-existent love life. And Finn and I have the most epic roasts. Our banter back and forth is one of my favorite things to do. He's funny and always down to call me on my shit when needed. He's one of the few people I can be myself around. Finn scoots closer to see my screen. Our shoulders touch and heat curls low in my stomach at his warmth. And he smells so good, too.

I swipe to a bio that reads: Looking for my forever fishing partner.

Finn groans. "That's every guy in Wisteria Cove."

Another proudly calls himself The Crypto King.

I deadpan, "Oh yes. Nothing says romance like fake money and zippered hoodies. All he needs is a thick gold chain around his neck."

"Oh, he has one!" Finn says excitedly, pointing to the next picture and throwing his head back and laughing.

"Oh my gosh." I groan and laugh.

"Swipe left. Now," Finn instructs, jabbing a finger at my phone.

Mack wanders back just in time to witness our chaos and lifts a brow. "If you two spent half as much time flirting with each other as you do with chasing these poor souls on an app, you wouldn't have to worry about swiping."

"Go away, Mack," I tell him, but I'm smiling. Mack loves to give us shit.

The door swings open and in saunters Marilyn and Vanessa, aka the mean girls of Wisteria Cove, wearing matching leggings, crop tops, and ponytails. Of course, they spot us and Vanessa leans toward Marilyn and says loud enough for the entire bar to hear, "Still no permit for the witch."

I set my burger down with care. My smile goes flat and sharp.

"Hey, Marilyn and Vanessa," I call sweetly to them and am met with glares.

Finn's jaw tightens. He keeps his voice gentle as he practically growls, "Rowan."

"It's fine," I tell him and keep my eyes on the two of them. "How's your Pilates studio coming along? I can't wait to see it."

Killing them with kindness. That's what I tell myself as I stand there smiling like the calm, collected business owner I'm trying so hard to be. On the outside, I'm polite. Pleasant. The picture of someone who believes in community collaboration.

On the inside, I'm two seconds from throwing my beer all

over their stupid designer leisurewear and watching it soak into their matching handbags. I can practically hear myself saying, "Acting like Grade-A bitches at forty is embarrassing. It was pathetic in high school too, sweethearts."

I smile though, teeth gritted together so I don't voice what I really want to say. My jaw hurts from the effort, but I do it. I remind myself that I'm running a business now, not casting curses behind the bleachers. I remind myself that losing my temper gives them exactly what they want.

When I'm with Finn, the restraint drops. With him, I don't have to pretend. I can say what I actually think. And what I think is that if they push me much harder, I'm not above putting them in their places.

He doesn't even flinch. He knows this version of me and he likes her. He's the only one I let see her without apology.

Marilyn gives me a thin fake smile. "We're trying to create a welcoming environment."

"Same," I say sweetly. "Minus the mean-girl soundtrack that you two are playing on a loop. I don't know if you know this, but there can be more than one fitness studio in town."

Okay, so maybe I can't completely bite my tongue. Oops.

They huff and drift away. Finn shifts, narrowing his gaze.

"I really don't like those two," Finn mutters as he pushes his empty plate away.

"You and me both," I say, shaking my head. "I'm convinced they're in on it with Mayor Sammy Briggs about holding up my permit. I can't prove it, but I'm pretty sure they're sabotaging me."

"If I find out they are..." Finn bites out, shoulders tense as he trails off, letting me fill in the blanks of his warning.

"They probably are," I tell him. "I just have to do my thing. Let them do theirs."

"You're pretty calm about this," he says, eyes narrowed as he studies me.

I shrug. "I'm trying to be good. I'm a Wisteria Cove business owner and I want people to take me seriously."

"You eating okay?" he asks, changing the subject, looking down at half my burger still on my plate. "You were also picking at your lunch when I stopped by the shop yesterday."

There it is. The soft moment that he always has for me. "I'm fine."

"Want me to talk to the mayor?"

I frown and shake my head. "I can fight my own battles."

He nods, but his eyes say he's going to quietly fight them anyway.

We get back to the app. He critiques how I rarely make it to a second date until I remind him of his own dating issues. "Please, you never even make it to a second date with anyone either."

"Maybe I have standards."

"Maybe you just get bored," I say dryly.

He drags his gaze over my face and mouth, and right now, he doesn't look bored at all. After a beat, he looks away, focusing on his empty plate like it holds the secrets of the universe. My pulse races, and I pretend it doesn't.

"Oh, hey, I forgot your song for the day," he says as he slides off his stool. "I'll be right back."

I watch as he crosses the bar to the jukebox. He flips through songs and retrieves quarters from his pocket. He leans against the wall and waits for it to load. He has to jiggle the side of the jukebox, and why that looks sexy, I don't know, but it does. Finn is a big guy with wide shoulders, and I hate that when I look at him, I have all these feelings. Feelings I shouldn't be having and chase out of my mind every time.

*Don't Stop Believin'* fills the room and I laugh. Of course he'd pick that one. For years, music has been a thing for Finn and me. Every time we see each other, we take turns picking a song and either texting it to each other or playing it for each other. Finn usually brings a performance into the mix and sings it to me in his off-key voice. I pretend to be annoyed, but it's funny. From rock classics to silly pop songs, we pick songs we think the other one might like or that remind us about something in our lives at that moment. I've been compiling a playlist of all our songs since we've been doing this. It's a really long playlist now, but I listen to it sometimes, and each song reminds me of a memory of him.

Mack takes our plates and refills our beers as Finn slides in next to me.

"What do you think about your song?" he asks as he sings the lyrics, looking into my eyes. He offers his fist to me. "Here, hold my microphone."

"Stop it." I laugh and wave his hand away.

He continues to sing softly, tapping his boot on the bar stool to the song.

"It's a good song, a classic. I'll have to think up an even better one for your song tomorrow," I add, sipping my beer.

When it's time to head out, we slide off our stools, and the entire bar seems to tilt an ear as we head for the door, and it's not even subtle. Wisteria Cove never is. It's full of meddlers and nosy neighbors. On our way out, Marilyn says something snarky that I can't make out. Vanessa pretends not to look at us, but I see her side eyeing us. I give them both my brightest smile and pat Finn's chest like he's my trophy. He's busy talking to a buddy of his and doesn't seem to notice. Then his hand slides over my lower back and he guides me out of the bar. I almost trip because I can barely focus with him touching me.

Outside, we head down Main Street. His hands slide into his pockets. He walks me to the door of Wisteria Books &

Brews, where I'm living above my sister's bookstore in her loft apartment for now. I have a small cottage I rent where I grow all my plants and have a greenhouse, but I like to be closer to the shop. When the cottage kept getting mold and everything broke down inside, I turned it into a little micro farm instead of living out there. The heat was sketchy last winter and when Willa moved out to the tree farm with Tate, I took her up on her offer of staying above the bookstore.

Finn leans in and says, "Have fun on your date tomorrow night."

"You, too. Maybe you'll make it to a second date with this one," I tease.

"That a challenge, Maren?" he asks.

"Maybe. Let's see if we can both make it to a second date." Highly unlikely on my end, but he doesn't need to know that.

He steps closer, near enough that I feel the heat of him before I even register the movement. His chest brushes mine for just a second, light enough to pretend it did not happen, heavy enough that my breath stutters anyway. I can smell cedar and soap on his shirt. It wraps around me before I can blink.

He reaches past me to open the door, his hand near my shoulder, his arm practically caging me in. His face is close, and his voice drops just a little, warm and sure. "I'll see you at lunch on Saturday."

His words move across my cheek like a touch. I swear the air changes. I nod, but my fingers curl around the strap of my bag to steady myself. My pulse races.

He holds the door there, waiting, watching me with this soft, unreadable expression that sinks right into the center of my chest. For a heartbeat, I wonder if he feels it too. This spark, this pull, this thing we have spent our entire lives pretending we do not notice.

"Sounds good." I smile. "Hopefully, my date won't turn out like the last one."

That guy was super creepy. He asked me how big my toes were and kept staring at my feet. That was when I excused myself to the ladies' room and called Finn who somehow made it there in record time and pulled me out the window by my ass. We still laugh about that story. That night he played *Getaway Car* for me on repeat, and we laughed the whole way home singing at the top of our lungs.

"You won't win the worst date wager," I say. "I still hold that title."

"That's for sure." He nods and flashes a grin, the easy kind he uses when he wants everything to seem fine. "You never know. Maybe tomorrow night you'll find the one."

There is something in his tone that doesn't match the grin. It's light and teasing but edged with something I can't quite place. His eyes hold mine for a second too long, like he's waiting for an answer I don't know how to give. The words sound like a joke, but the look... the look feels like worry or something close to it. Something warm and complicated that tightens the air between us for a breath before he clears his throat and turns away.

And I tell myself I imagined it, even though I feel it settling under my skin.

"I challenge you to find someone worse than Toe Guy," I say, trying to ease some lightheartedness into the conversation.

We shake on it. His hand's big, calloused, and comforting. The second our palms meet, a spark races up my arm like a live current. My breath catches before I can stop it. His touch feels grounded, steady, but there's something electric underneath, something that makes my pulse trip over itself. I tell myself it's just the magic reacting, but deep down, I know it's him.

"Night, Carpenter Ken," I call as he walks away.

He half turns, that grin catching the glow of the streetlamp. "Night, Hexy Barbie."

The sound of his voice hangs in the air long after he's gone. I stand there, pretending the chill crawling over my skin is from the breeze and not the way he said it.

But as his silhouette disappears down the street, the lie settles heavy in my chest.

Because no amount of small talk or first-date smiles could ever make me feel the way his goodbye just did.

And I already know that I'm in trouble.

Want more of Wisteria Cove?
Scan the QR code to read Rowan and Finn:

# Hexes & Honeysuckle

Want more of Wisteria Cove?
Scan the QR code to read Rowan and Finn:

www.ingramcontent.com/pod-product-compliance
Lightning Source LLC
Chambersburg PA
CBHW011317310726
48973CB00011B/2969